CLUB RULES

Also by Andrew Trees

Decoding Love
Academy X

CLUB RULES

Andrew Trees

ST. MARTIN'S PRESS ✹ NEW YORK

CLUB RULES. Copyright © 2010 by Andrew Trees. All rights reserved. Printed in the United States of America. For information, address St. Martin's Press, 175 Fifth Avenue, New York, N.Y. 10010.

www.stmartins.com

Library of Congress Cataloging-in-Publication Data

Trees, Andrew, 1968–
   Club rules / Andrew Trees.—1st ed.
      p. cm.
   ISBN 978-0-312-57027-9
   1. Rich people—Fiction.   2. Social classes—Fiction.   3. City and town life—Fiction.   4. Domestic fiction.   I. Title.
   PS3620.R444C58 2010
   813'.6—dc22

2009040232

First Edition: March 2010

10 9 8 7 6 5 4 3 2 1

For my father, who taught me about golf and life,
not necessarily in that order

CLUB RULES

PROLOGUE

It was the fucking air conditioner that drove him crazy. The banging and wheezing and grinding. He didn't complain when they shoved him in that airless attic with the sloped roof, which forced him to crouch like a hunchback. And he didn't complain about the half-fridge with no freezer—even though it broke down regularly. And he didn't complain when they stored the fertilizer in the warehouse below, although in the hot summer months it filled his apartment with a rank stench. But when they stuck him with that used air conditioner, it was too fucking much! They spent $15,000 retiling the pool after a couple of members complained that the red tiles reminded them of blood. When he wanted them to replace his air conditioner, though, they went to a junkyard in Waukegan.

And that, as far as Miguel was concerned, was the last straw. So he would lie on his cot and listen to that fucking thing rattle and thump, and he would seethe. He dredged up old resentments. The fact that half the members insisted on calling him José and talking with a Spanish accent to him. Making jokes about burros and tequila, although he had lived in Eden's Glen for most of his life, longer even than some of them. So long that he had no family to return to, losing not just his parents but his wife and daughter, making a mockery of the promised good life working in America was supposed to bring them all and leaving him like some palsied actor condemned to repeat his lines long after the play has closed.

He watched them through his one tiny window. They would stroll by, laughing and kicking at the grass in their polished golf shoes, and he tried to remember why he had stayed. He never had a chance of becoming head groundskeeper. They didn't want some Mexican coming to the board meetings. They wanted a white guy with a degree in environmental science, even if he didn't know shit about how to keep the golf course in shape. That was some consolation at least. Seeing the brown patches and the weeds appear after he had retired because they didn't know what they were doing. He loved watching them come out and stand around poking anxiously in the ground, trying to figure out what was wrong. It was about the only time he felt happy anymore.

Deep down, though, he knew what had kept him there. All those promises they had made. Miguel, we'll take care of you, they crooned. Life will be sweet. And he had wanted to believe them because it was the only way to justify those years spent in the service of something as silly as tending grass. Nursing it like a loving mother so that the greens rolled true and the fairways were an unblemished carpet and the rough twisted itself angrily around the hosels of clubs to punish the wayward. He practically suckled that fucking grass until it drained the life from him. How could anyone justify a life like that—*pendejos*! And after all of that, they stuck him in this shithole. When he went to see one of the doctors from the club—part of his promised reward for all those years—the other people in the waiting room sneaked looks at him, and the doctor frowned unhappily and hurried him through his visit.

So he grew to hate them and their fucking golf course and their fucking club. He would lie in his bed with that air conditioner banging out its leering beat as if the fucking thing were inside his head. And eventually he grew to hate himself for believing their lies. He couldn't sleep because of the noise, and he lost his appetite and grew thin.

He could simply have bought a new air conditioner. He nearly did a dozen times. But then he would grind his teeth and glare at it and lie back down on his cot. It was the principle. The fucking *principle*! When he asked the head groundskeeper for a new one, the man had laughed and told Miguel to be grateful. Grateful! As if his forty-odd years working there meant nothing when he no longer tended their precious grass.

And so Miguel spent more and more time lying on his bed and listening to the air conditioner until one night he went down to the warehouse and mixed an herbicide into the fertilizer and then watched out his window as they spread it over the fourteenth and fifteenth fairways. The next night, he blew his brains out with an old service revolver.

The grass soon died and left those two fairways as barren as a moonscape. The members were in a panic. Out of desperation, a group went to Miguel to see if he could make any sense of what had happened. They would have come sooner if they could have smelled his decomposing body, but the odor from the fertilizer covered that up.

When the police searched the room, they noticed that the air conditioner had also been shot several times, although it continued to limp along, sputtering quietly. And they found a note, which they assumed was a suicide note, although it was only two words. It read in full, "Fucking golfers."

CHAPTER ONE

It was a glorious early summer day in the year 19–. A happy time. A prosperous time. A complacent time. Not that the town was untouched by the winds of change. The distant tremors of social upheaval had lapped gently against its shores. There were whispers that America might be losing its preeminent place. But it was hard to take those whispers seriously amid the bucolic splendor of Eden's Glen, and the whispers were too faint to scale the high, ivy-covered walls that girded the Oak Hollow Country Club, whose cathedral of trees seemed to buttress the very sky. As couples strolled side by side through the verdant paradise of the club's immaculate golf course to compete in the Benedict Cup, it was difficult to think anything but that God was in His heaven and all was right with the world.

The Benedict Cup was named for Arthur Benedict, who loved golf, if not his fellow man. He died a perfect death, collapsing from a massive heart attack on the ninth tee after hitting a four iron two feet from the pin. His long-suffering wife decided to show her appreciation to the golfing gods by endowing the Benedict Cup, an alternate-shot competition for husbands and wives. It was affectionately known to members as the Benedict Arnold Cup for the spectacular betrayals that

often occurred in the final holes as lifetimes of disappointments spilled over into heated shouting about missed putts or
shanked drives. Occasionally, the shouting stopped only when
the divorce proceedings made final what the Benedict Cup
had begun, which led to the competition's other nickname—
the Divorce Cup.

Preston Baird Winthrop and his wife, Anne, were well on
their way to an unprecedented third Benedict Cup. The
other couple making up their foursome, Bob and Margaret
Fairfield, were well on their way to a marital meltdown. It
had started auspiciously enough. They were all good friends
and had gone out to dinner only the week before. And Margaret wasn't a particularly good golfer, so it wasn't as if she and
Bob had started their round with any expectation of winning
the tournament.

Anne was wearing her favorite golf skirt that day, a light
blue wraparound that hugged her hips. When she wore the
skirt, she felt ten years younger. Her thin friends would ask
her where she got it, and her overweight friends would make
catty comments about how it looked a little short. Anne would
smile blandly and make a mental note to wear the skirt more
often.

At thirty-eight, Anne was still attractive. More than attractive, she was beautiful, but her beauty had begun to deflate
slightly. People who saw her for the first time always commented on how great she looked. But no one in Eden's Glen
was seeing her for the first time. They didn't see the beauty
that remained, only the beauty that had been lost. Her friends
noticed that the lines around her mouth were growing deeper
and that her brow had started to look furrowed. Anne knew
she wasn't the beauty she had once been. She would study herself in the mirror and wonder if it was time to think about getting a little work done. But she didn't need to look in the

mirror. She could see it in the way they looked at her. Not so much the men. She still caught them casting admiring glances when they thought she wouldn't notice. But the women—no, the women looked at her with sharp eyes ready to carve out and examine every imperfection as punishment for being more beautiful than they were. And after a while, she couldn't help seeing herself through their eyes. She had read somewhere that she was already at the age when her spine was beginning to compress so that she was becoming shorter with each passing year. And she wondered when her life had turned, when it had gone from a sense of promise to what it was now—a gradual shrinking, a failed struggle just to remain in place.

But Anne didn't feel that way when she was wearing her blue skirt. She felt young and sexy and athletic. It was all she could do to keep from twitching her hips as she leaned over her ball and prepared to swing.

Margaret wanted to wrap her driver around Bob's balding, fat, sweaty head. Did he think she didn't notice him leering at Anne the entire time? And what was Anne thinking wearing that skirt? It was *obscene*! How did Preston let her walk out of the house in it? And Bob sucking down Bloody Marys all day. She was surprised he could walk at this point, let alone swing a club. She already knew what the afternoon held. He would fall asleep on the couch watching television, wake up around five and begin drinking again, eat too much cheese and pâté, and then, as she brought dinner to the table, announce that he really wasn't that hungry.

Just how the hell was she supposed to look like Anne, anyway? She had three kids to take care of. God forbid Bob would lend a hand! It wasn't as though she had the time to primp and preen all day. Even with the oldest one in college, half of every day was spent in the car driving around to an endless array of lessons, doctors' appointments, and tutoring. She hardly had time to shave her armpits, but every time she bumped into Anne, the woman looked as if she had just gotten a facial and had her hair blown out. When was the last time *she* had a facial? Margaret knew she shouldn't complain. They had a good life, although somehow, no matter how much money Bob made, it never was quite enough. There were private school fees and now college tuition, the vacation house they had bought a few years before. Always something stretching them a little thin. By any reasonable standard, they were very well off, but they could never relax. Part of that was life in Eden's Glen, where a five-year-old car could raise eyebrows and annual dues at the country club trimmed almost $10,000-plus from their bank account.

It didn't help that she and Bob never had sex anymore. She would be in the middle of doing laundry or putting sheets on a bed, and she would find herself trying to recall the last time the two of them had done it. It was so long ago she had trouble remembering the night. Was it Bob's birthday or a few weeks before, when they had celebrated their daughter's college acceptance? Then she would start trying to remember what their sex life had been like when they were younger. Even then, Bob was hardly a Casanova. There were always the kids underfoot, and he worked such long hours when he was trying to make partner. Still, there had been a hunger to their couplings, an ache that demanded relief. My God, one time Bob had grown so impatient he had ripped her stockings right off her body. There was nothing like that now. Nothing hurried or eager. The slow fumblings of two people engaged in a desultory undertaking.

Not that Margaret felt very sexy these days. The last time she had taken inventory, she wanted to puke. Varicose veins. Stretch marks. Wrinkles. And what little sex drive she had left after taking care of the kids was pretty much snuffed out by menopause—or at least that was what she told herself. Heavy drinking and eating had done the same thing to her husband. Even on the occasion when the two of them bothered to go through the motions, it was rarely satisfying. The lack of sex wouldn't have been so bad. Only it had become an open secret when she made the mistake of confessing to a good friend after too many glasses of wine at lunch. The occasional stray comment from other friends revealed that her secret had spread through the town.

And now here she was at the Benedict Cup having to watch her husband ogle another woman's ass. A driver to the head was too good for him.

Bob knew his wife was angry, but he didn't give a crap. What did she expect when she let herself go like that? Always going on about their three kids as if that was an excuse. Anne had a kid and look at her. Her ass was unbelievable. Preston was one lucky son of a bitch.

He took another sip of his drink. Without bothering to look, he knew that Margaret was watching him with that expression she got when she thought he was drinking too much. *Of course* he drank too much when she went around with that sour expression all the time. It was damn depressing to deal with. And the nagging. Always the nagging. About his drinking or his eating or what he was wearing or how much time he was spending with the kids or whatever. The drinking blurred all of that, made it bearable, muffled her words until they were a slight distraction from the pleasant buzzing in his head.

And sex! She never stopped nagging him about sex. Why didn't they have sex? Did he find her attractive? Should they see a doctor? And on and on. Of course, he lied and said that everything was fine, stress at work, blah blah blah. The truth was he didn't find her attractive. *Not at all.* Not even a little bit. He dreaded the nights when he would come to the bedroom and the lights would be dimmed, and there would be candles on the dresser, and Margaret would be wearing one of her silk nightgowns. He used to try to do his duty—he would shut his eyes and think about that hot little number who worked in his office. Then she started insisting that he look at her while they did it. Told him it was more intimate. As if being married more than twenty years wasn't intimacy enough, wasn't more intimacy than any one man could stand. And all he could see were those saggy tits and the dark hollows under her eyes. In the candlelight they made her look monstrous, although of course he didn't tell Margaret that. He just tried to blow out the damn candles and turn down the lights. And then she would start nagging him about how he wasn't romantic.

Then one day he lost his erection. It was like letting the air out of a balloon. The damn candles were lit, and Margaret had on some silly lingerie—the kind of thing he used to buy her when they were first married. And he was pumping away with his eyes dutifully open when he glanced down and saw his hand on her leg. And there was something about the way her skin puckered under his fingers that made her seem so old. It as if he were fucking his grandmother, and just like that he lost his erection. He pretended at the time that he had come unexpectedly, and Margaret was delighted, thinking that she could still turn him on like that. The next day, she kept joking about how he had the self-control of a teenager. And of course that only convinced her to get more of those ridiculous nightgowns.

But Bob began to worry that it would happen again. And the more he worried, the worse the problem became until he couldn't even get an erection when she was in the room. At first she pitied him, which was humiliating. And then she grew angry. And through it all his member lay there in utter indifference. So Bob started to drink more to blunt the sting of her words, although he soon realized that drinking was a good excuse for not having sex. He eventually realized that it was an excellent excuse for just about anything at all.

He knew it wasn't healthy. He was drinking so much that it often took most of the morning before his head felt clear and he was able to get any real work done. And it didn't muffle only his wife's nagging. It did the same thing to the voices of his children. His daughter would call on the phone from college, and she would seem so far away. Bob was always struggling to remember the names of her professors or her friends as she would unspool some long, involved story to him, and then she would stop abruptly, clearly expecting a response. He would try to remember what she had told him and mumble some generic words of praise or condolence, and then there would be a disappointed silence. Now when she called, she didn't even bother to talk to him, just told him to put Mom on the phone. It wasn't any better with the younger ones. They would buzz around him and chatter away about some new friend from tennis or an annoying thing one of their teachers did, but he could never remember all those damn names. So they eventually stopped telling him their stories, until he was like a fogbound freighter slowly drifting past an unseen shore.

Still, Bob usually enjoyed these rounds of golf with another couple. Margaret kept her tongue under control in front of other people, and there was a chance to get another drink every few holes. All in all, it was a nice way to spend the afternoon. He knew he was going to get an earful when he got home, but as he set up over a short putt, he was almost happy. He must have had more to drink than he realized because he smacked the hell out of the ball and sent it rocketing past the hole so that the next putt was twice as long as the first one. Not that it mattered. They weren't in contention for any sort of prize.

"Nice putt," Margaret said. "Usually you can't get it up."

Bob gave her a horrified look.

"To the hole, I mean," she said with a smirk.

He noticed Anne and Preston exchange an uncomfortable look, and he had the appalling realization that they *knew*! That the whole fucking town *knew*! That his dumb fucking wife had told one of her stupid friends, and now the whole fucking town *knew*! And they were laughing at him behind his back, laughing at his sorry excuse for a prick when they should have been laughing at *her*! Jesus Christ, how could anyone expect him to fuck *that*?

He was so inflamed with rage that he felt dizzy and short of breath. He took a wild swing with his putter at his drink on the ground and sent the cup spiraling across the green, sending out little red flares of liquid that sparkled briefly in the sun.

"Bob, control yourself. It was just a joke," said Margaret.

He could see the hint of a sardonic smile at the corner of her mouth and knew that she was secretly pleased with his outburst, which only drove his fury higher. He turned and shook his putter at her as if he might hit her and then heaved it with all of his might into a small grove of trees, where it caught harmlessly in the branches.

"You fucking bitch!"

He saw Preston and Anne walking discreetly to the next hole, but he didn't care anymore.

"You ugly fucking bitch!"

And then it poured forth. From both of them. And in Bob and Margaret's fury, they said hateful things that before they had hardly dared to think silently to themselves. When their divorce was finalized a year later, it would have been difficult for either of them to pinpoint exactly where things had gone wrong. Bob certainly wasn't happy about having to move to a smaller house, and Margaret complained about losing her country club membership. In the end, though, the divorce proved far more amicable than their final round of golf together.

When Preston and Anne arrived on the eighteenth green without the Fairfields, no one was surprised. It wasn't the first time a couple had stalked off the course in the middle of a round. And when they held up the Benedict Cup to the applause of their friends, they experienced a thrill of pleasure at the victory, although Preston was somewhat peeved that the outburst had marred the afternoon. But he soon forgot about that in the hum of warm congratulations, and he put his arm around his wife and basked in the glow of their regard.

Of course, a number of people went home and grumbled that having the same couple win the trophy a third time was a bit much. And a few wondered whether Preston and Anne finished the hole before Bob and Margaret's fight and suggested that they sidled away quietly to avoid having to putt their own ticklish little three-footer. Not that they didn't like the Winthrops. Everyone liked the Winthrops. It was just that the sun always seemed to shine a little too brightly on them.

Preston and Anne put the Benedict Cup on a shelf in the den with their other trophies and forgot about it in a week or two, but everyone else remembered it for a little while longer and wondered if it wouldn't be such a bad thing for the Winthrops to have a slightly smaller share of the good things in life. Not that their friends wished them any grave misfortune. Well, maybe a few did. Mean-spirited people who could be happy only when those who were high were brought low. But most just wanted to see them fail in some small way, to stumble a bit like everyone else, instead of their seemingly untouchable perfection, which denied the ragged, imperfect humanity that is our common lot.

CHAPTER TWO

Preston Baird Winthrop III. Mr. Winthrop to bank employees. PB to older business associates (to differentiate him from Preston Baird Winthrop Jr., his deceased father). Preston to friends and associates. And occasionally during an intimate moment with his wife, simply Press. His son was Preston Baird Winthrop IV, and he looked forward to the day he would hold in his arms a grandson christened Preston Baird Winthrop V, ensuring the safety of the family name for one more generation.

Preston loved entering the bank on Monday mornings, walking past the imposing stone façade with the Winthrop name carved deep into the lintel and striding across the enormous hall where most of the public business of the bank was done. It was a weekly reaffirmation of his true identity. The nods from longtime employees. The quiet hellos from the young executives. New employees often got so excited that they would call out, "Hello, Mr. Winthrop," across the echoing marble until they were quietly pulled aside and told that such behavior was not really consistent with the decorum of Winthrop Trust. And while Preston could look stern when the solemn hush of the bank was disturbed, he smiled inwardly and, if it was a particularly comely woman, would offer an almost imperceptible nod to her.

From Preston's earliest days, life had spread its bounteous harvest before him with an unstinting hand. There were an array of trusts and financial interests set up in his name so that he received a never-ending flow of payments, some every other week ("fortnightly," as his father liked to say), some monthly, some quarterly, some yearly. Every time he received another payment it was as if he had suddenly come into a small windfall, a never-ending lottery in which he was always the winner. And because this was the natural order of things—even as a boy, the money flowed to him—he experienced no qualms or guilt or unease. Just a simple sense of abundance. Sometimes he felt like a latter-day Midas. Well, perhaps not Midas, whose golden touch had proved to be more curse than blessing. But a new and improved Midas, liberated from gold, which was rich in luster and poetic connotation but could hardly compare with the flickering electronic numbers at his fingertips, numbers that spiraled upward in unending flight.

Monday mornings were a confirmation of who Preston Winthrop was and what he had accomplished. President and chairman of Winthrop Trust at the age of forty-one. Of course, it was his family's bank, but it wasn't as if it had been handed to him. He worked in the mailroom as a teenager and then started his apprenticeship by rotating through the bank's major departments, a few years in loans, a few in the trust department, and so on. When his father died suddenly of a heart attack, he had been thrust into the presidency. Of course, the plan had been to give him a little more seasoning. To rotate him through all the departments. Despite his youth, though, he had been the unanimous selection of the board, and he hadn't limped into the role. He'd seized the opportunity, making the kinds of bold acquisitions that his more cautious father might have delayed or avoided altogether. He had already tripled the bank's size, aggressively buying up smaller banks and opening new branches throughout the region. If the numbers were a little disappointing, so what? He was building an empire. You couldn't be a bean counter and expect to become a Caesar. Perkins was always nagging him about return on investment and earnings per share, but if Perkins was running the bank, they would scarcely have grown. No, Perkins was a little man with little ideas. Perfectly acceptable as chief financial officer, but that was as high as Perkins would ever rise, at least if Preston had anything to say about it. And as Winthrop Trust's president and largest shareholder, he did.

As Preston strode across the lobby to the executive elevator, he experienced a rising exultation. A sense that the great chain of being remained unbroken. He rose swiftly to the fifth floor with its panorama of the city spread beneath him like a rich banquet.

Samuel Perkins was talking to Matt Crane, one of the loan officers, when Preston walked in. Matt whistled quietly.

"Look at him. A giant among men."

Perkins harrumphed noncommittally and asked a question—in a much more pointed fashion than he would have moments before—about why Matt had relaxed the bank's usual collateral requirements. He pretended to listen while Matt bumbled through a response—Perkins already knew the answer. It was his business to know the answer. The obvious truth was that the applicant had been a ripe young thing with most of her assets amply displayed on her person. And in a moment of what Perkins could only consider giddy irresponsibility, Matt had approved the loan.

While Matt blathered on about the girl's character, Perkins surreptitiously watched Preston stride across the hallway. You couldn't exactly call it a swagger. No, Perkins was fairly punctilious about such matters and didn't think exaggeration served any purpose. But the walk definitely had something *imperial* about it. Of course, it was his family's bank, Perkins thought irritably, not that Preston had done anything to deserve his sudden elevation. When the board had announced its decision, Perkins was stunned. He had assumed—not out of any sense of self-aggrandizement, just out of sound judgment—that he would serve as the bank's president, at least until Preston had more experience. Preston's father had practically promised him the job.

Matt's explanation finally petered out into a pathetic shrug of the shoulders. Perkins snapped the folder shut and gave Matt a long, cold stare. He had learned years ago that the unspoken threat was always more disturbing to underlings than the spoken one. The imagination, you know. Not that Perkins had much imagination. He considered that one of his strengths. Give me the numbers, he would say, not the song and dance.

As he walked away, he cast a scornful glance at Preston's back and experienced a fresh surge of resentment. Goddamned hair, he thought. In Perkins's darker moments, he believed that Preston's hair alone was the cause of his meteoric rise and the reason everyone remained so worshipful. It wasn't as if Preston had shown himself to be a young Morgan. The bank had overpaid for its acquisitions, which had hurt their numbers. Some of the new branches were struggling as well. Yet the board shrugged it off and gave Preston a raise. A *raise*! And that was after Perkins had suggested that the officers freeze their salaries for a year to help get the bank back on track—a suggestion the board had been only too happy to accept.

Perkins's own hair was a running joke at the bank. They liked to call him Potted Plant Perkins behind his back. He was almost bald with only a few wispy strands sprouting in odd directions, which Perkins combed over in a futile effort to stave off final defeat. As Preston stepped onto the elevator,

Perkins glanced at him one more time. The last thing he saw was Preston's hair—his wavy head of flaxen hair, just beginning to gray at the temples.

With Perkins gone, Matt breathed a sigh of relief and sat down at his narrow wooden desk nestled in its bullpen with the other loan officers. He was looking forward to his next appointment. He glanced over at Vicky and waved as he picked up his phone and called a friend to make lunch plans. He pointed at the receiver as if it was a major annoyance and gave her an apologetic smile. But the truth was he wanted her to wait. He wanted her to see him as a busy man who was making time for her out of the goodness of his heart. He looked down at her file. There was no way she was getting the loan, especially after that earful from Perkins. But he had drawn out the process as long as possible to make it appear as if he was working hard on her behalf. And now he was going to reap his reward.

There was no getting around the fact that she was a touch overweight. But that just made his job easier. Overweight women were so anxious about their appearance. Besides, she still looked great. In a different era, she would have been considered a great beauty. Yes, he was going to enjoy this, and she would be grateful for the attention.

Vicky Thayer hated the bank. Everything about it made her feel small. Her suit was several years old and looked like something her grandmother would have worn, with its faded yellow fabric and taffeta collar and boxy cut, which made her look ten pounds heavier. It didn't help that she had gained a little weight, so that the seams strained to contain her hips. And she hated the way she always had to wait. As if someone wanting a loan had all the time in the world, and it was only the loan giver who was busy and had things to do. And she hated the way she had to sit there in full view of everyone like a truant waiting to go into the principal's office. A young man in a suit walked in from the street and glanced briefly in her direction. She tried to sink into her seat and imagined him thinking all sorts of things about her—that she looked old, that she didn't know how to dress, that she needed to lose weight, that she needed money. Yes, that was it. The bank made her feel poor, which she was, although she certainly didn't like being reminded of that fact. She had to jump through hoops so that they might share a few crumbs with her. She didn't want that much, and they had stacks of money sitting in their vault. Even the small size of her request made her feel diminished.

Every time, as Vicky waited to meet with one loan officer or another, she wondered what she was doing. A bakery? Sure, she could tell you how it happened. She had talent. Everyone always said so. It was a running family joke. Well, her father would say, if everything else doesn't work out, you can always open a bakery. If everything else doesn't work out—is that what it had come to? At thirty? Had everything already failed to work out? She started selling a few baked goods during the divorce to help make ends meet, and she stumbled into a position at a bakery. After a few months, she realized she could do a better job than her employers. And now here she was at her fourth bank applying for a loan. She wished it were something more substantial and mainstream. She hated the condescending way everyone talked to her about the bakery. Telling her how lucky she was to do it. How much fun it must be. Sure, when you made cookies every couple of months, it was fun. But when you had to wake up at four A.M. and bake them, it was work. Hard work. It wasn't as if she were living in a fairy land with little elves running around pouring the flour for her. And everyone always made the same comment, some variation of "I don't know if I could work in a bakery. I'd gain too much weight." Then they would give her an embarrassed glance and look away—even the heavy ones! Yes, she had gained a little weight, but it wasn't because she was sitting around eating cupcakes all day! She was so exhausted from work that she had stopped exercising.

The worst part was that they didn't just say no and send her on her way. They would patiently explain the reasons they weren't going to give her the loan. They would remind her that she already had a lot of debt and that she had no real collateral to speak of and that her financial history wasn't great. Did they think she didn't know those things? Why did they think she needed a loan? And it wasn't as if they allowed her to explain her side of the story. She couldn't tell them that she almost had to declare bankruptcy because of the loser she married right out of college. That shiftless idiot who managed to send them into a financial sinkhole. And if she told them that her current debt was the result of having no health insurance and discovering a swollen lymph node one morning—which turned out to be nothing after she spent thousands of dollars on medical tests— they wouldn't lend her the money. Besides, she had her pride. She wasn't going to tell this weasel about her health scare. She already knew he was going to turn her down. Not that the bastard hadn't gotten her hopes up. He'd strung her along far longer than the others. At first she'd thought he cared, that he was going to find a way to make it work. But she'd eventually realized that he was doing it for another reason entirely. She had wanted to stop the whole charade weeks earlier, but she had no other options and decided she had to see it through, even though she already knew what he was going to say.

Matt finally got off the phone and waved her over to his desk. He was all polished surfaces and slicked-back hair and white teeth. She sat down, and he gave her the kind of smile you might give a dim-witted child right before explaining something you thought she wouldn't understand. She wanted to slap the complacent look off his face, but she controlled herself and returned his smile. And she kept the smile on her face as he patiently explained all of the reasons why the bank was going to reject her loan application. And then he spent several minutes telling her how hard he had worked for her and how he had gone out on a limb for her.

"Look, I feel really bad," he said. "But I think I can still help. I know a lot about the financials of running a small business." He pulled out a business card and scribbled a phone number on the back. "This is my cell phone number. I usually don't give it out, but you seem like a really nice person. And I want to help you. I really do. Maybe we can get together for dinner—my treat—and see if there are some ways I can help you get your bakery off the ground."

Matt handed the card to Vicky, and she hesitated a moment as she looked at it. Not because she was wavering. No, she had expected this from him. But she wanted him to experience his own moment of hope before she carefully crumpled the card and dropped it in the wastebasket.

"No, thank you," she said with a condescending smile. When she walked out of the bank, she was no richer, but she did feel she had regained a small measure of her dignity.

Matt thought of himself as a good guy. When he turned in his final loan reports, he was fairly mild. After he rejected loans, there was no need to be vindictive. When he turned in the final report for Vicky, though, he took great pleasure in giving her the lowest possible rating and adding a long paragraph detailing why the bank should never, ever lend her money. Not that it would make any difference. But it made him feel better.

CHAPTER THREE

Nancy Harcourt was admiring her slender figure in one of the mirrors when Anne Winthrop entered her store. She reminded herself to stay calm. Even after all these years, when she became nervous or excited, it started to leak out—the dark, rusty twang of nasal vowels and elided consonants. Her laugh became loud and braying, and the years spent struggling to put some distance between herself and her past would come rushing back and threaten to overwhelm her. When she realized it—or, worse, when someone commented on it—she would lash out viciously.

But she couldn't afford to be vicious, not with Anne. Not today. She had cultivated her for months, complimenting her taste and giving her special discounts on the clothing. And today was the day she was going to reel her in.

Nancy had started her clothing store as a lark. God knew she needed something to do. Frank worked all week and golfed all weekend. She wanted to play, but she couldn't stand the thought of looking ridiculous while she learned. So she pretended not to be interested and confined herself to the occasional game of tennis.

Then that storefront right on the town square became available, and it seemed like the perfect hobby. It had been fun

for a while. She came up with a great name for the store—
Measure for Measure—and had a whimsical sign painted and
hung above the door. She filled it with lovely furniture—
gilded chairs and sofas and gauzy fabrics draped over minia-
ture Greek columns. And she enjoyed buying the clothes. But
it gradually became work. *Work!* She had spent her whole life
trying to escape work, and then she had unthinkingly thrust
herself back into it. As if she hadn't learned her lesson long ago
working at the Woolworth's after school and then taking on a
second job during the summer. No time to do any of the
things she wanted to do, to be a cheerleader or just go to the
movies. And all those beauty pageants she entered were only
more work. A never-ending attempt to win another $500 or
$1,000 in scholarship money. After she escaped her sad little
town and went off to the state college, the work didn't stop.
Not schoolwork, but the real work of looking beautiful. Making sure that her hair was done and her makeup was just so.
And always, always working to erase that hill country twang,
which sounded to her ears like white trash. When she met
Frank, she knew that he could be hers. His family was not so
high up that the match would raise any eyebrows. And he was
inexperienced enough to be awed by her beauty and to feel
indebted for the occasional sexual intimacies she allowed
him. He was at best average looking. That was important. She
didn't want someone who was going to attract the attention of
other women, particularly any women as attractive as she was
with her auburn hair and handsome features. He was not rich,
but he was ambitious. Her only gamble was that his ambition
would be rewarded. And it was. Richly rewarded. They had a
beautiful house on the fashionable side of town, and they belonged to the Oak Hollow Country Club. Their only son was
going to Cornell. Of course, all of that cost money so sometimes it felt as if they were stuck on an accelerating treadmill

where Frank's salary barely managed to keep pace with their lifestyle, even after he made partner. Frank also wanted more children, but she hadn't escaped her old life just to repeat her mother's mistakes. And it took only a small lie. A tearful confession after a supposed visit to a doctor in the city. Frank never asked her about it again.

Everything had been fine. Better than fine, until she decided to open the damn store. Now she had to keep track of employees and total up receipts. Although people still told her she had great taste, she noticed that most of them never bothered to come to her store, and those who did rarely bought much. She wondered occasionally whether that girl who had worked so hard to escape had managed to get very far at all.

She hired a manager to take care of the grubby details, and everything was going along okay until Frank came home one night in a bad mood and declared that the store was losing too much money so she would have to close it down. Well, of course, if there was one thing that nearly twenty years of marriage had taught her, it was that you don't let your husband tell you what to do. That was not the deal she had made when she married Frank. Of course, nothing had been put into words explicitly, but she'd made it perfectly clear who was in charge. And Frank had been only too happy to acquiesce, bedazzled as he was by her beauty. She wasn't going to be ordered around like some Egyptian slave now! And then she made that ridiculous promise to turn a profit, so she had to fire her manager and start working more hours herself. And the store still lost money. Then Frank threatened to cut her allowance. Cut her *allowance*! Did he think she could look the way she did for any less? Frank could let himself go. He was a man. But it wasn't as if she could become a jiggly, hairy mess. That, to her, was practically a declaration of war. And the next time they had sex, she didn't pretend to enjoy a moment of it—just to let him know that two could play that game. He left the bed muttering darkly, and it was beginning to look as if their skirmish could actually turn into a protracted stalemate. But now Anne was here. And Anne could solve everything.

Anne glanced up at the Measure for Measure sign before entering the store. It was a ridiculously fey affair—a series of dresses hanging off a unicorn's horn painted in a loose, cartoonish style. Not very Shakespearean, she thought, as she stepped inside and immediately sensed Nancy's eyes on her. She had grown to hate coming to this store. She didn't like the clothes. They were too dowdy and conservative. But she would pretend to admire something simply to avoid insulting Nancy, and Nancy would announce that she was putting that item on sale for Anne. She would do this in a grand manner as if it were a great favor. Then Anne would feel obligated to buy whatever it was. She already had several items in the back of her closet that she didn't know what to do with. Perhaps a Christmas gift for an older friend?

"Anne, I'm so glad you could drop by," said Nancy, walking across the room and kissing her on the cheek. She never would have worn the blouse that Nancy had on, which was so busy and frilly that it took the attention away from her fine figure.

Before opening the store, Nancy had never been particularly friendly with Anne, which was no surprise. Nancy was one of the few women in town whose beauty rivaled Anne's, and experience had taught her that women who are used to being the most beautiful do not enjoy being almost the most beautiful. Although Nancy had recently become much nicer to Anne, she liked the old Nancy better than the new one. There was a grasping quality to the new Nancy, which made Anne uncomfortable.

"Nancy, so good to see you," Anne said.

"I got those new silk blouses I was telling you about, and I'm sure I can work out a special discount for one of my dearest friends."

Anne smiled weakly. She knew she would be walking out of the store with some hideous blouse. She only hoped she could escape without having to buy two. She allowed herself to be ushered to a couch, and Nancy began plucking items off one of the racks. Anne looked down in distaste at the Louis XIV couch with its elaborately stitched fabric. Hadn't Nancy been to any other clothing stores in the last ten years? What did she think she was doing? Re-creating Versailles? Nancy never talked about her past, and Anne sensed she shouldn't ask questions about it. As she sat there looking around the store, though, she couldn't help thinking that there was something so provincial about it, as if everything had been chosen by a young girl imagining what fashionable life would look like.

Anne came to the store only out of a perverse sense of duty. She thought of visits like this as one of the hidden costs of being Preston Winthrop's wife. There was a ceremonial aspect to her life, a constant, niggling list of responsibilities. Oh, they were never onerous. She was expected to serve on the important charity boards like the North Shore Botanical Garden and to help plan the winter auction to raise money for the high school. She had to be nice to certain people she didn't like. Or invite some bore to a dinner party because of a long-standing family tie. Or visit an irritating woman like Nancy. Over time, though, even those small duties began to feel constricting. Well, maybe constricting was too strong a word. But they did create a hidden reservoir of quiet discontent growing steadily with the regular drip of obligation. What made it worse was that everyone acted as if all of these duties were a blessing, as if she should feel honored to serve on the various boards, and at one time she probably felt that way, too. But you can only spend so many afternoons dealing with some mind-numbing drudgery having to do with invitations or seating before any sense of being honored disappears beneath the smothering mass of obligation. It made Anne want to break free and act as if nothing depended on her. Not that she dreamed of doing anything too irresponsible. Just wearing something inappropriate to a party or drinking too much or, God forbid, flirting a little with another man. It wasn't as if other women didn't flirt shamelessly with Preston.

Anne considered it her duty to visit Nancy's store to show that she was above Nancy's pettiness and snide remarks—a self-imposed duty but a duty nonetheless. Anne had so much social power over the small world of Eden's Glen that she went out of her way not to use it, particularly with those she least enjoyed—not hated, she liked to think that she hated no one. Sometimes she thought of it as a kind of penance, an atonement for having so many of the good things in life. Other times she told herself it was a way to ward off a larger misfortune by subjecting herself to a small one.

These habits had become so ingrained that she hardly thought about them. Ever since she had been a small child, she had been the prettiest girl, the teacher's pet, the one all the boys chased. And she'd quickly realized that if she was ever going to have any girlfriends, she would also have to be the nicest, to give them no reason to add to the envy they already felt. Her own mother would complain half-jokingly about how her father doted on her. Even with her closest friends, she could see the buried resentment seep out occasionally in a stray remark, something catty and pointed. Whoever said it would immediately laugh, as if whatever they said had been a joke. Anne sometimes felt as if her whole life had been a failed search for friends who did not resent her for something—her looks or her husband or her life. So she forced herself to be nice to everyone, even to a grasping, shrill woman like Nancy.

Despite her efforts, though, it often seemed as if she was at a slight remove from everyone around her. Although she had all the markers of popularity—she was a cheerleader and the homecoming queen—each triumph seemed to separate her a little more from everyone around her so that she felt like a butterfly trapped behind glass. Not with Baird and Preston, of course, but they were only a limited help. Baird was in that awkward adolescent phase. She had tucked him in with a hug and a kiss every night of his life, and now he shrank from any contact as if he were repulsed by her. And she hardly knew anything about his life anymore. He used to tell her about his friends and teachers, and now she could scarcely get anything out of him beyond a few grunted answers. She knew it was a phase. She had taken psychology in college and could come up with a whole list of reasons from Freud and Erikson about why Baird acted that way. Just because she understood, though, didn't make it any easier.

And Preston was no help at all. She had lived in Eden's Glen for half her life, but she still felt like an outsider. Preston never understood that. The charmed circle at the core of the town—the barons of pork and cattle and timber and finance who had carved out great parkland estates in this rural enclave to escape the crowds of the city—had lived here for generations. Preston had known these people his whole life. He had known their parents and, in a few cases, their parents' parents. He had never experienced the feeling of being an outsider or, worse, an interloper. There were several women among their circle who had been determined to marry Preston themselves. A couple of them had been his girlfriends in high school, and they had not been happy to see the town's golden boy snatched away. The men of the town were also a constant source of worry. It was one thing for Preston to flirt and banter with the wives of his friends. He had been doing it since they were teenagers, and no one thought anything of it. If Anne was a little too risqué with someone, though, it was sure to become the talk of the town. Then Preston would sit her down and have one of those quiet discussions with her that she dreaded because they made her feel that no matter how long she lived in Eden's Glen, she would never be one of them.

Nancy oohed and ahhed over her ugly blouses, and Anne murmured her approval, navigating a careful line between showing too little appreciation and being rude and showing too much appreciation and being forced to buy something. Why would anyone want to be festooned with gaudily painted flowers that looked vaguely clownlike?

Nancy seated herself next to Anne and leaned in. "As usual, your taste is impeccable," she said.

Oh God, Anne thought, she's really going in for the hard sell.

"You know, it's so helpful hearing what you think. Sometimes I feel a little overwhelmed by all of this, and I would love to be able to bounce ideas off of you."

A surge of sympathy shot through Anne. One look around the store revealed that this was too much for Nancy.

"Of course."

"That would be such a relief," said Nancy. "You really have no idea."

They both sat there happily for a moment, like two young schoolgirls who have discovered that they both enjoy peanut-butter-and-jelly sandwiches.

"I have a few ideas," Anne said timidly.

"Wonderful," Nancy said. She tried to look excited at this prospect and nodded encouragingly. Anne was soon twittering away about changing the look of the store. Oh, my God, Nancy thought with horror, she not only thinks she has taste—she actually thinks her taste is better than mine! Although her smile grew increasingly brittle, Nancy managed to keep up the façade. She just needed to get Anne on board! And she was confident she could do it. She bullied Anne into buying something every time she was here. This time she would bully her into buying half the store. How hard could it be? Preston was so rich that he wouldn't miss the money. And once that was done, she would know how to put Anne in her place. Anne would have to understand whose store it was. After Anne finished talking, she looked at Nancy with an excited smile.

"Those ideas are marvelous," Nancy cooed, "simply marvelous. Now, I don't know about you, but I'm thinking partnership. Of course, we would have to draw up an agreement, and there would be a modest financial outlay for you. And then—"

"Partnership?" Anne said. "You mean becoming part owner of the store?"

"Why, of course!" Nancy laughed, although her laugh seemed a little loud. "What did you think I meant?"

"Oh . . . I didn't know."

"Think of how much fun it would be. Buyin' trips and things like that," said Nancy.

"But, you see, I'm not really interested in owning a store," said Anne. "I just . . . Well, it's not for me."

Nancy's throat flushed with anger. Not for *her*! Was Anne trying to suggest that it was more appropriate for Nancy to run a store?

"I thought this might be a nice opportunity for you," she said in a clipped tone. "But perhaps I overestimated you. Perhaps this is a little too much for you. A little too scary. I understand. Some women can't handle too much independence." Nancy stood up. "I have work to do."

She strode back to her desk and ignored Anne until she left the store. She looked down at the papers in front of her and pretended to study them, but all she could think about was her allowance. She gritted her teeth in frustration and called her favorite spa and made an appointment for a full bikini wax (Frank loved that) and a manicure and pedicure. It was time to go to work, and she resigned herself to uncomfortable underwear and feigning a great deal of interest in sex over the next few weeks. She shuddered at the thought of Frank's sagging belly and his overgrown pubic hair (why couldn't he get a bikini wax?) and how he always pushed her head farther and farther down his veiny prick until she was almost choking. She would never forgive Anne. *Never.*

Anne was so relieved as she walked out the door that she didn't mind Nancy's rudeness. A few more minutes and who knew what might have happened? Not that Preston would have cared. He didn't worry very much about money. Still, the thought of working with Nancy made her shiver. Of course, Preston had hinted that the bank might drop Stein and Thurman as their legal counsel, which would take something out of every partner's wallet, including Frank's, and she knew that wouldn't be easy for Nancy. But mostly she thought about how she had escaped without having to buy a blouse. And after this afternoon, she could probably get out of ever having to buy something there again. She was so happy she wanted to skip down the sidewalk.

CHAPTER FOUR

If he could have had any superpower, Baird Winthrop would have chosen to be invisible. Not for the usual reasons boys wanted to be invisible. He had no desire to sneak into the girls' locker room or spy on people. Just an overwhelming desire not to be noticed. He would walk down the hallways between classes and imagine that no one could see him. When he was younger, he played a sport every season, and he was a member of half a dozen clubs. He didn't do any of those things now. He was not popular—certainly not like his father, whose picture still adorned the hallway as part of the long line of past student body presidents—but people liked him well enough. And although he was in that ungainly stage of life when his body was a loose collection of parts that often worked at cross-purposes, he was beginning to grow out of it and to show glimpses of the man he would become, tall and well built with the same chiseled good looks as his father. But all he could see when he looked in the mirror was a body and face that did not belong to him. And there was something deeper, a kind of subterranean ache that he could not begin to name. Baird only knew that it made him uncomfortable around everyone. So he gradually dropped out of his clubs and stopped playing sports. He moved to the periphery of groups and tried to go into a kind of hibernation in the hope that he would wake up one day and not be filled with so much uneasiness. And it would work for a time. He could slide through a day or even an entire week without a trace.

If he could have, he would have been invisible at home as well. His father was always pulling him into his study to talk to him about the future or making him walk down the long central hallway and listen to his stories about his forebears in the portraits. That was the word his father used. *Forebears.* Baird would listen silently and nod his head, but it was as if the breath were being squeezed out of him. My God, didn't his father look at him? He was never going to be anyone's forebear. And his mother still treated him like a little boy. She was always coming into his room when he was getting ready for bed and hugging and kissing as though he were five, and he would get this angry knot in his stomach and act sullen until she went away.

When he did excel at something, it only made him more miserable. He could still remember bringing home his first A plus in math the year before. He loved math, loved the way equations resolved everything into neat answers. It was a refuge from the rest of life, where everything seemed so complicated. His parents were so proud. They insisted on putting the test up on the refrigerator, although it looked sad there. A forlorn scrap of paper on the great stainless-steel expanse. And then his father pulled him into the study and started talking to him about the bank and how important numbers were and how he needed to cultivate his talents and on and on. Baird didn't enjoy math as much after that talk, and he made sure he never did well enough to draw attention to himself again. A steady stream of B's and B pluses. But it was too late. He could see the look of disappointment on his father's face when he got the report card. And he got all twisted up inside.

It was the same way with golf. Whenever he hit a good shot, his father would laugh and tell him how he was going to carry on the family tradition, and he would start talking to him about what he needed to work on until the fun was drained out of it and Baird couldn't wait for the round to end. Now he purposely missed shots so that his score wouldn't be too good. He didn't want his father telling him to join the high school team. But Baird loved the game. And when he went out by himself in the late afternoon, he found a peace on those undulating fairways that eluded him everywhere else in life. The graceful, slow rhythm of his swing and of the round itself. A long, unthinking stroll through a manicured landscape punctuated by brief bursts of intense concentration. A charmed green circle of eighteen holes, where he never worried about how to act but simply flowed from one shot to another as if the entire round were predestined.

No matter how hard he tried, though, he could never stay invisible for long. The high school stuff wasn't so bad most of the time. He couldn't help but stick out for the obvious reason. In a school filled with rich kids, he was by far the richest. And everyone knew that. Or if they didn't, they learned it soon enough. The cool kids didn't really know what to make of him. Occasionally they teased him. Other times, almost more bewildering, they would be overly nice. And then there were the random kids who would sit down with him at lunch one day and act as if everything he said were the most interesting thing they had ever heard. If he told a joke, they would laugh and laugh. But it was as if he were performing for them, playacting a version of Baird that they expected to see, and he would grow uncomfortable and withdraw into silence. They would drift away and pass him in the hallways as if they had never spoken.

Sometimes Baird worried that he was being too sensitive,

that high school was a place where no one could be invisible. People always whispered about each other. Friendships were made and broken and remade in the space of a few weeks. And then he would long to be part of the group again and to laugh at some stupid joke that had a swear word as the punch line or to throw pretzels at the girls sitting at a nearby table. But whatever way he felt, he knew that he wanted things to be different from what they were. Like with girls. He'd had lots of female friends growing up. Occasionally, he was the only boy invited to a girl's birthday party. But girls had recently become a complete mystery to him. He didn't know how he was supposed to act. Like his lab partner, Lizzy, with her dark eyes and crooked smile. He liked her. They got along well. Occasionally they sat together at lunch to work on the lab questions or whatever. And then other times she acted as if she couldn't stand him. Like the other day. They were dissecting a frog, and she was making all these jokes about the frog and how gross it was. And it *was* gross. He still couldn't get used to sliding the scalpel into the spongy body parts. He practically had to close his eyes, although he didn't tell anyone that. The boys joked about how the girls made them do all the cutting for the dissection as if it was no big deal, and he was not about to let anyone know how he felt about it. But then he would leave class and worry about what that meant. Was he lacking something that the other boys had? Why was he so squeamish about it? When he was younger, he had a pet frog, and his mother was always telling him to keep it out of the kitchen. So he would leave class and worry about it all day. And then if his parents asked him about it at dinner, his father would joke about how girls could never handle dissections, which only made him feel worse. Sometimes he would lie awake at night and feel shivery about whatever butchery he had performed, but it wasn't as if he could tell anyone about it.

And if the image of the greasy insides of some dead animal splitting open under his knife didn't keep him up, then thoughts of what the hell he was going to do with his life would torment him. He knew what he was expected to do. He wasn't an idiot. There was obviously a point to those walks with his father down the hallway with the family portraits. He was supposed to do what his father did. What his grandfather did. What his great-grandfather did. He would join Winthrop Trust, and one day he would run the bank. But he could never imagine himself doing that. He could barely bring himself to cut open a frog. How could anyone ever expect him to run a bank? The funny thing was that he had wanted to be a doctor as a little boy. He had worn a toy stethoscope for two years, and he would insist on listening to his parents' heartbeats every morning to make sure they were in good health. And now he could barely bring himself to cut open a fucking *frog*! It was like some great cosmic joke. He was such a loser. But what else was he supposed to do? Be a lawyer? He could just imagine the look on his father's face if he told him he wanted to be a lawyer. And if he did work at the bank, he could already imagine how it would be. He had worked there parts of the last two summers, and he hated it. Everyone treated him well enough, but he knew that wasn't how they really felt. A couple of times he overheard them talking about him, and not just talking but making fun of him and saying that the bank had grown too large to keep turning it over to the next generation. They made one thing perfectly clear—no one thought he was anything like his father.

Of course, he didn't need to think about the future to keep himself awake. It wasn't as if his daily life wasn't torment enough. As if the stupid frog dissection with his lab partner wasn't already a big enough problem. He still didn't know what he had done wrong. She had been laughing and making these stupid jokes about the frog and how she was going to kiss it and find her prince and saying how it would be better than kissing him. But laughing as she said it like it wouldn't really be so terrible to kiss him. And then he had tried to make his own joke about how he would help her kiss the frog. And all he had meant to do was give the thing a little poke so that its wide, flabby lips would gape open. Only he hadn't been able to control a shudder, and he'd ended up flicking the frog's eyeball, and the thing had popped out of its head like a grape coming off the stem, and it had rolled across the table until it came to rest against her notebook. She screamed and nearly fell off her stool. The teacher ran over and started yelling at him about respecting the natural world. Before the teacher even said anything, though, he was already overwhelmed with shame as if he had desecrated the frog, which was so stupid because it was a *frog*. Watching that eyeball roll around bothered him so much that he instinctively reached out and grabbed it and threw it back into the tin tray, where it bounced around like a tiny marble. Then his lab partner screamed again and shouted, "I can't believe you touched it!" And everyone looked at him. The boys were laughing and giving him thumbs-up signs. But Baird thought he was going to be sick. He washed his hands, but for the rest of the day he felt as though he still had something oily clinging to them. And he would sniff his fingers and think that he could smell the eyeball, which was ridiculous because it wasn't as if he knew what an eyeball smelled like. And his mind would circle in this twisted direction, and he would ask himself, So, Baird, what does an eyeball smell like? And this Baird he didn't recognize would give a cocky smile and say, Well, Baird, it smells a lot like chicken.

After the teacher left, he noticed that the eyeball had left a faint brown smudge on the edge of her notebook. Lizzy saw it, too, and then she looked at him in a way that made him want to slink out of the room. "You're *disgusting*," she said before turning away and refusing to talk to him, even though it was a double period lab, and he was forced to do the rest of the work alone.

If there was one student Piggy hated, it was Baird. He wanted to punch him in the face every time he saw him. Or better yet, smash his skull with a rock. He couldn't stand how stuck-up he was. You could just see it oozing from him. He held himself aloof from everyone and everything. *Aloof.* That was the word. Piggy learned it recently in English class and immediately thought of Baird, who didn't hang out with the cool kids, although he could have. He even thought he was too good for them! He would take his lunch over to a quiet corner away from the scrum of tables at the center of the room that served as the de facto court of the popular crowd. *De facto*, that was another phrase Piggy had learned recently, and it seemed to apply to everything around him, to describe the whole world of high school, where some kids were, *de facto*, cool, and others were not. Where teachers, *de facto*, favored some and disliked others. Where Tim Trevaline, *de facto*, had become Piggy. There had been nothing all that great about being Tim. He wasn't popular or athletic or smart. But there was nothing particularly bad about it, either. And then, *de facto*, he had become Piggy and been thrust to the far edges of high school life. When his social studies class learned about the different castes in India and discussed the untouchables, Piggy thought, That's me. I'm an untouchable. It was strangely comforting to find out that his condition was not some peculiarity to his high school, that it existed all over the world and in far more unpleasant versions than his own personal hell.

Piggy would have killed to hang out with the cool kids. A

few of them occasionally said hello to him. His father was rich, and he saw them at the country club. But it wasn't like he could sit at their lunch table or stop by their locker and say hi. Not that he hadn't tried. If there was no one else around, they would ignore him or tell him to fuck off. But if he made the mistake of doing it when there were too many other people, they would turn on him and taunt him. *Fatty four-eyes! Blubber boy! Piggy! Piggy! Piggy!* Or worse, dumping the contents of his backpack into the crowded hallway and laughing while he scrambled around on the floor trying to pick everything up. Or pushing him down. Or worse. And there was Baird, just sitting by himself half the time. *Alone.* It was like social death to most kids, the idea of eating lunch alone. But it didn't seem to bother Baird. And it was obvious that he could have sat with the cool kids, obvious that girls liked him, which made the spectacle of him sitting alone even more infuriating. It was bad enough being stuck at the bottom of the social ladder, but to see someone who could have been at the top simply removing himself altogether practically drove him into a frenzy. As if Baird was above it all and had nothing but disdain for the rest of them.

And there he was—*Piggy.* Everyone called him that. Ever since eighth grade, when they read *Lord of the Flies.* Fucking book. He was a little overweight, but it wasn't like he was fat. Not like that girl Beth or that kid Arnold. They were *fat!* One time he made the mistake of defending himself by saying that he was big-boned, and that became a running joke for months. Everyone started calling him Big Bones, which eventually got shortened to Boner. For months. Even a couple of his teachers accidentally called him Boner once or twice. It was almost a relief when they went back to Piggy. If only they hadn't read that fucking book! Or if his fucking eyes weren't so bad. Or if he didn't have such a round fucking face. Or his cheeks didn't stick out so much. He could still remember that day he walked into English class with his new glasses, and one of the boys had pointed at him and said, "Hey, look! It's Piggy!" And that had been that. He had been Piggy ever since. Only adults bothered to call him Tim anymore. It was like he didn't have a Christian name, as if the nickname had blotted out that other person.

He got teased all the time, especially in the locker room after gym class when they were supposed to take showers. At least once a week, someone would grab his towel, and everyone would laugh and point, and people would slap parts of his body and talk about how long it jiggled. Piggy would stand there impassively and try to imagine that none of it was happening to him. He found that they stopped sooner when he didn't react. *Impassive* was another word he had learned recently. He liked to imagine himself in various situations being impassive. Not like when he got pushed around in the shower or when his mother was telling him to clean up his room but in heroic situations. Like being tortured to reveal state secrets and remaining impassive. Or sitting in a plane that was about to crash and staring out the window impassively. Or seeing Baird fall to his death and watching impassively. He dreamed that this was how he would be when he grew up. Impassive. And skinny.

He didn't hate the kids who teased him. That was high school. Plenty of kids got teased. And Piggy was perfectly happy to turn around and point the finger at someone else when the chance came. But he hated Baird. Baird never teased him. And that drove him crazy. It was as if Baird thought Piggy was so pathetic that he couldn't take it. Sometimes Baird stood up for him and told the others to stop or handed him a towel. And that was worse. Impassive people did not need pity. Piggy did not need Baird's fucking pity.

Their mothers were close friends, and when the two boys were younger, they had played together all the time. But then things had changed between them. Piggy always told his mother that Baird dropped him when he became fat. That wasn't the reason, but it was easier than explaining how it happened, the embarrassing stuff Piggy had done on that sleepover.

Baird had it so easy. Even in the locker room. Piggy would watch Baird undress out of the corner of his eye. His long, lean frame. His flat stomach. His smooth, unblemished white skin so unlike Piggy's freckled body. His hair falling over his eyes just so. And Piggy would feel something knot in his stomach. A weird, strangled feeling that his vocabulary workbooks had not yet given him a word for, and he would want to smash Baird's fucking face in.

CHAPTER FIVE

Norman Bond was proud of his house. He knew he shouldn't be, but he was. He did make a decent show of hiding it. When he talked about the move with people at work, he stressed how good the schools were, and if he happened to mention the size—4,500 square feet, thank you very much—he did so with a shrug of his shoulders, as if he was the victim of some whim of his wife's. Not that he didn't wish a few things were different. The houses on either side were too close, and his own house was on a measly half acre. The whole subdivision was so new that there were not a lot of trees or much landscaping. But those were small matters.

His wife thought the house looked too new, but for him that was part of its appeal. It was new! No one had dinged up the walls or left greasy stains in the kitchen. And it was *his*! The freshly laid sod was like a plush carpet under his feet. He smiled to himself as he surveyed his domain. A three-car garage. My God, they had only one car at the moment. It was almost decadent. And when you entered the house, it took your breath away. No dingy, narrow corridor with rooms jammed off of it like malignant growths. A vaulted ceiling that went right up to the roof! A giant round window with a fleur-de-lis above the door. A wooden staircase winding up one wall to the second floor. God, it made him proud. Really and truly proud. A man's home was supposed to be his castle, and he had finally found his.

And he deserved it, didn't he? All those years working his ass off for this moment. Why shouldn't he be proud? He had gotten here faster than he had dreamed. Thirty-two and it was all his. His mother and father had gone to their graves in a rinky-dink duplex. His father spending his whole life as an insurance agent writing policies to protect the few meager possessions his neighbors had managed to acquire. His mother baking the same brownies year after year for the church bake sale and content to do so until the end of time. Norman could still remember his horror when his father talked to him about taking over the insurance office, as if he were doing Norman a great favor. Norman could barely conceal his contempt. Before he left for college, he already knew he was going to do everything he could to get as far away as possible. And he had done exactly that. Majoring in finance, going to business school while working at a brokerage house. And now he was standing before this goddamn beautiful house!

Of course, Norman had his own worries on that score. The size of his mortgage had woken him up in a cold sweat more than once, but he reassured himself with the thought that he was still on the up-and-up. In a few years, he would probably look back at his worries and laugh. Hell, in a few years he would probably move to a bigger house on the more fashionable side of town.

Norman walked across the lawn like an emperor approaching his throne. When he reached the front door, he stopped for a moment and experienced a pleasurable rush as he imagined his friends standing outside waiting to ring the doorbell, awed by the round window and fleur-de-lis and whispering to themselves about how he could afford to live there. He imagined his friend's wife giving her husband a sidelong glance and wondering if, in the race of life, she had bet on the wrong horse.

He reached for the door handle—a big, solid brass number that felt substantial—and gave the door a push. It stopped after an inch, caught on the threshold. He gave the door a sharper push and only succeeded in wedging it more firmly. He looked angrily at the offending doorstep. He'd shelled out $300,000 for a house and the front door didn't open? Who the hell did they think they were dealing with? Some hick from Skokie? He was not going to put up with this! At the very least, $300,000 should pay for a working front door! Goddamn them! A rage rose in him as in a child who finds his favorite Christmas toy broken in its box. He clenched his fists and turned around toward the plush lawns surrounding him. Calm yourself, he thought. Just calm down. It's a new house. These sorts of problems happen in a new house. You tell the builder, and the builder fixes them. Just calm down. He took a deep breath and walked around to the three-car garage. He tried to regain his sense of ease, but the feeling was gone.

He walked into the garage, which usually puffed him up with pride, and stared at the wreckage of the move. Boxes filled the entire space, although they couldn't quite cover a small crack he had discovered on the floor. He had found it the night before when he'd walked around the garage, imagining the two new cars he would buy to fill the empty stalls. Actually, three new cars because in his mind their current clunker had already been exchanged for a new station wagon. And then a sports car for the weekend and another car as his train car. He loved thinking of it as his train car. A car dedicated solely to taking him to and from the train station a couple of miles from his house. It was so luxurious. He couldn't actually afford to own it, of course, not with the size of that goddamn mortgage. But there were great deals on leases. He was pretty sure he had read somewhere that it was better to lease. His wife wanted him to get a Chevy, but he rebelled at the thought. He didn't want a Chevy! Plenty of his friends at the office had Chevys.

But that crack! That damn crack! For a moment, Norman wondered if he had been had. Why didn't he listen to his wife? Why did he make the bid without taking any of the usual precautions? They hadn't even seen the house in daylight before he made the offer, but when he drove up at dusk and saw the lights casting a warm glow over the lawn and then walked through the front door—how the hell had they opened the door that night?—and saw the ceiling vaulting above him, he knew he had to have it.

He pushed the boxes away from the crack and inspected it more closely, barely resisting the urge to drop to his knees and begin scrabbling at it like a rat, as if he could uncover its full proportions and relieve his terrible fear that it revealed some deep and fundamental flaw in the house, a rottenness that had already shown itself on the surface and was slowly eating through the entire thing, eating through his very lifeblood. Goddamn house! What the hell had he been thinking?

"Norman, what are you doing?"

He reluctantly turned his eyes from the crack to his wife standing in the doorway. Her long brown hair was held back by a bandanna. He almost laughed when he saw her. From the neck up, she looked as if she'd walked out of a 1950s poster on housekeeping. She was wearing old blue jeans and a dirty T-shirt with a buxom woman holding a stein of beer printed across the front. He frowned and turned away.

"Nothing," he said.

"Well, if you aren't doing anything, come in and help me.

These boxes aren't going to unpack themselves. And Norman Jr. is starting to act up."

"I'll be there in a minute."

"But, Norman—"

"Goddamn it, Paige, I said I would be there in a minute."

He heard her sigh and shut the door. He looked down at the crack, but it no longer enraged him. Goddamn his wife! Why did she have to do that? She knew he hated those jeans. They made her ass look huge. The thin, sexy woman he had married seemed like a mirage beside that matronly figure. Of course, she was a mother now, and she had put on some weight because of the kid. That was only natural. He had put on a little weight himself, although he thought it made him look more substantial. But he had begun to fear that she would never be thin again. She still had a great face. Those plump red lips and full brown eyes. Should he buy her a membership at a gym, or would that be insulting? Maybe he should say something. She might appreciate it. His eyes drifted back to the crack.

And that *shirt*. He had bought it for her as a joke when they started dating. They had sex for the first time in her tiny studio apartment in Lincoln Park and were lying naked on her futon with the sheets twined around their bodies. They could hear drunken fraternity boys singing songs at the bar across the street, and the light from a streetlamp shone through the window and glowed on her skin. He pulled off the sheet to expose her to the light, but she grabbed it from his hand and drew it up around her neck. When he asked her what was the matter, she admitted shyly that she thought her breasts were too small. And he pulled away the sheet and kissed them tenderly and told her that they were perfect and that she was perfect. And then he pulled her into his arms and held her as the two of them fell asleep.

He bought her the T-shirt the next week as a joke. She was upset at first. She thought he was making fun of her and started arguing with him and spouting all this feminist crap. He hadn't really given the T-shirt much thought. It was meant to be funny. That was all. But when she got so angry, he knew he couldn't leave it at that, so he told her how he bought it for her because he thought her breasts really were perfect. There were a lot of other parts to the explanation he made up on the spot. In the end, Paige forgave him. It was the first thing he ever bought for her.

Initially, when she wore it, they laughed and would flirt with each other as if she were a sexy waitress trying to pick him up. "Come here often?" she would ask in this throaty voice that got him all worked up. He would slap her ass, and she would put on skimpy shorts and parade around, and as often as not, they would have sex. But now she wore it as a work shirt. And all he could think about as he looked at her in it was how small her tits were. And how the armpits were stained yellow. My God, what man wanted to look at his wife's pit stains? How was that sexy? He sighed and ran his foot along the crack.

CHAPTER SIX

Costas Galanis's chest was getting tight as he looked over the accounts from the golf shop. He was sitting in his small office crowded with dusty trophies and faded photographs and old issues of golf magazines. *Fuck!* All these rich bastards, and he could hardly turn a profit. He overcharged for everything—balls, shirts, golf clubs—and he was barely keeping his head above water. Nine dollars for a goddamn sleeve of Hogans, and he still couldn't make any money. *Fuck!* He looked at the mass of paper littering his desk and wondered for the thousandth time if he should hire a real store manager. It was crazy to keep his ex-wife around. Not after everything that had happened. But she worked for so little. And if he had to pay someone else's salary, he might start losing money. *Fuck!*

He reached into his desk drawer and pulled out a bottle of vodka. He poured himself two fingers and gulped it down.

"Maria!"

His ex-wife stuck her head into the cramped room.

"Yes, Costas?"

"Maria, these goddamn books! We're barely making money!"

Maria shrugged. Costas could feel his heart rate go ratcheting up. Why the fuck had he ever kept her on? *Fuck!*

"What about those shirts? All the members are wearing them. Why didn't we make more money on the shirts? We only made"—he dragged his finger down the page but couldn't find the entry—"hardly anything! How could we make so little?"

"Because you priced them too high, and no one bought them. They only bought them after I put them on sale. And the sale price was only a little above our cost."

Costas felt as if his chest was going to explode. Those fucking shirts were gorgeous! He had the club insignia stitched on them and some other beautiful shit. Those shirts were fucking works of art! And those goddamn cocksuckers wouldn't buy them until they were on sale! They drove cars that were worth more than his house, and they wouldn't buy his fucking shirts unless they were on sale!

"Goddammit, Maria!"

"What do you want me to do? I can't make them buy the shirt."

He knew it wasn't her fault, but he yelled at her for a while anyway. What was he supposed to do? He couldn't yell at the members. So he took it out on Maria until he made her cry, and then he felt guilty, so he gave her $50 out of the register and told her to take the day off and get herself something nice. *Fuck!* He didn't have $50 to give away! His goddamn temper!

He locked himself in his office and vowed to look through the books and go through every goddamn receipt until he got to the bottom of it. But he did what he always did. He glanced at the columns of numbers for a few minutes and then got frustrated and poured himself another drink and stared out his small window and wondered where his life had gone wrong.

Sometimes he blamed his troubles on Maria or some member he thought was out to get him. But most of the time he thought about what would have happened if he had made it through Q school and gotten his card. Three fucking strokes! That was all he had missed by. Three! Fucking! Strokes! It wasn't that he would have made a fortune on the tour. But he could have had a nice living, gotten a few endorsement deals. And how much more would he be worth to a club today if he had been on the tour? He might even have won a couple of tournaments. All it took was getting hot for a week. Hell, that could have happened. He leaned back in his chair and thought about himself waving his hat to the gallery and accepting the oversize check from the sponsor and saying a few modest words for the TV camera.

What Costas didn't remember was that he had putted out of his mind all week and that if he hadn't, he would have missed the cut by more than ten strokes. And he didn't think about those friends of his who were better golfers and had gotten their cards and had lived out of their cars for a couple of years as they drove from tournament to tournament before washing out without making anything.

But daydreaming about the tour would relax him. By lunchtime, his chest wouldn't feel as if it was going to explode, and he would get a cheeseburger and fries from the grill and drink a few beers. The rest of the afternoon would pass in a comfortable haze. He would give a couple of lessons and maybe hit a bucket of balls and then call it a day and head home and forget about his troubles until he found himself back in his office the next morning, staring at the books and feeling his chest get tight again.

CHAPTER SEVEN

Paige washed the breakfast dishes, wiped down the counters, fed Norman Jr., and then stared at the remaining boxes waiting to be unpacked. The wreckage of a decade of marriage. Somehow the grand casting-off they promised themselves they would do when they moved never quite happened, so that random gadgets and unworn flannel shirts from Norman's parents and old, mismatched china had accompanied them to their new house. Now she was looking forward to going through it because it would give her something to do when the baby was napping.

She gazed around anxiously at the house. Without Norman to keep her company, it made her feel out of place and lonely. She'd never wanted such a big house. She hadn't even wanted to move. They were so cozy in their old apartment. Not that it wasn't a little cramped, but it was home. When they eventually had another child, they would have had to move, but they could have stayed there until then. Norman wouldn't hear of it, though. He kept insisting that property values were going to go up and that they were already too crowded. And he would go on and on about the problems with living in the city, the same city he used to brag about when they first met. But she was used to letting him have his way, and when it came to things like property values, he did know better than she did.

But she missed it already. Her little coffee shop on the corner. She loved to go there in the late morning and sit in a booth with the bright sunlight streaming through the window and read a magazine or just watch the people walking by on the street. The nearby park where she could meet friends who had their own babies. She knew so many women with babies in the city. There were friends who had children a few years older who helped her figure out what to do when he wasn't latching on to her nipple and who gave her a steady stream of clothes and toys. Friends she made at Lamaze class or the doctor's office who had babies the same age and could commiserate about the sleepless nights and make joking reference to the death of their sex lives. And friends with their own quickly expanding stomachs who would call her up to complain about their nausea. Would those friends come out here to visit her? They used to struggle to get together regularly when they lived a few blocks from one another. And now she was so far away.

She wandered around the house with the baby in her arms and wondered how long it would take before she felt at home there. She stared down the long hallway. A shudder ran through her, and she turned away. What was she supposed to do? What did other women do? She imagined impossibly beautiful women dressed in white slacks playing tennis on a grass court and laughed to herself at the ridiculousness of the image.

She was never going to meet anyone by staying in the house, so she went into the bedroom to change. Let Norman open some of the damn boxes. He had hardly lifted a finger the entire weekend, just stood in the garage muttering. She put the baby on the bed and opened the door to her walk-in closet. She did like that. No more clothes stuffed on the top shelf in the kitchen or shoes buried underneath the bed.

She noticed her T-shirt from the other day in the laundry hamper and experienced a slight pang at the sight of it. She wore it only when she wanted to annoy Norman, and she always felt a little guilty afterward. When she thought back to that night, though, it still made her angry. She had shared her greatest insecurity with him, and he'd turned around and made a joke about it. Later, when he saw how upset she was, he was very smooth explaining how he didn't mean anything by it, and she had forgiven him, sort of. But she could see how he really felt. He thought she didn't notice when his gaze lingered a little too long on some woman's chest, but she did. And she knew how much it bothered him when she wore the T-shirt. So she wore it when she was fed up with him. Not often. Still, she experienced a pang when she did. The funny thing was that breast-feeding had finally given her a decent-size chest, but she had never felt less sexy in her life. And the thought of Norman pawing at the same breasts she used to feed the baby filled her with disgust.

Of course, the other mothers warned her about how the baby would crowd out everything else in her life, and it was true. It was as if she were caught in some strange reality where time moved backward, where the baby had come first, had always been there, and Norman appeared later, a ghostly, peripheral figure who was essential to the baby's arrival, even though he came after. When he was absorbed in something else—which was nearly all the time with Norman—she would stare at him and try to remember what had drawn her to him in the first place. Often, it was hard to remember. No, that wasn't right. She could remember, but it was hard to see the Norman she fell in love with in the man standing in the garage and muttering to himself.

The Norman she fell in love with still had a boyish earnest-ness about him that she found endearing. Of course, he tried to present himself as some big-city sophisticate, but the truth constantly leaked past his bluster and only made him more charming to her. The first time he had taken her out to an Italian restaurant, he'd mispronounced Chianti, confidently calling for CAY-anti, and the waiter had replied discreetly that he would be happy to bring a bottle of Chianti. Norman had blushed, but after the first bottle, the two of them had laughed about it. Norman entertained her with stories about his father's insurance practice—the comically inept tales of insurance fraud, where a stolen truck would be parked only a few blocks away in a cousin's garage. And there was a drive about Norman she admired after dating so many boys in col-lege who didn't seem concerned about anything but the next party. She herself had drifted into adulthood without any real plan, working for a while at a department store and then later as a secretary. But Norman had enough drive for both of them, its relentless quality like a stiff breeze that forced her to brace herself and set her face firmly in one direction. Only now Norman seemed to have been taken over by his drive, although it seemed unfair to think that. You couldn't marry a man for his ambition and then complain that he was too am-bitious. Still, she missed those stories about his boyhood. He never talked about his parents or his childhood anymore, as if they were no longer a part of him.

She fingered a navy blue pantsuit she had always loved, but she knew it wouldn't fit. She hadn't lost all of the weight from the baby, and like a great many other things in her closet, the pantsuit would remain on the hanger until she did. She put on a pair of jeans and a tan cotton sweater and turned to Norman Jr.

"How do I look?" she asked. It was a little game she played.

Norman never noticed what she was wearing anymore. She couldn't really blame him. Since they had the baby, she hardly noticed him, either. So she had begun a daily ritual of discussing her outfits with the baby. Soon she had him dressed and strapped into the child seat in their station wagon, and she pulled out of the driveway feeling as if she were going on a treasure hunt.

She didn't know where she was going at first. She drove through their subdivision, which was filled with houses that looked much like her own. Norman insisted that their house was different. *Very* different, he kept saying, although from what she could see, a large entrance hall and a three-car garage were pretty common.

Then she drove around the outskirts of Eden's Glen. It wasn't a large town. That was part of the appeal for Norman. She couldn't remember how many times he had called it an "exclusive enclave." Of course, it was true. The town had managed to keep the surrounding suburban sprawl at bay, a Shangri-la increasingly hemmed in on all sides by strip malls and squat office buildings with cheerless black glass façades. A large forest preserve bordered the south side of town, so she drove to the highway that ran along the western edge of Eden's Glen, passing what had once been farmland. Over the past decade, the cornfields had been plowed under, though, and sprouted with subdivisions much like their own. Then Paige drove through the north side of town, an odd jumble of forests and fields covered in prairie grass and the occasional stray office park tucked back discreetly from the road, as if the town plan had petered out before it reached this spot, leaving it to catch whatever washed up from the town proper. And finally she wound her way through the tree-lined streets on the east side of town. The fashionable side, as Norman always said. The houses were much larger and were set on several acres of wooded land. Large gates flanked the driveways, as if the owners were worried that people might steal up to the house and press their noses against the glass. Many of the estates were so large that she couldn't see the houses from the road.

It was as if Paige had slipped into another era, a simpler time when things had been clearly demarcated and everyone knew his place, before the dislocations and confusions of civil rights or feminism or Vietnam or gas lines. She knew she shouldn't think like this, that some of those changes were good things. Hadn't she herself benefited? No one questioned whether Paige should go to college or not. Her more daring friends were still single and working away at their careers, although they complained constantly about how the men made crude jokes to them and swatted at their behinds after they drank too much at lunch. Despite all that, though, she couldn't help feeling that America had lost a certain innocence, not unlike the boyish earnestness of the man she fell in love with. A state of grace that couldn't really be appreciated until it was gone. And behind the well-fortified walls of these houses—mansions, really—she couldn't escape the sense that they had somehow managed to preserve that innocence, that the vast, well-tended lawns were a kind of moat that kept the rest of the world at bay. And what was wrong with that? The news of the world so often only seemed to bring tidings of death and destruction. Still, it was a ridiculous thought, the idea that the sort of innocence she had in mind could be preserved or had ever existed in the first place, and she smiled at her own fantastical notions.

At last, she found the entrance to the town's beach and drove down a steep road to a sandy oasis that stretched for miles along the shores of Lake Michigan. She could see a boatyard in the distance studded with tall white masts. The beach in front of her was filled with bodies lying in oiled perfection, but she didn't get out of the car, worried that she would look ridiculous pushing a stroller past them in jeans and a sweater, as if she were an interloper from a chilly corner of Wisconsin.

She drove back through the quiet streets and smiled to herself as she entered the town proper. A small square surrounded with quaint little shops around a village green that had a fountain at one end and an American flag at the other. It was like a vision out of a Norman Rockwell painting.

There was a parking spot in front of a cute store called Measure for Measure, and Paige soon had the baby in his stroller. She was fumbling for quarters when she realized with the delight of a longtime city dweller that there was no meter to feed. She pushed Norman Jr. down the sidewalk and began to enjoy, for perhaps the first time, her new life. She found a small coffee shop just off the square and decided to treat herself before exploring.

She ordered a large coffee with a lot of milk and, at the last second, also bought herself a brownie. Norman was always dropping hints about her weight, although it wasn't as if he hadn't let himself go a bit. Portly was probably the nicest way to put it, which made his five-foot-eight-inch frame look squat. His sandy-colored hair was thinning on top, and even his nose seemed fleshier than it had been when they first met. She would never have said anything to him about it, though, so she didn't like it when she caught him staring critically at her as she took her clothes off at night.

Paige maneuvered the stroller to a table by the window. She looked at the other customers and tried to imagine herself as their friend. But she couldn't. Who were these women? And where were their kids? And what were they doing getting coffee in the middle of the morning? They all looked six feet tall and had perfect, straight blond hair and were thin and well dressed. She looked down at her own outfit and noticed that her tan sweater was starting to pill where the diaper bag rubbed against it. She finished quickly and hurried to push the stroller back onto the street, nearly running over a woman on her way in.

"What's your hurry, honey?"

The woman had a slow, sugary voice. Paige glanced up and smiled when she saw the kind face looking at her.

"Oh, I'm so sorry," she said, disentangling the stroller. "I'm new to this place. I just moved here."

"Don't worry. No harm done. I've been run over by worse than a baby stroller," she said, leaning down. "Look at you, you cutie. Look at you!"

She began playing with Norman Jr., who gurgled happily.

"I'm Leanne," said the woman, extending her hand. "Welcome to Eden's Glen."

Paige shook her hand and smiled. "I'm Paige."

"If you're not in too big a hurry, why don't you let me buy you a cup of coffee and welcome you properly?"

Paige felt awkward, as if she was back in high school. "Okay," she said shyly.

They went back inside and found an empty table.

"What can I get you?" Leanne asked.

"Oh, nothing. I had something already. I'll just sit."

"Well, that's no good," Leanne said, "I'll have to surprise you."

As Leanne waited in line, Paige studied her. She was tall and blond but not like the other women. She wore too much makeup to cover up a bad complexion. Her hair was haphazardly dyed, and one of her front teeth had a smudge of dark red lipstick on it. Each imperfection reassured her.

Leanne came back with a large coffee for herself and two brownies.

"They're really good," she said. "They have chocolate chips in them."

"I know! I had one before I bumped into you. I really shouldn't. I'm trying to lose my baby weight," Paige said, pulling a large piece off one of the brownies.

I think I've made my first friend in Eden's Glen, she thought happily.

CHAPTER EIGHT

Maria looked around the room while Rob Samuels grunted above her. It was a nice bedroom. Not exactly her taste. A little too floral and feminine. Lots of frilly pillows and a colorful blown-glass vase and little pewter bowls filled with potpourri. She let her hands roam idly around his back. It was hairy, which was unpleasant. But only mildly. Every couple of thrusts she would let out a moan, even though she was already bored and wished he would hurry up and get it over with. She began moaning more quickly, as if she were on the verge, and dug her fingernails into his back, which did the trick. Rob quickened his thrusts and let out a low sigh as he came. He rolled off and gave her a satisfied smile.

The truth was that none of these men could fuck worth a damn. They had it too easy. There was none of that air of desperation she seemed to need to get her really excited. Not that it mattered much. She had plenty of ways to get off when she went home. Besides, Maria didn't do it for pleasure.

It hadn't started off that way, of course. The first time she had been sad and lonely, and she thought the man—a club member, naturally enough—cared for her. And she loved him. Not the way she once loved Costas. She didn't think she would love anyone that way again. It was more like gratitude. But it

was still love of a sort. He convinced her that he was going to
leave his wife, and she allowed herself to imagine a time when
she wouldn't work in the golf shop but would walk in as a
member. Then, of course, it had all gone to shit. He had no
intention of leaving his wife and certainly not for a forty-
something divorcée who worked in the pro shop. She hoped
for a while that his wife would leave him if she found out
about it. And Maria made sure she found out about it. Nothing
too obvious. A few phone calls. Sometimes hanging up. Sometimes making up an excuse for her call. Later, after he made it
clear to her that it was over and that the phone calls would
stop *or else*, it was obvious that it hadn't been the first time and
that his wife had no interest in leaving him or the life he provided. Not that the wife didn't find ways to extract revenge.
The woman found a weekly excuse to stroll through the store
and unfold half the shirts on display. Maria sometimes thought
she did nothing but refold those shirts, as if, in some twisted
way, she had been forced to become the woman's maid.

Maria was so humiliated by the whole experience that she
would never have done it again, except for one thing—it drove
Costas crazy. He wasn't really jealous of her. If she had met
some guy and remarried, it wouldn't have bothered him.
What infuriated him was that some member banged his ex-
wife. After a lifetime of suffering small indignities at the club,
he had to suffer this final outrage. And what made it worse
was that because she was no longer his wife, he couldn't even
do anything about it. He just had to choke on it. After years of
putting up with his infidelities and feeling powerless, she had
finally turned the tables on him. So she kept on doing it.
Simply for the pleasure of watching him suffer.

She was discreet. Not because she was worried about her
reputation. But because it was better if Costas discovered it on
his own. She could always tell when he found out about

someone else. She would see him seething quietly. That was when he had developed his temper. He had always been volatile. *I'm Greek,* he would say in defense of whatever tantrum he had thrown, *what do you expect?* But he hadn't been an angry man. Not then. Now he was. He was angry all the time. She could see it just below the surface.

Sometimes she seduced a member because she knew it was someone who would really bother Costas. Like Preston. Not that she wasn't attracted to him. Even naked, when most men looked a little ridiculous, Preston was still so handsome. And that hair—yes, there was nothing unpleasant about seducing Preston. But what had made it even better was that Costas and Preston played golf together. Costas actually liked Preston. And she loved the thought of Costas spending four hours with Preston and having to pretend to have a good time while he burned on the inside.

Not that it didn't have its downside. She had caught a couple of STDs, and one of those bastards had given her genital herpes. But she had turned that to her advantage as well. When a member was particularly obnoxious and leering, she would wait for an outbreak and then seduce him. She loved to imagine the look on his wife's face when her OB-GYN told her what she had.

Rob was chattering away beside her like an excited schoolboy, and Maria was murmuring replies and hoping he would shut up. The poor guy clearly hadn't done it in a while, but Maria couldn't really blame his wife, given what she had seen that afternoon. She actually liked Rob's wife and hoped she didn't find out about it. Not that it mattered much as long as Costas eventually found out. It might take months to get back to him. And then one day he would walk into the pro shop, and there would be that look in his eyes. She could see the manly pride just leaking out of him. That was one of the few things that made her happy. That and stealing Costas blind at the shop.

Why wouldn't Rob shut up so she could daydream in peace? He rolled over and pressed himself against her.

"Care to try again?"

She was impressed. At his age, most men needed a good night's sleep before thinking about another go. She could already feel the sticky and insistent throb of him against her leg. Poor bastard. She patted him gently and somewhat condescendingly on the head.

"I'm afraid you've worn me out," she said.

He broke into a huge smile.

"We'll have to plan another occasion," he said.

Doing it once to get back at Costas was one thing. Doing it a second time was something else entirely.

"We'll see," she said lazily.

"You enjoyed it, right?"

The smile faded from his face, and he had the look of a hurt schoolboy.

"Of course, darling," she said, laying a hand on his belly. She reached down and gave him a reassuring squeeze. "Another time."

Rob gave her a sheepish look, and she already knew what he was going to ask. She knew because too many men had asked her the same question. It was so pathetic. Didn't they realize that? Didn't they have any pride?

"Was I . . ." He looked at her, hoping that she would finish the question for him, but she wasn't going to let him off the hook so easily. She was going to make him ask the question himself. She waited. "Better?"

"Better than what?" she asked, although she already knew.

"You know . . . than Costas."

You would think that the son of a bitch was Casanova, not

a goddamn country club pro. He hadn't even played on the tour. And still they asked. Hell, he wasn't even that good-looking anymore. And still they asked.

The truth was that sex had never been their problem. Even when Costas was fucking around on her, they had sex all the time. Not just tired, boring, married sex, either. Good sex. Great sex. Costas was passionate. You had to give him that. He could be rough with her. These assholes were almost apologetic. Nothing that ever got her heart racing. She could still remember that day when Costas had broken the course record and taken her back into his office and shoved her against the wall and done it to her right there. They were thumping away so hard that every picture fell off the wall. God, she had loved him. And every time some guy asked if he was better than Costas, she remembered how good Costas had been. Every single time. This was always the moment that made her want to quit the whole thing and move somewhere else. Why did they have to make her remember? Occasionally, if she had enjoyed it—which was pretty rare—she would say something about how she couldn't really tell after one time. Enough of a challenge so that they would want to do it again, if only to prove themselves. But the thought of doing it again with Rob was repulsive, so she told him her usual lie.

"You were great," she said, "much better than Costas."

CHAPTER NINE

Norman boarded the train with his newspaper and brief-case and sat next to one of the windows where he looked out with satisfaction. My God, even the train stations were beautiful here, he thought exultantly as the imposing brick structure receded into the distance. He was sure that would come back to bite him in property taxes, but he didn't care. It was worth it. Send a man off to work with appropriate pomp and circumstance. He leaned back in his seat and smiled. No sour smell from a homeless man on the corner. No scrambling to catch a bus. No unfocused stare to avoid meeting the eye of the crazy-looking man across from you. Just rolling vistas of well-kept lawns and sparse woods and picturesque towns.

And his stop was the fairest of them all. He wanted to seek out the commuters who had stepped onto the train with him and shake their hands and laugh with them and make jokes about the stock market and how politics was going to the dogs. Eden's Glen! My God! He lived in Eden's Glen! Norman Bond, son of Hank Bond from Kansas, who never had more than a few thousand in the bank. Hank Bond, who thought really living was buying imported beer and watching football on New Year's Day. And now Norman was living in Eden's Glen. As the train stopped at the towns closer to the city, his exultation grew. It didn't feel like a commute. It felt like a coronation. Norman Bond had arrived.

Sure, there were some kinks to work out. That was to be expected. You couldn't move from a cramped two-bedroom in the city to a house in a place like Eden's Glen without a few growing pains. That was natural. The first thing he needed to do was get his own car. He didn't like having his wife drive him to the station. He didn't like it one bit. It was like having his mother drop him off at school. Where was the dignity in that? He didn't want her fussing over him in front of the other men, especially not at that time in the morning when she never looked her best. It wasn't that he was ashamed of her, but he didn't want to parade around with her on his arm at seven-thirty A.M. No, that was priority number one. A new car.

That and the Oak Hollow Country Club. He looked out the window and thought about the endless expanse of well-tended grounds strung out on the bluffs above Lake Michigan like an emerald necklace. Of all the town's many plums, that was the sweetest and the most difficult to grasp. Norman still had to content himself with the occasional round of golf on a municipal course with his buddies. Plodding affairs that lasted five or six hours. Guys wearing T-shirts and cutoffs. No clubhouse to speak of, just a couple of crappy rooms with mildewed carpet where you could buy an overpriced beer. When he became a member of the Oak Hollow Country Club, though, all that would change. He would be a part of the most exclusive membership in the entire metropolitan area. Hell, in the entire region! That was the kind of place he should be playing golf. Of course, it would cost a fortune to join, but it would be worth every penny. The business contacts alone would justify it. Norman stared out the window and imagined himself holding forth on an intricate foreign currency question while other members listened with rapt attention—

until an overpass blotted out the landscape and ruined his daydream.

He picked up his paper, carefully folded the business section into quarters, and held it in front of him. He pretended to read but secretly watched himself out of the corner of his eye in the train's window and admired how he looked. When the train pulled into the station an hour later, he grimaced as he stepped off. He had to pick up his pace to avoid being jostled, and he could feel a weariness descend on him as the grind of it all began again. He was hurried along the pavement by everyone around him, and his skin prickled with the morning heat and humidity of the early summer.

He walked through the revolving door of the sixty-story glass tower on Wabash Avenue with a sigh of relief. He entered the elevator, was wedged into the corner by some goddamn delivery guy, and glowered at him in silence as he rode up to the twenty-third floor. He shoved his way out and walked to the end of the hallway where "Harkness & Hames" was emblazoned on the glass door. No, it was not the most prestigious financial firm in the city, but it had as much goddamn hustle as any of them. And the better firms didn't just throw open their arms to welcome someone like Norman, although he knew that it was only a matter of time before he pushed his way past their polished glass doors as well. Harkness & Hames was only a stepping-stone for him on the way to greater things. He pulled open the door and arranged his lips into a confident smile.

"Good morning, Marjorie," he said, winking at the receptionist. Good morning indeed! He didn't mind a little flirtation with her when he had free time on his hands. She always wore tight tops, and her skirts never reached her knee. And when she laughed, she opened her mouth too wide. Still, it was harmless fun.

He strode through an open room of cubicles and called out greetings to his colleagues. He experienced a brief pang at his separation from them. He had once been their ringleader, the loudest and funniest guy in the room. There had always been a crowd of people around his desk whispering the latest gossip. But that was a small price to pay for his own office. He smiled as he walked through the open door and looked out across the city. Yes, Norman Bond had come very far indeed.

CHAPTER TEN

Preston stood on the first tee, looked across the perfectly manicured greens and fairways, took a deep breath, and smiled. This was the happiest moment of each week. He felt like Adam looking out over Eden and seeing God's bounty. Almost a religious feeling.

An uneasy thought suddenly tugged at the corner of his mind. How long had it been since he had gone to church? Not that he needed to. His moral compass remained as true as ever. But the boy . . . He should have some religious training. Go to church occasionally. Get familiar with the whole Episcopalian way of things. Not too religious, of course. He didn't want him becoming a Holy Roller. He vaguely remembered reading about some kind of connection between religious fervor and homosexuality. Still, the boy should spend a little more time in church, learn the liturgy, that sort of thing. Preston struggled to remember the Nicene Creed but found himself unable to get past the only begotten son part. Not that it mattered. He remembered the broad outlines, which was the important thing.

He thought back to his own boyhood, sitting on the hard wooden pews and listening to the liturgical murmurs on the occasional somnolent mornings when his father made him go to church. Shy glances up at his father in his dark suit, his neatly trimmed mustache framing a mouth that was forever pursed, as if the man behind that mouth disapproved of the world in some fundamental way. His father would take in the service through disinterested eyes, giving his son no idea of whether or not he was concerned about the state of his soul. But there was no reason to worry about that sort of thing anymore. The world Preston inhabited had been sanctified by an easy affluence that pushed away dark worries about the hereafter.

As he took a few practice swings with his driver, he made a mental note to increase his donation to the Episcopal church and to have the priest and his wife over to dinner. They seemed like nice people. Not too religious. Perfectly pleasant at a party and not shy about knocking back a few drinks with their parishioners. Maybe he should invite him to play golf some weekend. Not on a Sunday, of course. And wasn't that more in the spirit of true Christian fellowship? Not that stuffy kneeling and reciting in church. He took a deep breath and looked out again at the lush landscape before him. The giant oaks that flanked the twelfth fairway swaying in the breeze. The sunlight shimmering off the lake by the second green. There was something calming about it. Almost spiritual. And how could that be a bad thing? How could God want anything but that feeling for all His creatures? His playing companions joined him on the tee. Preston smiled at them benevolently. Yes, it was a glorious Saturday, a magnificent day for golf.

Jim was already nervous, and he hadn't spoken one word to Preston yet. It was a stroke of good luck that he had ended up in his foursome this week—usually John played in this group, but he got stuck taking his wife's brother out for a round. So

Jim got the call. He wished he had had more notice. At least a couple of days to gather what information he could on Winthrop Trust's legal issues. But he could get up to speed later. The important thing was to get Preston on his side by the end of the round. If he could land the account, he could breathe easier about things.

Money—the getting of it and, especially, the spending of it—was always nibbling away at him, pulling his thoughts from whatever it was he was supposed to be doing. His wife would be talking to him, and he would realize with a jolt that he had missed the last couple of minutes of what she was saying because he had been thinking about what the mortgage payments were going to be when the rate reset after seven years. It was expensive as hell to live in Eden's Glen. Houses were expensive. Property taxes were expensive. The county club was expensive. And then there were these extras he hadn't anticipated. Like private school. What a financial debacle that had been. Eden's Glen had some of the best public schools in the state, but once he got into the club, he realized that no one from that set sent their kids to the public school until high school—and even then, some of them went away to boarding school. So that was added to the cost of living there. What irony that he and his wife had convinced themselves that the move was worth it if only for the public schools, then turning around and sending them to the private school with scarcely a moment's hesitation. With two kids at more than $10,000 per, that was no joke. And the cars! How could he not have known about the cars? He had a perfectly respectable Honda. He never thought twice about it since the day he bought it. When he drove into the club parking lot the first time, though, he realized that they would have to get new cars as well. And not just a nicer Honda but something German. And on and on it went. He was drowning in a sea of red, and the only way out was to make partner. It had looked like a lock until last year when Paul snagged that big insurance account. He'd thought he was going to be sick when he heard about that. If he could land Winthrop Trust, though, everything would be fine.

That was the whole point of clubs like this, Jim reminded himself. So that he could rub elbows with someone like Preston Winthrop and get a leg up on that asshole Paul, who was always needling him about moving to the suburbs, as if Jim was semiretired or something. Jim still remembered the phone call telling him he had been accepted at the club. He thought he had finally arrived, that all those years of hard work were paying off at last, but he had hardly had a good night's sleep since that day. He would wake up in the middle of the night sweating, his heart hammering away, the numbers spinning around in his head. He had to get that account!

Jim was the first to tee off, and he was more nervous than the first time he had argued a case in court. He fingered the club warily, as if it might suddenly decide to turn on him. He told himself to relax as he settled over the ball, but he could feel the swing go wrong from the moment he started it. He yanked the club back much too far. And his downswing was a frantic slash. The ball took a wicked slice and scurried into the prairie grass that flanked the right side of the fairway. He reached into his pocket for another ball.

"What do you say we play it clean today, Jim? No mulligans," Preston said breezily, as if he hadn't just watched Jim shank one into the weeds.

The others agreed—Todd even had the nerve to smirk at him—and Jim put the ball back in his pocket. Fucking Preston! Hadn't *he* taken a mulligan the last time they played after he knocked his drive in the bunker? The goddamn nerve! He wouldn't have minded needling Preston about that and hitting the mulligan anyway—as if he needed some sort of permission! It was galling. But he needed that account. So Jim swallowed the anger that was welling up inside of him and walked meekly back to stand beside his caddy.

When he joined the club, he thought his days of kowtowing were behind him. He had finally scaled the ladder and could relax and be himself. But he had been wrong, terribly, terribly wrong. Being a member of the Oak Hollow Country Club was one long exercise in deference and self-abnegation. He had to scrounge for tee times and a locker and playing companions. He had to treat the pro—that peacocking, gold-chained, bronzed, fat fuck of a pro—as if he were a goddamned Arabian prince. And each time he was forced to suffer through some small humiliation. He never got used to it. Every time it happened, it was as if another small corner of his dignity had been sanded down. In his darkest moments, he dreamed of quitting the club (good-bye $50,000 membership fee) and starting anew in another suburb where he wouldn't always be at the bottom of the food chain. Someplace like Schaumburg, where he could hold his head high and tell anyone he pleased to fuck off.

But Jim couldn't think about that now. He had to stay focused. He had to have that account. And if that meant he put up with a little shit from Preston, so be it. He would smile his biggest shit-eating grin, and he would laugh, and by the end of that round he would have the Winthrop Trust account if it fucking killed him.

Preston attempted to shake off his irritation as he drove home. He had played well, and the round passed pleasantly enough. Still, he was annoyed. That damn new guy, Jim. He couldn't stop dropping hints about the bank's legal account all day. Then in the locker room, pressing him like that. It was outrageous! The whole point of the club and of being so damn selective about the membership was so that people like him weren't badgered for business by people like Jim. He couldn't put his finger on it, but there was something he didn't like about Jim. Oh, he was perfectly polite. But there was still a little too much hustle about him, something that clung to him from the hard scramble up. Not that Preston thought about it in precisely those terms. If he was pressed to say how he felt, he would simply have said that some people were the right sort and others weren't the right sort and leave it at that. He was a man of action, not a philosopher.

Still, Preston was annoyed. It wasn't as if Jim didn't bring it on himself. I mean, my God, he shanks his drive and then immediately reaches into his pocket to take a mulligan. Of course, it was customary to do that, but he didn't so much as glance at the rest of them. As if he had been a part of their foursome for years when he had been a member for only a year or two. So Preston put him in his place. He didn't say anything offensive. But he made it clear that someone like Jim couldn't reach into his pocket for a mulligan any damn time he felt like it. Of course, Jim's face showed that he understood. That big grin as if he were a kid caught with his hand in the cookie jar. The fact that he accepted Preston's suggestion without a whimper showed what sort of man he was. Contemptible allowing himself to be cowed like that.

Preston could see how angry Jim was when Preston took his own rolling mulligan on the sixteenth tee. But that was different. Todd sneezed in his backswing. And Preston wouldn't have taken a mulligan if Todd hadn't told him to take it. You see, that was the difference. Preston didn't presume. Of course, he had glared at Todd until the offer was made. But the idiot had sneezed in his backswing! How hard was it to hold it in for another couple of seconds? Todd was a jackass.

But it was what happened after the round that really bothered him. As if the dozen hints on the golf course hadn't been enough, Jim insisted on giving him this whole *pitch* as Preston sat in front of his locker and changed his shoes. Preston played golf to get away from thinking about the bank, and the last thing he needed to be reminded about on a Saturday was changing law firms. He wasn't even planning on changing firms. He had only started the damn rumor so that Stein and Thurman would feel some heat and lower their fees, not so that people like Jim would hassle him on the golf course. Besides, Jim wasn't a partner. Preston would never deal with anyone except a partner. Jim wouldn't stop bothering him, though, so Preston told him to arrange a meeting with Perkins. He smiled when he thought of how Perkins would treat Jim. He would be willing to bet that Jim would be a little less presumptuous the next time they played golf together.

Of course, thinking about Perkins only got him annoyed again. That idiot would never see the big picture. Just a bean counter. He opposed every single thing that Preston wanted to do. Like this whole law firm thing. Now that the bank was so much larger, it had every right to throw its weight around, and Preston didn't see what was wrong with using its size as leverage to get a discount with their old firm. It wasn't as if Stein and Thurman hadn't made plenty of money from the relationship. They had been the bank's firm from the beginning. But did that mean they were supposed to grow fat at his expense? No, he had had enough of their complacency and their inflated fees. Unsurprisingly, Perkins hated the idea, even though the man loved nothing more than saving a dollar. My God, if Preston let him have his way, people would have to requisition one pen at a time. But when Preston tried to sell his idea by appealing to the bastard's cheapness, Perkins just kept repeating that the legal bills were so high because of the acquisitions. As if the bills were Preston's fault! It was infuriating. If Perkins was in charge, they would still be the same small-time bank they had always been. Creeping along and opening one new branch every couple of years. As if that was any way to build an empire. Goddamn bean counter!

An enormous sense of relief washed over Jim as he drove home. It wasn't a done deal yet, but he had the meeting with Perkins. That was the important thing. Preston wouldn't have set that up if he hadn't been impressed. Of course, the round of golf had been torture. Preston seemed determined to stick it to him every chance he got. Like that fucking putt on the sixth. All these guys giving each other putts right and left, and then they make him putt out that dinky little three-footer. Even though it didn't mean anything! The hole was already decided, and they just stood there and waited for him to putt as if it were the goddamn PGA tour or something. And when he missed it, Preston laughed, and then Todd jumped in and said, "Well, now that you've done that, we're going to have to make you putt them all." Fucking Todd giving him grief about his putting! The guy had the yips so bad that he used a belly putter. It had been like that the whole round. And then Preston had taken that mulligan on the sixteenth tee. What the fuck? Jim could have a single-digit handicap if he started giving himself a fucking do-over in the middle of the round. But he had kept his mouth shut and smiled blandly as Preston re-teed. It took all his self-control, but he held his tongue. And hadn't he been rewarded? He put up with their shit, but he closed that fucking deal in the locker room. He stood there and sold the hell out of himself, and now he had a meeting with Perkins, the number two guy. Rich guys like Preston were like that. Sometimes they made you put up with a ton of shit to see if you could take it, and then if you passed the test, you became one of the gang. Hell, Jim wouldn't be surprised if he became a semiregular member of the foursome, and then one day he could take his own rolling mulligan on the sixteenth. It cost a fortune to be a member of the Oak Hollow Country Club in more ways than one, but if it helped him land the Winthrop Trust account, it would be worth every penny.

CHAPTER ELEVEN

Behind a high, ivy-covered wall and gates topped with spikes stood Winthrop Hall. At one point, the Winthrop grounds had covered hundreds of acres and much of the east side of town. Preston's father had turned it into a semiprivate park and stocked it with exotic wildlife. Guests would spend hours walking the footpaths, and they could almost imagine that they were seeing it the way it had looked before the first white settlers had crossed Lake Michigan. But an environmental group had started talking about how there was a rare breed of deer in the park, an endangered species, and government officials came around and discussed how the use of the land would have to be regulated and monitored. And no goddamn government bureaucrat was going to tell Preston Baird Winthrop Jr. what he could do with his private property! The week before government inspectors were scheduled to come out and do an official survey, he hired a group of professional hunters and slaughtered the deer. Every single goddamn one of them. It was a good thing, too, because property values exploded in the coming years as the merely wealthy flocked to live beside the obscenely rich. By the time he had sold off the last parcel to a developer, he had substantially increased the family fortune. Of course, there was some awkwardness afterward, since the town had originally been named Deer Park. But it was a small matter to change that to Eden's Glen. A far smaller matter than letting some goddamn paper pusher tell Winthrop what he could do with his property.

Today, the Hall sat on twenty acres of lakefront property. From a distance, it looked like a Greek temple, a Parthenon on the shores of Lake Michigan. Its masonry seemed built to withstand time itself. According to property records, it was one of the largest private residences in the state. And even with the diminished grounds, it was still a magnificent setting, especially on the night of the annual Winthrop summer gala, always held the weekend after Memorial Day ever since Preston's grandfather had thrown the first party more than half a century ago.

After passing through the gates, cars followed a long, curving driveway through a copse of woods before emerging beside the formal gardens that bordered the grounds. The centerpiece was the lawn itself, a sea of perfectly mown grass that looked as if it hardly knew the touch of human feet. It took an entire afternoon—typically Tuesdays, unless it was raining—for one of the gardeners to cut the grass with a massive green tractor mower typically used on golf courses. He would patiently sweep back and forth across the vast expanse, neatly decapitating uncountable blades, each cut stalk spilling its life in the service of a higher cause. An infinitesimally small loss, a mere intimation of mortality. A testament to the beauty that could be wrought from so much harsh pruning.

On the afternoon of the party, caterers swarmed over the grounds with the single-minded focus of ants, setting up tables and piling dishes high with smoked salmon and caviar and rack of lamb and shrimp and oysters. Others set up tents and tables and chairs. Several bars covered in yellow cloths had sprouted around the grounds like summer dandelions.

And a swing band could be heard warming up on the flag-stone terrace overlooking the lake.

The guests arrived in the golden light of the early summer night, and even those who had been coming to the party for years found themselves overwhelmed with the splendor of it. The life-size ice sculptures. The gift bags crammed with expensive wine and truffles and scented candles. The sheer bounty of it all.

Baird stood off to one side of the patio and hoped that no one would notice him. He was growing so fast that his mother had to buy him a new tuxedo every year, so he was never comfortable in any of them. It was as if his clothes could never quite catch up with his body. This year, his shoes were too tight, and the sleeves of his jacket were a bit short. He put his hands in his pockets and hoped no one would notice. Catching sight of his reflection in one of the windows, he saw that his bow tie was already askew. He was afraid to fix it because the whole thing was threatening to come apart. He wished he could wear a clip-on, although the look on his father's face when he had made that suggestion shut him up quickly enough. The way his father had gone on and on about the importance of tying your own tie—by the end of it, Baird would have been happy never to wear a bow tie again. It was only seven o'clock, and Baird was already dreading the long night ahead.

The party was well under way when Norman and Paige arrived. Strings of white lights twinkled around the estate, and the crowd twirled and mingled under the stars, sipping Champagne. And the glitter from their smiles and their diamonds matched the glitter of the lights and the glitter of the stars and the glitter from the waters of Lake Michigan. It was dazzling, Norman thought. Absolutely fucking dazzling.

He still couldn't believe he had wrangled an invitation to this party. Not that it hadn't cost him. He had basically bribed one of the senior partners by giving him the commission on that currency swap. But it was worth it. Norman walked through the entryway and stopped to stare at the marble staircase sweeping up each side of the large hall. He couldn't help but think of his own entranceway and staircase, which suddenly struck him as puny and insubstantial. The wooden balustrade seemed like a child's plaything compared with the heavy polished surface of the marble.

Paige tugged at one of the straps on her dress. It was too tight, and she was self-conscious. She should have bought a new dress but had vowed not to buy any new clothes until she lost all her pregnancy weight. She worried that everyone was staring at them. They should have come earlier, but Norman had read some stupid book about New York socialites last year and now insisted on arriving late wherever they went. He told her it was distinguished, that Gloria Vanderbilt was famous for arriving at parties only as they were ending. What was he doing reading a book about socialites? For a while, he had also stopped wearing a watch, despite having bought himself a very expensive Rolex the previous Christmas. When she asked him about it, he simply replied that if you were important enough, people would wait for you.

John Duggins walked over to Mark and Sylvia Blake, who stood near one of the bars in the entranceway. He noted with pleasure that Mark's tuxedo was a little tight. Sylvia leaned over to kiss his cheek. She wore a shimmering black dress that clung loosely to her body, and her blond hair fell across her face quite becomingly as she leaned forward.

"Good to see you, John," Mark said, holding out his hand.

"How's the golfing dynamic duo?"

"Fine, just fine," Mark replied.

Mark looked at Sylvia with a tight smile. He couldn't remember when it had started. Years before. When they were first married. All of the older couples seemed to live separate lives. He and Sylvia promised each other that would never happen to them. Could never happen to them. And that was how it began. Their weekly golf game. Proof that their relationship was never going to be like other people's. And now they had to play. Every week. Every goddamn week. Because it was their thing. And because people knew it was their thing. And if they didn't do it, people would talk. They didn't invite other couples along anymore or take caddies because they both had grown too afraid of what the others would see. But it was too late to change anything. Continuing the charade was really the only answer, although it pressed on Mark more heavily with each passing year. But no, no, there was nothing to be done.

He tried to remember when things had begun to change, when the game had become his weekly torment. Or when Sylvia had started to take such malign pleasure in it. Every wayward drive, every lost ball, every shank, occasioned a comment. One of those snide remarks she had become so adept at. He had been a fairly good golfer before he married her, but under her withering stare he rarely broke eighty. And she had become a stronger player, seeming to feed off of his own diminishment. She was the scratch golfer now. He could see her smile to herself every time he skulled a chip shot. He swallowed the rest of his drink and tried to focus on what John was saying.

"Well, John, we should let you mingle," Sylvia said. "Poor Mark keeps finishing his drink."

She gave Mark a patronizing pat on the back.

"Eases the pain, right, Mark?" John said with an ambiguous smile. He gave Sylvia another kiss and let his fingers slide down the bare skin of her back. Then he licked his lips and walked away.

Anne stood in front of the mirror and looked herself over carefully. Even she had to admit she looked perfect—or at least as perfect as a thirty-eight-year-old woman with a child could look. Sitting down to touch up her makeup before going downstairs, she could see Preston moving around in the walk-in closet behind her, putting on his tuxedo.

She smiled to herself as she thought about her first party here—how nervous she had been. She hadn't eaten all day and had almost passed out when she was walking down the stairs. Not that she needed to worry. Everyone liked her from the start. Of course, Preston's father could be a little overly friendly when he had too much to drink, and she grew to resent the casual hand he would rest low on her back or the wet lips he would press against her cheek to greet her, although at first those attentions had reassured her.

They lived in the gatehouse then, but she had taken her things over to the Hall and dressed in one of the bedrooms. Preston looked so dashing in his tuxedo. She thought she had never seen a man look so handsome. He came to get her before they went down and helped her zip up her dress and then tried to persuade her to unzip it, although she was too nervous for anything like that.

She missed those early years in the gatehouse. It was such a cozy place. Old stone walls and mullioned windows and a big fireplace in the living room. It was nestled in a small grove just inside the gates, and during the summer, the leaves hid the house so that you could imagine you lived in a magical forest where nothing bad could ever touch you. Not that the

Hall wasn't wonderful on a night like tonight, but most days it felt cold and empty. She supposed it would have been different if she had had as many children as they had hoped for. They would have filled the Hall with noise and life. But the complications from Baird's birth made that impossible. Now the gatehouse was shuttered. Such a shame, really. When they moved out, Anne had brimmed with ideas on how to make use of it. Perhaps as housing for a few local students on scholarship at the college or as a children's library for the town. It was a crime to leave such a charming house empty. But Preston found something to object to about each suggestion, and Anne eventually dropped the idea. Sometimes she thought Preston missed it as much as she did, and she would fantasize about the three of them moving back there, although she knew that cramming themselves into that little house with its tiny kitchen and old wiring was absurd when they had the Hall to live in, like Marie Antoinette playing at being a peasant girl.

No matter how long Anne lived in Winthrop Hall, though, she felt as if she didn't quite know who she was in this vast expanse of columned hallways and stately rooms. Her own life hadn't prepared her for anything like it. Her father was a successful executive for IBM, and they had a comfortable life. Renting cottages on the Jersey shore for the summer. A new car every few years. But nothing like this. And her father had been content with quiet, domestic comforts. At night, he used to play checkers with her. But it was impossible to imagine Preston playing checkers. Not that she had any right to complain. She had everything she could wish for. More than everything, in fact. Besides, hadn't her mother always said that it was the wife's responsibility to mold herself to her husband's wishes? And that was what Anne had done. She had been a dutiful daughter. And now she was a dutiful wife, although occasionally she wondered if she was too dutiful, too yielding. But look at what she had won. Preston was the great prize, wasn't he? How could she view it any other way? And what good would it have done her to be less dutiful? It would only have made everyone around her unhappier, including, she suspected, herself. The things she had given up had cost her no great pain. Of course, she would have enjoyed a project like making the gatehouse into a children's library. It would have been great fun to wander down and help with the various programs, to sit there in the soft light of late afternoon and read *James and the Giant Peach* to a group of rapt children and then pass out candy and send them home with a small gift. But she could understand Preston's objections. People driving in and out all day. The insurance risk.

Still, Anne missed those early years in the gatehouse— quiet nights by the fireplace listening to Preston talk about the bank and then lying in each other's arms and sharing low whispers about starting a family. Life was filled with endless possibility, and now—well, now it seemed filled only with routine.

Not that she could complain. Everything had turned out as they had hoped. Preston was running the bank. They had a wonderful son, and yet—it was just that life became more complicated as they grew older. Preston didn't talk in the same way about the bank. Not with the same enthusiasm. He was always worrying about the new branches or Perkins or something. And their own relationship had become not exactly cool but somehow perfunctory. Diminished by time, instead of enriched.

And their son—she loved him, of course. In fact, she adored him, but she knew Preston was worried about him. Not worried. That was too strong a word—but concerned. Baird would be the one who would have to carry on all of this, and

Preston had his doubts about whether he was up to it. She was always reassuring to him, but she knew what he meant. Baird wasn't like Preston. He wasn't going to be the class president. He didn't command attention when he walked into a room. She often thought he looked as though he wanted to hide. But he was a teenager, and teenagers were awkward. And Baird had other, quieter virtues that she cherished. He would turn out fine. If only he wasn't an only child. It was too much pressure to put on him. Too many expectations. She would have to talk to Preston about that. She worried about the way he talked to Baird—as if Baird wasn't a teenager, as if he should be ready to step in and run the bank at a moment's notice. Of course, she couldn't really blame Preston, not after the way he lost his father. But she would speak to him.

"Preston, will you zip me up?"

He came in, still struggling to get his cuff links attached.

"Here, let me." She threaded them through and then adjusted his bow tie and looked up at his handsome face. She chided herself for her ungenerous thoughts and for the vague sadness that occasionally enfolded her in the afternoon when she was waiting for Baird and Preston to come home. Yes, she reminded herself, I am very lucky. She turned and presented her back.

Preston looked at Anne's face in the mirror and smiled. She was a good wife. He was a lucky man. He reached down and zipped her up and remembered the first time he had done that in this house many years ago. God, he could barely restrain himself. She was like a goddess. He could still remember the first time he had seen her at one of his fraternity mixers. "Who is *that*?" he had asked. And when he was introduced to her, she laughed—this tinkling little laugh that banished any worry—and he thought, I would like to hear that laugh for the rest of my life. She was still a beautiful woman, and he often reminded himself of that, although he couldn't help noticing the places where her skin was mottled from too much sun as he zipped up her dress. They never worried about getting too much sun when they were young, and now they both slathered on suntan lotion before a round of golf as if their very lives were at stake.

That was life, he thought. You lived your life one way and then everything changed and you had to live your life a new way. When he had been young, he had thought he would be perfectly content with taking over the bank one day from his father and raising a son to take over from him. And now he was doing exactly that, so why was he sometimes so dissatisfied about it all?

Alone at night in his study, he would occasionally stare up at the dour portrait of his father on the wall and wonder if he had worried about his legacy, worried that people would look at his life and think he hadn't accomplished enough. But his father had died long before Preston had started thinking about those sorts of things. Now he was surrounded by young M.B.A.'s, the whiz kids, he called them, who chanted the same mantra that a business must grow or die. Preston had come to believe them, had started to think that if he didn't build the bank up, it—and he—would fail. But he also had Perkins in his ear constantly nagging him about the numbers, and he sometimes worried that he had made a mistake. Maybe he wasn't building the bank up but destroying it under a mountain of debt. Maybe he had already failed miserably, but the failure wouldn't become visible for years as the folly of his purchases worked their way through Winthrop Trust like a cancer.

And then there was Baird. He wished they had more children, that the complications with Baird's birth hadn't made that impossible. An heir and a spare, wasn't that the saying? He liked Baird. He really did, but the boy was so damn shy and sensitive. It was hard to imagine he could ever leave all of this in his son's hands. If not Baird, though, who?

He loved Anne, but he sometimes thought that all of this would have been easier in an earlier time when there were plenty of things a wealthy and powerful man could do to deal with the problem of succession. Like Henry VIII—not that he would ever do anything like that. But in those days he could have found a number of ways to have more children. That didn't mean he would love Anne any less. He dimly remembered some lines from Shakespeare about a dull, stale, tired marriage bed, and it was true. There wasn't the same passion, the same intensity. How could there be after all these years? He didn't blame her. It was a fact of life. Anne seemed happy enough, though, and he was a good husband, even if the bonds of matrimony chafed a bit. He knew he had nothing to complain about. His life was blessed. He didn't want any sort of drastic change. If only he could have felt the old enthusiasm about things. That would have been enough.

"What's the matter?" asked Anne.

He looked at his frowning face in the mirror and rearranged it into a smile.

"Nothing, darling, absolutely nothing."

When they finally descended the broad marble steps hand in hand, the hundreds of guests burst into spontaneous applause, moved by the abundance of it all, the dizzying plenty. It was like a glimpse of perfection. No, more than that—it was as if for one night under the dying stars, all could rest content, dazzling in the reflected glory. Preston squeezed his wife's hand and realized that his worries were foolish, that he already had everything any man could hope for and that nothing would ever breach the high stone walls of Winthrop Hall to disturb his domestic idyll.

Norman had intended to stay in the background. Technically, he hadn't been invited to the party, but as soon as he saw the Winthrops, an overpowering desire to meet them swept over him. By the time he was halfway across the giant entrance hall, in his mind he had already sold his house, moved to the east side of town, and become good friends with Preston.

"Stop tugging me! Why are you dragging me across the floor?" asked Paige, but he hardly heard her. He managed to push his way to the front of the stairs just as his hosts alighted on the floor.

"Norman Bond," he said, thrusting his hand in Preston's direction.

He could see the look of confusion on Preston's face.

"Good friend of Chase Smythe," he added.

"Ah, well," said Preston, shaking his hand, "nice of you to come."

"This is my wife, Paige."

"It's a pleasure," said Preston. "This is my wife, Anne."

Norman wasn't sure he had ever touched a hand as soft as Anne's, and he pumped it vigorously.

"We're new to town," he said, "so we're very grateful to be invited and meet people like yourselves."

Norman noticed that his voice had taken on a deferential tone, and he despised himself for it. He was trying to be this man's friend, not his manservant. He could see Preston's attention drift to another part of the room, so he pressed on.

"By the way," he said as casually as he could, although he felt as nervous as a schoolboy, "you wouldn't happen to know if anyone here could talk to me about joining the club?"

"Sure, just have a word with John," Preston said genially, pointing to a man with a polka-dot bow tie by the bar. "He's on the membership committee."

"Thank you," said Norman, bowing slightly before he realized what he was doing. But it didn't matter. Preston and Anne had already drifted off to say hello to another couple.

Damn annoying fellow, Preston thought, but what could you expect when you had a party this size? He imagined this was how the lord of the manor felt when the village descended on his castle for a feast day, although he couldn't picture a peasant walking right up to the lord and grabbing his hand as if it were a cow's udder. Still, the man was a guest, and his wife was not half bad-looking. A little plump but that almost made her more appealing. He sometimes wondered if Anne didn't keep herself too thin. Not that he could have convinced her to gain any weight given the way her crowd felt about that sort of thing. But it made her face look a little haggard. He experienced a twinge of guilt for thinking such thoughts and smiled down at his wife reassuringly.

Anne looked up at her husband and knew exactly what he was thinking. She had seen that flush on his face as they descended the stairs, that same flush he used to get when they were first married, when she would catch him looking across the room at her and beaming with pride. She worried sometimes that he was losing interest in her. Well, not losing interest. She knew he still loved her. It was silly to worry about it. They had been married for eighteen years. She couldn't expect him to look at her the same way he had in the beginning. Still, it was reassuring to see that she could still make his pulse race a bit.

Of course, it didn't hurt to have him see her next to that plump little woman. Cute in a fifties sort of way but hardly the kind of thing to catch Preston's eye. And that toad of a man was quite repulsive. The way he shoved himself in their faces. Did he really think he could join the country club? It was unimaginable. To the wife's credit, she seemed embarrassed by her husband. Anne caught herself midthought and was ashamed at her own snobbishness.

Costas already had quite a bit to drink by the time Preston and Anne made their entrance. Maria kept warning him to slow down, but it was the only thing that helped him keep the slow burn in his gut from raging out of control. He placed a proprietary hand on Maria's arm and was grimly pleased that she let him keep it there. She looked fucking gorgeous. In the soft light of the summer evening, he was reminded of how she had looked when he first met her. When she had made his blood boil and his breath come in short, ragged gasps.

And look at him. Fucking potbellied mess. It was hard to imagine that he was the one who had asked for the divorce, that she was the one who cried and begged him to stay. Now he would gladly have taken her back, although even through the boozy vapors, he knew that wasn't really true. He would never be able to stop thinking about the men she had slept with. All he would be able to feel would be fury at her betrayal.

Maria was giddy with excitement. She had waited for this night for weeks. She kept catching Costas leering at her but pretended not to notice. She let him keep a hand on her and experienced a pleasant warmth from the familiar touch, although she didn't show it. Costas stayed interested in her only because she pretended to be so uninterested in him. She had been made wise by too many reconciliations, too much tearful forgiveness after Costas's latest affair. There would be several wonderful weeks, sometimes months, when she would think that he had really changed. Until the familiar signs re-appeared. Late nights, drinking too much, attending some ridiculous golf pro conference in the winter. It was always the same. One thing Costas couldn't be accused of was too much cleverness. But she savored these small moments when she could imagine that nothing had ever happened to change things between them.

Preston composed his face as he approached Costas. He could see that he'd had too much to drink, and he regretted inviting him. Of course, he had never intended to invite him, but he had been talking to one of his friends about the party in the locker room when Costas walked by. Then Costas just stood there, staring at him. It was a damn awkward moment, and as gracefully as he could, Preston invited him to attend. He thought Costas might refuse, but he had been disappointed in that.

It wasn't that Preston thought of him as the hired help, al-though of course that was what he was. They were certainly friendly, playing golf together and sharing the occasional drink afterward in the clubhouse. But he missed the old distinctions of his father's world. It had always been Mr. Winthrop at the club and yes, sir, and no, sir. Now here was Costas at the party, and it didn't feel right, like inviting the maid—actually, the help were invited to the party. It was an old family tradi-tion, but they knew enough to show up early and leave dis-creetly soon after darkness fell. He was always Mr. Winthrop to them.

And then there was Costas's temper, which grew worse each year. Perhaps it was the drinking. Whatever it was, though, it was damn unpleasant. Swearing and tossing his clubs. And the way Costas was always grasping to take their money on the golf course and falling into a sullen silence on the rare occasions he lost. With the outrageous prices he charged in the golf shop, it was hard to imagine that Costas had any money worries.

Just before he reached Costas, Preston noticed Maria, and he wondered why that damn fool brought her. The woman wasn't even his wife anymore, and she had slept with a good portion of the membership. Of course, Preston reminded himself, Costas didn't know any of that. Why shouldn't he bring her?

Anne noticed her husband stiffen almost imperceptibly as they approached Costas. She knew he had become increasingly reluctant to play golf with him, but she hadn't known that things had grown quite so bad.

When Costas leaned forward to kiss her cheek, his hot, boozy breath filled her nostrils. He pressed her tightly and let his lips linger a little longer than she liked. She was reminded of that night a few years ago when they had all been at the end-of-summer bash at the club, and Costas had followed her down the hallway when she had gone to the bathroom and pressed himself drunkenly against her. She had pushed him away, and she still remembered the look on his face—like a little boy about to be punished. She had never told Preston. He would have had Costas fired. She wouldn't have minded that, but Maria would also have had to go. Anne had always admired Maria, the way she had weathered the divorce and Costas's abuse. Of course, Anne had heard the rumors, but she tended not to believe them. She thought a lot of it was simply envy about the way Maria looked, and Maria herself always went out of her way to be helpful. Anne enjoyed their brief chats whenever she was in the shop, and she often thought that in a slightly different world, the two of them could have been great friends.

"Maria," Anne said warmly, "I'm so glad you could come."

They chatted awkwardly for a few minutes, trying to ignore Costas's looming, sullen silence.

"Yes, well, I won't let Costas keep you from socializing with your other guests," said Maria, trying to make a joke out of it.

They chuckled weakly, all of them except for Costas, who was busy swallowing the last of his drink. Preston and Anne excused themselves, but before they could step away, Anne could hear Costas muttering something about Preston. She wasn't sure what, but she saw Maria give Costas a sharp glance, which shut him up.

She enjoyed the party that night. She always did, although there was an uneasy knot in her stomach from the encounter with Costas and Maria. She wondered if she should reach out to Maria and help her find something else to do, something away from Costas.

Norman stayed late, far later than Paige wanted. If he had his way, they would have stayed to the very end, and he would have found an opportunity to share a quiet moment with Preston and Anne and show them that he was far more polished than that brief first encounter might have indicated. As he drove home, he was upset that his wife hadn't let him bid his hosts good night, which she should have known was only simple good breeding. Of course, he also wanted another chance to chat with Preston, if only for a few seconds, but if good manners and his own self-interest went hand in hand, what was the matter with that? Paige had insisted, though, pointing out that Preston was surrounded by his friends and didn't want to be bothered with people saying good-bye. And he was. Standing at one of the bars with six or seven men around him, all of them laughing and smoking cigars. Couldn't she understand that was what Norman wanted? He longed to be a part of that group with their cigars and their brandy, all of them circled around Preston Winthrop.

In spite of that disappointment, though, the night had been a triumph. An absolute fucking triumph! He met someone on the membership committee and arranged to come to the club for a round of golf. He had pressed the flesh as the politicians liked to say. He must have handed out two dozen business cards. Thank God he'd remembered to bring them. No one else seemed to have any, and he wondered how they could be so unprepared. He wished he had remembered to hand one to Preston. He had a beautiful gold case, and he liked to produce the card with a small flourish that always impressed people. At one point in the evening, he found himself at the bar next to Anne and had exchanged a couple of remarks about the weather in a casual tone, as if the two of them were old friends. Yes, he thought, this was the beginning of a whole new way of life.

When Anne saw Maria kiss Preston good night at the door, the knot in her stomach tightened. It wasn't that there was anything in the kiss, but there was something about the way her hand rested on Preston's neck that made her uneasy. To push away the thought, she became giddy. She drank too much and flirted with the men who remained at the party. And by the time she and Preston walked up the stairs hand in hand, she had almost forgotten.

As she undressed in her sitting room, an immense weariness stole over her. Perhaps if she hadn't had so much to drink, she wouldn't have allowed that niggling thought to creep back into her mind, and she would have hesitated before calling out to Preston in the bathroom.

"I was surprised to see Maria tonight."

———

Preston looked at his face in the mirror and experienced an overwhelming sense of relief. Another successful party. Another year when the family tradition had been renewed, the family's place in the town reaffirmed. Not to mention that near debacle with Costas and Maria. Good God! He would never invite Costas to another party, no matter how awkward the situation. He heard Anne call out to him from the other room.

"What was that, dear?" he asked, entering and beginning to undress.

"Maria," she continued. "I said I was surprised to see her tonight."

Her face was flushed. She had had too much to drink, and she had flirted more than usual at the party. Preston had noticed all of this and planned to speak to her about it. Now was not the time, though. He wanted to let her enjoy the night. He knew these parties were as stressful for her as they were for him. Even after all these years.

"Yes, I was surprised, too. She and Costas have an unusual relationship."

"I had no idea that things between you and Costas had sunk so low."

"I'm hoping that inviting him to the party might help fix that."

Yes, tonight had been particularly unpleasant. Costas's belligerence. His surliness. Preston had put up with it for about as long as he could, but if things didn't change soon, he would have to do something. Perhaps speak to the golf committee. Maybe it was time to bring in a younger, more deferential pro. He sometimes worried that Costas knew about Maria and him, that his little mistake was at the root of it. But he didn't see how it was possible. He knew Maria would never say anything, and he obviously never said anything, except for a stupid joke he had made one time at a party after drinking too much. That could hardly be it, though. One joke was hardly a confession. No, Preston was confident that no one knew about his little misstep.

"I wonder if Maria has something to do with it," said Anne. "Costas has always had a bad temper."

That wasn't really true, but it had been true for the last several years, long enough that everyone had forgotten about the easygoing Costas.

"I hear things, you know, things about Maria."

Preston turned away from Anne and pretended to be struggling to get his cuff links off.

"I wouldn't listen to that kind of idle gossip."

"I guess you're right." She paused. "You haven't heard anything, have you?"

He forced himself to laugh and turned to face her. "No," he said, chuckling, "you women talk about that sort of thing much more than men do."

He pulled Anne to her feet and hugged her.

"And why would I concern myself with any of that when I have you waiting at home? The most beautiful woman in Eden's Glen."

Anne was glad for the hug, glad to be able to bury her face in Preston's shoulder, glad to be able to hide a little longer from the fear that Preston had slept with Maria. Sometimes, she thought, you knew your partner too well, too intimately. For years, she had always known when Preston was lying to her because he would make this forced laugh to cover it up. She never told him about it. She liked knowing what he was really thinking. She could ask him if he was worried about things at the bank, and when he laughed and said no, she knew he was worried. Things like that. Things a wife should know. Now she wished she had told him. What was she supposed to do? Maybe she was wrong. Maybe he really was laughing. Maybe it was all her imagination.

Baird was relieved that the party was over, although he felt uneasy, as if he still needed to be on his best behavior. It was always this way after one of the family's parties, as if all those people left behind little pieces of themselves that echoed down the long hallways like ripples from a pebble that continue to lap against the far shore long after the stone has sunk to the bottom. He pulled the sheets more tightly around him and waited for the ripples to end.

In some of the best houses in Eden's Glen that night, men emptied their pockets on their dressing tables before going to sleep. In the morning, bleary-eyed, they found a business card from Norman Bond among the coins and keys and money clips. A thick, expensive card embossed with gold filigree. They would have to think for a moment about where it came from, and then they would remember the bumptious little man handing out his cards—at a social occasion no less—with a ridiculous flourish. It became a running joke, and after that night a few of them started pulling the golf ball out of the hole after a particularly nice putt and presenting it with a flourish. It became known as the Norman salute. Years later, long after almost everyone had forgotten where the salute came from, members continued to offer the Norman salute to one another in mock deference to a golfing triumph.

CHAPTER TWELVE

Baird always experienced a slight sense of dread before a round of Sunday golf with his father. So often something went wrong. Normally his mother played, too, so he had someone else there. But she had stayed in bed this morning and sent them off alone.

He gripped the driver, and for a moment he felt flush with promise. In one fluid motion, he coiled his body, paused, and then unleashed a perfect drive, his ball carving a high arc over the corner of the bunker on the dogleg first hole. He watched it disappear from sight and smiled at its perfection.

"Nice drive," said Preston.

They walked in silence down the first fairway. Baird's ball had come to rest 220 yards from the hole. He took out his three wood and with an easy grace floated a high, soft shot right at the flag. His father looked at him with a raised eyebrow. By the time he was standing over his ten-foot putt, he knew it was going in before he finished his stroke.

"An eagle!" shouted Preston.

Baird grinned sheepishly.

"You keep playing like that, and you're going to make the varsity next year!"

Baird shrugged.

"You know, it's not too late to do a summer golf camp. I could make a few calls on Monday. What do you think?"

They had reached the second tee, and Preston was still talking about it and about how Baird was going to have to start practicing more and maybe find a good swing coach in the area. A rising anger gripped Baird. Why couldn't his father just let him enjoy the hole? He turned his left hand far past his usual grip on top of the club and snapped his drive into the woods.

"You can't hit them all perfectly," said Preston.

He suppressed a sigh and patted Baird on the back. He didn't know what he had done wrong, although he could tell that Baird was upset. Teenagers were always angry about something—although he couldn't remember ever being angry with his father. Too busy being afraid of him. If his father had seen a look like that on his face, Preston could imagine how he would have reacted. Maybe it was just a stage, although what kind of boy gets angry after an eagle? And then to hit such a terrible drive. It almost seemed deliberate. And what had Preston done but be supportive and encourage the boy to make something of his game? Was that a crime? To be supportive? Anne was always telling him not to push Baird too hard, but what if that was the problem? Perhaps he needed to push him harder. Baird seemed content to drift through life. Hell, he was going to graduate from high school without making any sort of mark at all. And any time Preston offered the slightest suggestion, like the golf school idea, Baird reacted as if he had been punished.

Preston wondered again if he had made a mistake not sending Baird away to boarding school. Anne had won that argument in the end. It was hard to tell a mother that she had to send her only child away four years earlier than she had expected, and Preston had assumed it was only a matter of time before Baird found his stride. With each passing year, though, Preston became more doubtful about whether or not he would. That this nondescript, unprepossessing teenager was going to grow into a nondescript, unprepossessing man. He blamed Anne in part. Too much coddling. Always hovering over him and smoothing away any problems. But Preston also worried that he was responsible in some obscure way. No Winthrop before him had any difficulty producing not just a son but the necessary sort of son. How was Baird ever going to be ready if he kept on like this? And there was Anne telling him not to push the boy! When what he needed was pushing. And not a gentle nudge, either, but a hard shove in the right direction.

Maybe he wasn't strict enough. He knew what his father would think about this new age child rearing. He would snort and say it was a load of crap. Preston once had to sit through a dinner party next to some woman who spent the entire evening telling him about what a special child she had and how his misbehavior was really nothing but misunderstood creativity, and all Preston could think was that the child needed a good spanking. But how was he any different? He had never spanked Baird, never even grounded him.

If he only knew how to talk to the boy. He tried to encourage him. But something always went wrong. If Baird had been more like him, he would have known what to say. It wasn't that he didn't love Baird, but goddamn it! It was time for the boy to start growing up. When was he going to take some responsibility? He was happy to drift along and take everything as it came. Like his golf game—the boy had talent. Preston could see that. It was as if he didn't care about it, though, or didn't want to cultivate it, to *work* at it. Sometimes Baird seemed to play poorly to spite him, although he knew that was crazy. Didn't the boy realize the future of the family rested on him? Preston tried not to think about that, but some nights he couldn't fall asleep because of it. Although he tried not to show it, he was afraid that Baird would turn out to be a disappointment, that he was already a disappointment.

Baird eventually found his ball and, for good measure, sent the next shot sailing across the fairway into a creek that ran alongside the hole. And he hated himself as he hit the shot. He could see his father pretending to look for a club so that he wouldn't have to say anything. Baird wanted to make his father happy, but any time he did anything well, his father started talking to him in a way that made him feel like a lab rat being trained to push a button. It made him sick. He wanted to throw his clubs into the creek and run away. Once, he had tried to talk to his father about it. He couldn't remember what he had said. He'd mumbled a few words about feeling pressured, and his father had given him this look. As if he were stricken or something. It was as if he were looking at him and wishing Baird weren't his son.

CHAPTER THIRTEEN

An immense sense of well-being filled Norman as he drove his Volvo to the train station. A new Volvo as his train car! Of course, he still needed to replace the old station wagon, but it was fine for now. Paige and the baby could use it to run errands. He admired the unblemished dashboard and ran his fingers along the pleather seats, and a small sigh of contentment escaped him.

Norman pulled into the station parking lot and assembled himself for the train. Brand-new leather attaché, freshly pressed coat removed from a hanger on the backseat hook, quick buff of the shoes with a cloth he had placed in the door pocket, and a careful inspection of his reflection in the side window.

As he walked to the train, his sense of well-being curdled. He didn't mind the Mercedes station wagon parked next to him. Someone using it as a train car and a family car. That was fine. Next to that, a BMW, an Audi, another BMW, a Porsche. By the time he reached the platform, Norman was convinced that the Volvo was a second-rate car. How had he ever let himself be bamboozled by that salesman? It was ridiculous. You took one look at that thing, and you could tell it was a piece of crap. Where was the so-called European styling? The flair? And now that he thought about it, he could swear that the

engine was making a funny sound. Goddamn it! They had
sold him a lemon! Well, he would just see about that! He knew
the law! They couldn't stick him with some fucking lemon! Of
course, he would probably have to pay a penalty to get out of
the lease, but what of it? He wasn't going to risk the life of his
wife and child on some junker!

He tried to read the paper while he waited but found himself
having imaginary conversations with the dealer in which Norman showed him in no uncertain terms who was who and
what was what. At last, the train arrived, and Norman collected
his things and tucked his newspaper under his arm. He noticed
that a number of the men were crowded around the doorway of
a car toward the back of the train, and then he realized that
the car didn't look like any of the others. For one thing, it
wasn't a double-decker. It was low, and there was only one set
of windows. It looked as if it was from another era. Norman
wandered over to the group just as Preston disappeared inside.
Excitement surged through him. So this was the car that Preston Winthrop rode in! He had to restrain himself from shoving
past everyone else and hurrying up the stairs.

A tall black porter stood at the doorway, nodding at the
men as they ascended. Norman held out his ticket.

"I'm sorry, sir. You need a different ticket to ride this car."

"I'm happy to pay whatever the difference is," Norman
said, reaching for his wallet.

"I'm sorry, sir. I can't sell it to you."

"Well, where can I get it?" Norman was starting to get
anxious. Did he have time to run back to the station and buy
another ticket? He had to get onto that car. Preston Winthrop
was in there!

"Sir, this is a private car. Members only."

Norman experienced a thrill of excitement. A *private* car!
On a public train! He didn't even know such things still ex-

isted. It was like being back in the world of the Rockefellers and the Gettys. To ride in that car would be nothing less than an ascension, a coronation as a captain of industry!

"Well," Norman said, trying to seem somber and not let his giddiness run away with him, "who do I speak to about membership?"

"It doesn't really work like that," the porter said, waving a hand to another porter a few cars away in preparation for their departure. A rising sense of panic gripped Norman.

"I'm sure we can figure something out," he said, shoving a $50 bill into the porter's hand.

The porter glanced nervously up the stairs.

"All right, sir," he said, "but once you speak to someone, you'll have to leave the car."

"Of course," Norman said, confident that once he set foot in that car, he would never leave it again.

When they entered, Norman had to stifle a cry of excitement. My God! It was like stumbling into El Dorado! There was a minibar in one corner and two bridge tables at the other end and real leather seats. And not a lot of them. A row against each side of the train. There was so much room. No jostling elbows with some sweaty clerk. You didn't even have to fold your goddamn paper over!

"That's the one you speak to," the porter said, motioning to a man buried behind a *Wall Street Journal*.

Norman walked over to him and coughed delicately. The paper lowered.

"John!" Norman cried with relief. "Remember me? We met at the party the other night."

John Duggins glanced up from his paper and tried to remember who the man was. He looked vaguely familiar.

"I'm sorry . . ." He looked at him uncertainly.

"Norman. Norman Bond."

He thrust out his hand, and John offered a limp return.

"Remember—the other night at the party. We talked about me joining the country club."

"Ah, yes, of course," said John.

"I don't know if you kept my card," said Norman.

John couldn't resist watching him do his flourish again.

"Actually, I was looking for it the other day and couldn't seem to find it."

"Not to worry." Norman reached into his coat and produced the case with an exaggerated sweep of his arm, popping the lid just in front of John's face.

"Thank you!" said John, winking at a friend across the aisle when Norman looked down to replace the case.

"So," Norman said, dropping into the seat beside him, "what are the possibilities of taking care of this train car membership today? I'm happy to pay whatever the extra cost. Don't worry yourself on that score."

"That is certainly a relief," John said dryly.

"All right, then," said Norman, "where do I sign?"

"I'm afraid there is one problem," John said with a sigh. "You have to be a resident for at least two years before you can apply. Otherwise, any Johnny-come-lately—not someone like yourself, of course—but any Johnny-come-lately could start badgering us for admission."

Two *years*! Two fucking years! Norman couldn't wait two years! It was like waking up on Christmas morning and being told that the presents were postponed until next Christmas! It wasn't fair.

"I'm sure exceptions can be made," said Norman.

"I wish they could," said John, "but the rules are really quite strict."

Norman wanted to argue. Maybe he could bully John into it. He looked around the car, and everyone was staring at him. And there was something so settled about John's response. He was temporarily cowed. John seemed well-disposed toward him, though. That was something. It would help with Norman's membership at the club, and after that, he could always try again.

"I guess if that's the rule, that's the rule," said Norman, taking his newspaper out from under his arm. At least he could ride in the car today, he thought. Maybe trade a few remarks with some of the other men and show them what a good fellow he was.

John nodded imperceptibly to the porter.

"Excuse me," the porter said to Norman, "I'm afraid you are going to have to leave."

Norman turned with pleading eyes to John.

"I wish I could help you, Norman, but I'm afraid I have no power over this man. Train regulations."

"Fine," he said, standing up and walking to the door.

"Oh, Norman, I should let you know one other thing," John said. "There is a long waiting list for membership on this car, so you'll have to go on that list after your two years of residency."

The porter closed the door on Norman before he had a chance to reply.

"John, you old devil," said a red-faced man on the opposite seat. "Two-year residency requirement! Ha!"

"Yes," John said, chuckling, "well, when the barbarians are at the gates, you've got to do something."

CHAPTER FOURTEEN

Sunday morning was agony for Anne. She pretended not to feel well so she could stay in bed and send Preston and Baird off to the golf course without her. She thought if she could just keep busy until he went to work on Monday, she could sort through things. So she found a number of errands to run after they left and then insisted that they see a movie that night and tried to crowd everything out of her mind. But she realized later that she bought the wrong things and lost the receipts so she couldn't return them, and she couldn't remember what the movie had been about by the time they got back to the house.

She lay unsleeping in bed that night, grateful that Preston hadn't been interested in anything more, then worried that he hadn't been, and all along wondering what she should do. At last, she went to the bathroom and took one of the sleeping pills the doctor had prescribed for them when they had taken that overnight flight to Europe. She woke up late on Monday morning, feeling dull and sluggish. Preston and Baird had already left for the day.

She got up and made herself some fresh coffee and sat down to think, *really* think. But soon she was wandering down the long hallways and entering various rooms and rearranging things and then putting them back the way they had been in the first place. What did she really know? Nothing. She was being ridiculous. She should ask Preston. Maybe Maria had slept with one of their close friends. Surely that was it. Preston was trying to be discreet. If she could just stop brooding about it. If she could get out of the house and clear her mind, it would all pass. She decided to go into town for lunch.

As soon as she made her decision, a desperate urgency seized her to be out of the house immediately. She threw on a pink polo shirt and khakis and left without putting on makeup. She parked on one of the town's side streets and decided to eat at a small sandwich shop she'd never noticed before. She couldn't remember the last time she had lunched in town alone. Except for a gray-haired woman behind the counter, the shop was empty. Anne ordered a sandwich and sat down to wait. The small Formica table felt sticky under her forearms, and the salt in the shaker had frozen into an immovable block from the humidity. When the woman brought over her sandwich, Anne found that she had no appetite, despite the hollow feeling in her stomach, and she threw the sandwich away after a couple of bites.

As she was walking back to her car, Blanche Trevaline, one of her closest friends, started waving to her across the street. Anne forced herself to smile and wave back, and Blanche hurried across to meet her.

"What a party!" Blanche kissed her on the cheek and then drew back in mock horror. "Look at you! No makeup. Sunglasses. Someone still hasn't recovered from her big night."

Anne smiled weakly. Blanche rubbed her arm encouragingly.

"Don't worry. I was feeling a little worse for wear myself on Sunday. We're not the young girls we once were."

"I suppose not."

"By the way, you looked fabulous at the party! And Preston! My God, he gets better looking each year. He's like a movie star. I was joking with Rick that if he doesn't start losing weight, I'm going to clone Preston and dump him." She laughed.

Blanche was one of the few people whose marriage Anne envied, which made the encounter almost unbearable. She felt faint and rested a hand on her car to steady herself.

"Anne, what's the matter? Are you all right?"

"I think I ate something that didn't agree with me," she said, getting into her car. "I'm sorry, Blanche. I'm really not feeling well."

As she drove away, she could see Blanche staring after her, and she had a sickening thought. What if everyone knew? What if people gossiped about her the way they used to gossip about Bob and Margaret?

She didn't want to go home, and she didn't want to see anyone, so she drove aimlessly around town, although that left her feeling trapped and exhausted, every road leading back to familiar places or ending in a cul-de-sac in some anonymous new development.

CHAPTER FIFTEEN

Norman couldn't believe how much it had cost him to get out of the lease on the Volvo. Goddamn shysters! He had driven the thing for only a few days. Still, what could he do? Now that he was on the Von Hoffman lot with its gleaming Mercedes sedans and BMWs, he already felt better. He had looked at the other license plates, and this was where people in Eden's Glen bought their cars.

Not that he was some sap. He was wearing an old sweatshirt and jeans—no need to flash his wealth around here. A salesman approached and held out his hand.

"Just looking?"

Norman couldn't help noticing the slightly mocking tone. He was glad he had worn his gold Rolex, and he stroked his chin with that hand.

"No, I'm here to buy, Sandy," he said, reading the man's name tag.

"That's great, and what would you like to test-drive?"

He wanted to test-drive the new coupé, but with all the money he had spent recently, he could barely afford the pokiest sedan on the lot. As they drove around the town, the salesman talked about the advantages of a Mercedes, and Norman nodded his head absently while picturing himself pulling up to the train station in this car. Yes, this was the one. He could hold his head up proudly in a car like this. He hoped he wouldn't have to keep a car seat in it for Norman Jr. He couldn't stand the thought of the baby spilling Cheerios and raisins everywhere.

By the time they were seated in Sandy's office, Norman had decided exactly what he was going to pay, and he knew he was going to get it. Christ, he negotiated prices all day long. And what kind of a name was Sandy? A girl's name? He thought he remembered a cute girl named Sandy from high school. Yes, Sandy was going to give him exactly what he wanted.

But Sandy proved tougher than he looked. As the haggling dragged into its second hour, and Sandy left him alone once more to talk to his boss, a rising fury gripped Norman. He wasn't there to be yanked around and screwed with like a goddamn yokel! They weren't the only Mercedes dealership. He had already gone $1,000 over the price he had decided on.

Sandy returned with an apologetic look.

"I'm really sorry. I talked to my boss—"

"I've been sitting here for over an hour!" said Norman, his voice rising. "And I'm not going to sit here much goddamn longer!"

There was a knock at the door. Norman looked up and saw Preston on the other side of the glass. Look at that head of hair! It was as if he had walked right out of the pages of *Gentlemen's Quarterly*. Norman hoped he hadn't heard him swear. He jumped out of his seat and followed Sandy out the door.

"Mr. Winthrop," Sandy said, "what can I do for you?"

"Sandy, my wife says her—"

Norman thrust his hand out. "Preston, great to see you!"

Preston gave him a confused look.

"We met at your party the other night. Remember? I'm Norman Bond."

Damn! He should have brought his business cards.

"Ah, yes," Preston said uncertainly, "good to see you. Now, Sandy, about my wife's car."

"Yes, of course. How can I be of service?" he asked, ushering Norman back into the office and shutting the door.

Norman sat down with an enormous grin. He was shopping for a car at the same dealership as Preston Winthrop! He knew this was the right place to come. Goddamn! That Von Hoffman plate was probably worth $5,000 alone. It might even help him get into the club!

Sandy hated being a car salesman. It was as if everyone had a license to treat him like crap. No one thought twice about calling a car salesman a liar, but he had to put up with the same bullshit from them. All the whining and pretending that if they went any higher, they would have to throw poor Granny out on the street. If money was really so tight, what the hell were they doing buying a Mercedes? And Preston Winthrop—talk about a fucking shark! The guy didn't even wait for Sandy to leave the room and pretend to talk to the manager. He left the room and got the manager himself, and by the time he and the manager finished chuckling over some idiotic story about when Preston's father had come in to buy a car, Sandy half expected Preston to be given the cars for free. That's right. *Cars!* Matching his and her coupés, one in silver and one in black. He had hardly made anything on two cars with a combined sticker price of almost $50,000! How the hell was he supposed to earn a living if he didn't get a big commission on a sale like that?

Without saps like this guy in his office, he would never make any money. You could see him coming a mile away. Sandy had a pretty good idea about how this would play out— he got one or two like him every month. The guy probably just moved to town, maybe owned an old Chevy, perfectly happy with it, never thought about it from one day to the next. And then he pulls into the train station for work that first day and looks around, and what does he see? Sandy knew what he didn't see—guys like Norman didn't see a six-year-old Chevy with 120,000 on the odometer parked there. Thank God for that train station. He owed half his commissions to that place.

It didn't hurt that Preston Winthrop had shown up at his door. Sandy could see the way Norman slobbered all over him. Hell, that little visit might be worth at least another thousand.

"So do we have a deal?" Sandy asked when he returned to the office.

"The price . . ." Norman sighed.

Sandy wanted to laugh. Before Winthrop had shown up, Norman had yammered on about how outrageous the price was. Now he just sighed. Sandy was going to make a lot of money on this sale. Maybe celebrate over a nice dinner with that cute receptionist who worked out front. A little flattery for Norman, and Sandy was home-free.

"Mr. Bond," said Sandy, "you seem like a smart guy. You know that you could buy this car more inexpensively somewhere else. But you know what you would lose? The Von Hoffman name. And that name means something. That's what brought you here. Why have Eden's Glen residents been buying their cars here for the last fifty years? Because they know we are a name they can trust."

"But if you could just come down a little—"

"I'll tell you what, Mr. Bond. I won't come down, but I will come up! I don't want to give you less than you deserve. For that price, I'm going to give you the extras. I'm going to upgrade your stereo and toss in rust protection and floor mats. Hell, those things alone would run you a couple of grand if I wanted to nickel-and-dime you. But I don't want to do that. I don't want to sell you a car and then tell you that you need to pay more for floor mats. That's not the way we like to do business here at Von Hoffman."

"I don't know. Rust coating—"

"I can see you are a man who values quality. That's why you're here. You know that trim package you were interested in? Same one that Preston Winthrop picked out for himself."

He thought he might have gone too far until he saw Norman flush slightly.

"That's right. Mr. Winthrop was in here buying a car from me not too long ago, and we had reached about the same point. And you know what he does? He reaches across the table and shakes my hand. So what do you say, Mr. Bond? Do you really want to keep haggling, or do you want me to take care of you?"

Sandy barely had the last words out of his mouth before Norman thrust his hand across the table.

CHAPTER SIXTEEN

Y ou slept with her, didn't you?"
   That was how it began. Anne had been thinking about what she was going to say for days, and then she just blurted it out one afternoon after Preston had come home from golf. Preston gave her a confused look, which only made her angrier.

   "Didn't you?" she repeated more loudly.

   "Slept with whom?"

   Even the punctilious way he said it made her angry.

   "With Maria. That's *whom*."

Preston resisted the urge to correct her. He knew whom she was talking about from the moment the accusation had left her lips. There was something about their encounter with Costas and Maria at the party that had left him uncomfortable, a slight disturbance that continued to hum inaudibly through the household.

   "That's ridiculous."

   "Is it?"

   "You know it is."

   He had been stupid to sleep with Maria that time, but he was drunk, more drunk than he had been since his college days. He had won the club championship that afternoon, so the drinking started early. Then there had been a bachelor party at the club. And by the time that had finished, he had been drinking for nearly eight hours.

He had gone down to the golf shop to sleep it off on one of the couches. It was late, and he didn't want to wake up Anne. The light had been on in the office. Maria was in there doing something with the books. He slurred an apology and stumbled off to the couch. She followed him and laughed when she saw how drunk he was. He couldn't get his studs undone. She sat on the couch beside him. Her small, delicate hands unbuttoned his shirt and untied his shoes. Then she reached up and ran her fingers through his hair. And that was how it happened.

When he had awakened the next morning, there was no sign of Maria, and he had hurried up to the locker room to take a shower and change clothes. That damn fool he sometimes played with when he was desperate for a partner saw him and gave him a lewd wink as if he already knew all about it.

As time passed, though, it was as if nothing had happened. Maria never mentioned it again. Costas treated him as if he didn't know about it. No one said anything to him in the locker room. He began to think of it as a bad dream.

"I'm not sure what I know anymore," said Anne.

Preston wanted to hug her and reassure her, but she was standing on the other side of the kitchen island with her fists clenched and pressed against the stone countertop.

"You know you can trust me," said Preston.

Anne wanted to trust him. She wanted what he was saying to be true, wanted it desperately. But she had to know. She had to be sure. She didn't want to be one of those women people talked about, the ones whose husbands were always having

affairs and who stumbled around drunk at cocktail parties
with glassy eyes.

"She told me. Maria *told* me."

For a moment, a flicker of fear licked at his heart, but it passed.
He knew that if Maria had wanted to say something, she
would have done it a long time ago. He tried to smile reassuringly.

"Anne, darling, you know that's not true."

If they hadn't been married for almost twenty years, that probably would have been the end of it. She would have let him
come around the island and take her into his arms and whis-
per how much he loved her. But Anne knew everything there
was to know about Preston, knew him in the way that only
devoted and attentive care over years can let you know a person better than that person knows himself.

She knew what his lucky shirt was when he had a big
match and how he had a special way of combing his hair that
his father had taught him, how he always kept his hands at ten
and two on the steering wheel. She knew that he thought he
didn't like almonds but would eat them if they were put in
front of him. She knew that if he drank two beers after golf,
he would take a nap in the afternoon and that if he had more
than two cups of coffee at breakfast, he would be snappish
later. She knew the difference between his real laugh and his
business laugh and the way he held his face when he was feigning interest but secretly bored. And she knew, when she saw
that brief flicker of fear, that he had slept with Maria.

She had known before, of course. That was what she told
herself later. She had known since that moment at the party,
but she both knew and didn't know. Or knew and hoped she
didn't know. She wanted desperately to be proven wrong, so

her knowledge was a tenuous thing, ready to go away with the right reassurance. But now she *knew*—knew on some deep, fundamental, unalterable level. It was as if a key suddenly turned in a lock, and all the complicated gears meshed into place, and it could never be undone.

And everything changed—or seemed to change—in her mind. It was as if she had been looking at her marriage in a fun house mirror that had made it seem normal and happy, but now she was standing in front of the real mirror. Or maybe this new mirror was the fun house mirror. Her mind was spinning, and she wasn't really sure. Anne only knew that everything looked different, distorted and ugly. Everything from their past came rushing back at her but from a slightly different perspective, as if she hadn't really seen what was happening the first time but only now understood the significance of long forgotten moments, understood fully the real meaning behind various remarks and gestures and silences, a knowledge so clear as to be almost unbearable. Those nervous smiles when he would return from a business trip or the furtive glances when she would ask him about an odd expense on the credit card or those times when she tried to call him in his hotel room, and the phone rang and rang and rang. It was as if she suddenly learned that everything about her marriage was based on a lie.

After hoarding her fear for days, it cracked open like a rock splitting after a winter freeze. She screamed terrible things at him with this new knowledge. Words poured forth that she hadn't known were in her. Awful things. Hateful things. About the lie their relationship had been, about their life together, about her, but most of all about Preston. Ugly things about him. Things designed to wound him as only one's most intimate lover knows how to wound. Words meant to unman him, to annihilate him, to make him disappear from her sight. Words meant to destroy their years together in a single furious blow.

Preston stood there in horrified silence. When Anne finished, when her fury was spent, and she glared at him silently across the countertop, he turned around and walked out of the kitchen without a word. He crossed the terrace and descended the steps to the lake through dark woods and branches heavy with leaves crowding down on his head and the occasional glint of sunlight. He took off his shoes. The sand was warm under his feet, but a cool breeze was starting to come off the water, which made him shiver.

He began to walk down the beach but stopped when he came to a steel erosion barrier. A small, plastic triangle was poking out of the sand. He pulled it out. It was a toy airplane, the once bright red dulled by the sun. There was a small figure glued into the cockpit. He vaguely remembered a day years ago when they had brought Baird down to play at the beach. Baird lost the plane—his favorite toy at the time—and cried and cried. Preston must have spent an hour scrabbling through the sand and searching in the water trying to find the damn thing. Had it been here all along? Or had it washed onto shore after years in the water?

He turned it over in his hands and studied it. He could imagine the surprise and delight and laughter at dinner if he suddenly pulled it out and placed it on the table. Or at least the delight that they would have had if this hadn't happened. Now what was the point? He took a last look at the plane and threw it as far as he could into the water. It made a small splash and sank slowly out of sight.

Preston walked the beach for hours until the sand grew cold beneath his feet. He tried to find a place in his world for the terrible things Anne had said to him, but he couldn't. He had made a mistake. She had a right to be angry. But to speak to him as she had—it almost seemed worse than what he had done. She acted as if there was nothing between the two of them but lies and unhappiness. It was as if her words had been the culmination of years of accumulated misery, not anger at one brief infidelity.

And what right did she have to be angry? Look at her life, at what he had given her. And it wasn't as if he didn't have his own disappointments, his own secret unhappiness due to her. Like having only one child. He wouldn't have been so worried about Baird if they had only had another boy or two, and he would have loved a daughter, loved to spoil her and lavish pretty things on her the way he couldn't with a boy. It wasn't fair to blame Anne for that, but it certainly wasn't his fault. And the way she still held herself aloof from Eden's Glen as if she weren't sure she was really happy there. He had made her the queen of this world, and still she would look around her as if she longed to be somewhere else. As if there were something wrong with his world, as if there were something wrong with *him*.

As he thought more about it, Preston's heart hardened against Anne. By the time he finished his walk on the beach, he felt as if he were the injured party, that what Anne had said was unforgivable. Well, perhaps not unforgivable but close to it. Very close to it.

After Preston left the kitchen, Anne sank to the floor and cried. She cried loud, wet tears that ran down her face and puddled on the red Spanish tile. She cried about Preston and Maria and about what she had said and about Preston leaving without saying anything. But mostly she cried because she felt as if the Anne she had known, the Anne she had been, had died and gone forever, and she didn't know who was going to take that Anne's place.

When she finished crying, she stood up and poured herself a glass of water and waited for Preston to return. She was no longer angry, just exhausted. And there was a nagging sense of guilt about what she had said to him. Then she was angry at herself for feeling guilty. And it was in this spirit that she went to look for Preston.

She couldn't believe he had just left the room. It was so cowardly. She hadn't planned to say those things, but she was upset. And she had every right to be upset. He was supposed to stand there and listen, to let her say whatever she needed to say. And then they would talk. That was how it was meant to go. Preston wasn't supposed to storm off like a little boy. It was as if he didn't care.

When Preston finally climbed the stairs back to the house, Anne was waiting for him on the patio.

"Where have you been?"

"I went for a walk."

She waited silently, but he turned his back to her and stared out over the water.

"Is that all you have to say?" she demanded.

"Anne, what do you want me to say?" he asked wearily.

"You could start with a goddamn apology! You could start by saying that you were sorry for sleeping with that whore!"

Anne's words ignited the hurt and anger that Preston had been nursing during his long walk on the beach.

"Fine," he said, "I'm sorry. There. Does that make you happy?"

He looked at her with defiance. Her face slackened as if she had just been slapped.

"Well? Are you happy now?"

He could see she was about to cry, but he didn't care anymore. Rage welled up inside him. Where was *his* apology? Why was he the only one who was supposed to feel remorse?

Before either of them realized what they were doing, they were shouting. Their voices clanged against each other and echoed out over the vast, silent waters. Blaming each other for real and imagined disappointments. For being boring in bed or a bad parent or shallow. A host of grievances, many that hadn't existed until they were named, all spilling out in one long, continuous screed.

Preston slept in one of the guest bedrooms that night. They both assumed it would be for one or two nights, but in the yawning silence after their fight, a night became more than a week as they clung to their grievances both real and imagined. When Anne announced abruptly one night that she was moving out of the house, Preston was not surprised. He was not even upset. All he felt was an enormous sense of relief.

CHAPTER SEVENTEEN

Anne told herself she couldn't bear to live another night in Winthrop Hall, although she had been telling herself that for more than two weeks without doing anything about it. She kept waiting for everything to go back to normal. Surely Preston would apologize at some point, and they would move on. But he never did. Worse, he went around with an aggrieved air, as if she were the one who should apologize. And with each passing day, it extracted a heavier toll, until she decided that she *had* to move. Only she didn't. He should be the one to move, she thought, but that would never happen. Preston Winthrop was not going to move out of Winthrop Hall. But where was she to move to? The difficulty of that question left her lying awake in bed at night until she was forced to take a sleeping pill. And when she awakened from her restless sleep, she was more exhausted than when she went to bed. She could have moved into the gatehouse, of course, but that held too many painful memories. And she couldn't stand the thought of living in the shadow of Winthrop Hall. She could have gone to stay with her mother, but the thought of that was unbearable. Her mother adored Preston, and Anne could just imagine the lectures she would get about how she should fix things. As if it were all *her* fault! Any number of friends would have taken her in, but that would be so public and demeaning. She still believed that with a little luck they would figure things out before anyone found out about it.

That left her to look for a place to live, but there weren't many houses to rent around Eden's Glen—that was the way people wanted it. Besides, getting a place in Eden's Glen would have made the break so permanent and public. A declaration that she was setting up her own residence. As if moving out was the prelude to an actual divorce. And even as she moved out, Anne didn't really think *that*. She thought of it more as a temporary escape from the agony of living alongside her husband but no longer living *with* him. Unbearable to lie in their bed at night and think of him down the hallway. Trying to put up a reasonable front around Baird, although their dinners were silent, hastily eaten affairs on the few nights Preston didn't come home late from work. The torment of Preston's rigid politeness. He never said a harsh word, but every gesture, every word, was delivered with a chilly correctness. She couldn't stand it anymore. She couldn't stay in the house one more night.

Not that Preston showed any signs of strain, Anne thought resentfully. Of course, he had never been one to give way to feeling. He valued propriety too much. That had been part of what attracted her at first. It made him seem mature compared with the other boys she had dated. He never lost control, never drank too much or swore or took liberties on the dance floor. But she had always assumed that his reserve would disappear over time, at least with her. In those confused days drifting listlessly through the Hall, she found herself wondering if Preston had always been cold. Perhaps the warmth she had thought existed between them was her own invention, a veil she had thrown over their relationship to hide the painful truth. Winthrop Hall had always struck her as an inhospitable place, but maybe it wasn't the Hall. Maybe it was Preston himself. Then she would remember some moment in their marriage—like the time Preston hired a chef from a local restaurant to cook her a surprise Valentine's Day dinner—and she would wonder if, in truth, the marriage had been full of warmth. Occasionally, she would catch herself thinking of the marriage as if it was already in the past, and she would burst into tears and hide in the bedroom.

But after a couple of weeks, it all became too much to bear, and she forced herself to get in her car and drive to nearby towns to look at places. The accumulated misery of those wearying days convinced her that moving out might somehow fix everything, that she just needed a little space. Perhaps it was the lack of sleep or the never-ending emotional strain, but she never considered the possibility that moving out would widen the breach. She simply knew that she could not spend one more night in Winthrop Hall until things between Preston and her returned to normal. So she overcame the lethargy that had paralyzed her since the day of the fight and began her search. But the houses she visited were dank, drab affairs that left her feeling hopeless. As she hurried from place to place on that steamy June day, Anne grew increasingly frantic. Having stumbled on the belief that moving out would fix things, she clung to her conviction until her failed search began to seem like some dreadful omen, a presentiment that things were already irretrievably lost.

At last—it must have been the ninth or tenth house—she saw one that she liked. It was dusk, and the evening light cast a warm glow over the small house. It wasn't big, but she hardly needed much space. It was only her, after all, and she didn't imagine that she would be there for very long. She just needed a little time alone to collect herself and sort everything out. Some time for Preston to miss her. The house was furnished, and it was clean, which was more than could be said about the other places she had seen. If she had visited it first, she might have been more critical, but she had seen it last. Last on a long, enervating day. The couple—a young academic and his wife, who were going away on sabbatical for a few months—didn't ask her to sign a lease, which made it all seem so wonderfully temporary. One day soon, she and Preston would talk things through, and he would acknowledge that he had acted badly, and they would walk out hand in hand and leave this all behind as if it never happened. At the time, she was so grateful she could have cried, although regrets and doubts crept in soon after.

In the cold light of her first morning there, she started noticing things she hadn't seen the first night. Nothing terrible. The backyard was lovely, and she could look out her windows and see the small flower garden at the far end of the yard. But a large oak tree shadowed the house and kept it in semidarkness for most of the day. At Winthrop Hall, she usually spent summer mornings sitting on the terrace bathed in sunlight. And the furniture was not entirely to her taste. Oh, it was perfectly nice. Better than she had hoped to find. An Ethan Allen dining room set. A gray couch. After she moved in, she noticed that the couch had a stain on it. Just a small, dark circle on one of the arms. It wasn't as if her family room couch didn't have a stain or two, but somehow this was different. She knew where those stains came from. The time Baird had dropped a piece of pizza, for instance. And somehow those stains gave her a cozy reassurance. They were artifacts of their shared past. Nothing like this unknown stain. This small, dark spot that was a constant reminder not of a shared history but of her presence as an interloper. This is not *your* couch, the stain seemed to suggest. But it went even deeper than that. Although she sometimes found Winthrop Hall oppressive, she had grown accustomed to the many daily comforts of living there. She always pooh-poohed them. She liked to tell herself that she didn't need any of that, didn't even want it, that she would be happy living much more simply somewhere else, but she found that she did miss it. She had always believed that she wasn't one of *those* people, those calcified souls who pronounced life positively unlivable anywhere but Eden's Glen. And now here she was. Missing life in the Hall. Missing Eden's Glen. The quiet afternoons sipping iced teas with friends at the club, the sedate parties with white-coated waiters offering to freshen your drink.

It added to Anne's unhappiness to think of Preston sleeping comfortably in their bedroom—the Egyptian cotton sheets and the custom-made bedspread and the dozens of other careful touches she had added to make the room comfortable. Living happily in the rooms *she* had decorated! She would try not to think about it, but then she would see that small, dark stain on the couch. She did love one thing about the house—the bathtub, an old claw-foot model. Deep and large. She sometimes felt as if she spent most of every day soaking in the bath. Occasionally, she would slide under the water's surface and shut her eyes tightly and enclose herself in perfect stillness, almost like being in the womb. If only she could have held her breath until everything returned to normal around her, but eventually her aching lungs would force her back up, and she would look around and think, No, not back to normal.

After her bath—always so long that it left her skin pruned and translucent white like a gutted fish—she would dress herself listlessly. She had moved all of her clothes in one frenzied afternoon. Armfuls tossed haphazardly on the backseat of the car. And a large, rolling suitcase filled with her makeup— realizing how small the three closets cleared out for her use were only when she started trying to put everything away. It left her feeling defeated, and she soon gave up the effort to get organized, leaving piles of clothes strewn on the bedroom floor. And there was no room for all of her makeup in the small cabinet above the bathroom sink, so tubes of lipstick and bottles of perfume spilled across the floor and rolled around underfoot. She soon realized that she could have left most of it at home anyway. She had taken clothes to dress herself for a life she no longer led. She had outfits for the club and for nice lunches with her friends and more formal clothes for evenings out. But she didn't want to do any of those things. The idea of going about her usual routine filled her with revulsion. Most days, she pulled on the same old pair of khakis and a T-shirt. Sometimes she wore the same clothes for two or three days in a row.

She didn't have to live like this. There was plenty of money sitting in their various accounts, and Preston wouldn't have said a word. But pride kept her from taking more than a bare minimum as if the money itself were tainted. She could have hired a lawyer and forced Preston to pay her maintenance. But getting a lawyer was so final. She wasn't ready to take that step. No, Anne thought, this is all temporary. Soon everything will go back to normal.

And then there was the overwhelming guilt she felt about deserting Baird. What had he done to deserve this? So overcome with her own misery, she hadn't given enough thought to him. She realized that now, although she wasn't sure what she could have done about it. To protect Baird, she would have had to stay, and that would have meant a tacit acceptance of what Preston had done. She had thought that she could still take care of him, even if she wasn't at home. She planned to return to the Hall every afternoon to spend some time with him. And that was what she did. At least at first. She would get in her car and drive to the Hall and make some sort of snack for him to eat when he came home. She hated doing it, hated having to enter the Hall every day as a stranger. She no longer belonged in her own house. But she did it for Baird. Only it didn't work out as she planned. It just wasn't the same, her coming over like that. There was nothing casual about it. In the past, if she had asked him about his day and he didn't want to talk, Baird would grunt some reply and go up to his room, but now they would sit awkwardly at the kitchen table and make stilted conversation in a failed attempt to act as if nothing had changed. She longed to explain the reasons why she had left, but she knew she couldn't do that. How could she tell Baird about what Preston had done? For all of Baird's awkwardness, she knew that underneath he worshiped his father. So she fell back on vague answers—Preston and she were simply taking a break, sometimes adults needed a little time away from each other—that did nothing to address the confusion in Baird's eyes. These awkward encounters made her feel as if she were somehow in the wrong. Although they never spoke about it, her visits gradually became more infrequent, which was both a relief and a lacerating source of shame. She told herself that when this was all over, she would find a way to make it up to Baird.

With each passing day, though, the longed-for clarity that physical separation was supposed to provide only seemed further out of reach. She had imagined that Preston would repent and ask for forgiveness after a few days of separation. A week at the most. In Anne's darker moments, she worried that even this would not be enough, that she would realize some crucial piece of the relationship had been destroyed by his infidelity, leaving unsolvable the puzzle of why one person falls in love with another. But moving out only mired her more deeply in confusion. She had cut herself off from everything that was familiar and found herself without any sense of how to take the next step or even what that next step should be.

My God, she had never held a job, never even graduated from college. She could still remember the argument she had with her father about that. One more year at Bryn Mawr and at least she would have had a degree. But Preston was older and ready to get married, ready to move back home, and she was afraid of losing him. No, not just afraid. Terrified. Preston was her whole life, and the thought of being apart from him was unbearable. And it wasn't just the physical attraction, although he was so very handsome in those days. There was also something about him that was deeply comforting. He was so sure of who he was, of his place in the world. At ease with himself. It wasn't that she was flighty. Well, perhaps a little bit in those days. But she had no clear plan and certainly no settled idea about who she was. Being with Preston anchored her. It was as if she discovered who she was only when she found him.

So she had left Bryn Mawr and married him. And now at thirty-eight, what did she really know how to do except be a wife and a mother? She used to be proud of that, but now it seemed like a terrible failing, something to be ashamed of. Her life had unfolded like a fairy tale, and she had glided from one success to another. Nothing had prepared her for this, for the crippling self-doubt that left her paralyzed with indecision. How could she go back to Preston on these terms? She felt weak and pathetic. So her thoughts went round and round as one day slid into the next.

She would go for a walk and tell herself that she was going to think—really *think*—and figure out what to do. When she returned home, though, she couldn't remember what she had thought about—just fragments of memories from her marriage or childhood, as if the answer were to be found in some forgotten corner of her mind. And whatever she was looking for remained out of reach.

CHAPTER EIGHTEEN

Baird spent most of his time in his room. He didn't like to walk around the house. It was like a tomb. His mother had always provided most of the noise of daily life—the conversation and the laughter and the questions about when he was going to do his homework. His father was a more remote figure. Even when they were throwing a ball around or watching television together, there was a distant air about him, as if he were trying to solve a thorny problem.

He thought of his family as something that just *was*. Like in geometry class when the teacher had talked about how the triangle was an essential shape in math and nature. That's how he thought of their family, as a kind of triangle. His father was the base. His mother was the side providing the warmth and comfort. And he was . . . well, he wasn't sure what he provided. Baird supposed he represented the future or some crap like that. But now that his mother was gone, it was as though the triangle had collapsed in on itself, and his home felt alarmingly large and suffocatingly small at the same time.

At first, he didn't know anything was going on. He could tell that things were off. He wasn't stupid. Like at dinner. Normally there was a pattern to things. His mother would ask about each of their days and then tell them about hers. It had become a family joke between him and his father. They would groan and roll their eyes at each other and then dutifully recite the highlights. But one day his mother didn't ask about their day, and most of the meal passed in silence. And then on another day, she asked him about his day but didn't ask his father. And the food was different, too. His mother would forget to make gravy for a dish that had always had it, or she would leave something out of the salad dressing. His mother usually prided herself on her food. That had become another running joke in the family. When she was really excited about something she had made, she would start talking about what she had done differently for that particular meal, and his father would laugh and offer commentary in this deep announcer's voice as if he were narrating a cooking show. And then he would pretend to interview her.

"Well, Mrs. Winthrop, that was quite a coup, using rosemary like that. Can you tell us what gave you the idea?"

And his mother would get this serious expression on her face and say, "That's a good question, Dan"—she always called his father Dan when they did this—"I suppose it came together when I was reading *Gourmet* magazine last month and looking at a recipe for lamb."

"*Gourmet* magazine," his father would say in an exaggerated voice, "that sounds quite fancy. How does a woman like yourself stretch the budget to cook items from *Gourmet* magazine?"

"Sometimes it's a struggle, Dan. But the clever home chef is not without her tricks."

At some point, his father would turn to him.

He might say, "We have here a noted food critic. Well, Baird, what do you think?"

And Baird would try to say something thoughtful. He had loved this game as a young boy, although lately he found it a little corny and occasionally didn't play along, which seemed so childish now, when he would have given anything to find himself sitting at the dinner table with both of them and pretending they were all happily taking part in a cooking show.

His mother came to talk to him before she left. But Baird could hardly remember what she said. She kept asking him if he had any questions, but he hadn't known what to ask. She sat too close to him and kept hugging him and crying, and he remembered feeling uncomfortable and wanting her to leave. Then after she left, all he wanted was for her to come back. And once she was gone, he started to think of questions to ask. Like, Why are you leaving? Or, Do you still love each other? Or, When are you coming back? When he did see her, though, he would feel awkward and shy and wouldn't ask anything. He wondered if he should have said something to make her stay that day in his bedroom, that maybe she was looking for something from him that he had failed to give her.

He would think back over the days leading up to that teary farewell in his bedroom to try to remember some crucial detail that might explain things, but nothing struck him as unusual. One time, he thought he might have heard his mother crying in the bedroom, but he wasn't sure. And his mother always had days like that when she would sit at the table and stare vacantly out the window. If he asked her what was wrong, she would say something like "Oh, I'm just not myself today." One time he asked his father about it and was told that women were more complicated than men and that you couldn't worry too much about every little change in their emotions.

His father didn't seem to want to talk to him at all. He would sit in his study at night, drink in hand, and stare out the window at the darkening landscape. Baird tried to ask him once about what was going on, but his father told him it was nothing to worry about. And when he tried to ask again, his father got stern and sent him away.

He couldn't escape the feeling that it was all *his* fault—that if he had only been the kind of son his father wanted or if his birth had been easier and his mother could have had more children, everything would have been fine. Even at school, he felt different after his mother left, as if he were marked in some way. He couldn't actually tell if the other kids knew. No one said anything to him. He could see people whispering, though. But people were always doing that in high school. So maybe it was nothing.

He hurried through his days as if the simple passage of time might resolve everything. He would come home from summer school and go straight to his room. He had told his parents he wanted to take a few extra classes to strengthen his college application, but the truth was he dreaded the idea of working in the bank another summer. He would do his homework and watch television or play video games. Around six, he would listen for his father's arrival. Sometimes his father went to his study and didn't come out for the rest of the night. Other times he would come out again after a drink or two and call Baird down to dinner. They would sit there silently at the small table in the kitchen. His father wouldn't eat much and would stare out the window most of the time. Every once in a while, he would rouse himself to ask a question about school, but he would be staring out the window again before Baird finished talking. Baird didn't know what to ask his father about. He knew he wasn't supposed to ask about his mother. And he had always been taught not to talk about business at the dinner table—not that he would have known what to ask about anyway. So they mostly ate in silence. Baird would sit there tensed as if something momentous might occur, but it never did. At a certain point, his father would push his plate away, tell Baird to do his homework, and disappear back into his study.

One afternoon when no one else was at home, Baird pulled down the trapdoor in the back hallway ceiling and climbed into the attic. He hadn't been up there in years, but he knew exactly what he was looking for—a few old boxes in one of the far corners that held yearbooks and football equipment and a tiara studded with rhinestones that spelled out "Queen." A year ago, one of his friends had taken him down to his basement and pulled out a similar box, and the two of them had laughed at the old pictures of the boys' parents. In one of them, they held a small baby—obviously the boy himself— and they looked so awkward and happy, as if they had received a wonderful gift but had no idea what they were supposed to do with it. Baird remembered feeling as if this glimpse into their past was almost too intimate to bear, and he turned away and suggested that they do something outside. But now here he was on his knees, scavenging through old photos and flaking pages of newsprint containing tales of triumphs from long ago. If anyone had come upon him and asked him what he was looking for, he wouldn't have known how to answer. An obscure sense that somehow the answer might lie *here*. That he would find some clue that would explain things. Perhaps a picture that would reveal a latent unhappiness or a forgotten letter containing words to dispel his deep sense of unease. But he found nothing and grew tired of scrabbling through the musty pages, which offered only glimpses of happier days, like a kind of highlight reel that made his parents recede further and further from him until they were like characters out of a movie. Distant and remote and impossibly perfect.

He stood up and walked over to a small round window that

faced out across the lake. From this vantage point, he could see across the tops of the tallest trees to the endless expanse of gently rolling water, cerulean in the fading sunlight of late afternoon. He used to escape up here when he was upset as a child. He would stand on a chair and stare out the window and watch the undulating water until whatever was bothering him had passed, but now the view brought him no comfort. The hidden depths of the lake, the unseen far shore—it was as if the world itself had become a mystery whose simplest puzzles remained unknowable.

CHAPTER NINETEEN

Mark's breath was ragged as he ran up the final steep embankment before the trail leveled off and the forest ended abruptly to reveal a long stretch of rolling meadows filled with high summer grasses and wildflowers. This was his favorite part of the run. He could linger in these fields for an hour or more. Most of the time, he didn't bother to run. He would watch butterflies or lie on his back and listen to the wind. Anything to stay out of the house until Sylvia had a chance to down a couple of cocktails.

Of course, this, too, had become a source of complaint. At first she nagged him about how long his runs were. He didn't know why she complained. It wasn't as if she took any pleasure in his company. But gradually she turned her attention to his weight. How can someone who runs for so long be in such poor shape? she would ask. She made snide remarks about his waistline, and if he wore sweatpants, it was the main topic of conversation all night. Sometimes he was tempted to tell her. To spit his drink in her face and say that he was pretending to run so he didn't have to spend one more fucking minute with her than was necessary. But then she would know, and he might lose even this. So he shrugged and said that he must have a slow metabolism.

Sylvia was in fantastic shape. Of course, she didn't do anything, so she had plenty of time to exercise. Three hours. Every day. That included a little time in the steamroom and a shower and a salad with her girlfriends. He had to admit that she looked great, although he wished she didn't look quite so good, that she showed her age a little more. It was like a competition. As if she was trying to show him up in one more area of their life. To show him what a disappointment he was.

The only reason she stayed married to him was her sister, Mary, with her perfect husband, Tim. If not for them, maybe everything would have turned out differently. Mark and Tim had both gone to work for their father-in-law's company after they married into the family. Mark's work was fine, but Tim was a superstar. After a few years, it became clear which one of them was going to run the company after the old man passed away. And that was when things began to change with Sylvia. The way she looked at him shifted. There was a hint of contempt in her eyes. That was also when the teasing had started. About his weight or his hair or his golf game. It didn't really matter what. And then there had been the babies. He and Sylvia had two girls. Tim and Mary had two boys. Every time the old man pulled Tim aside and started talking to him about the boys, he could see Sylvia tighten up. So Sylvia wasn't going to let her sister best her in marriage as well. No, sir. In front of her family, it was all love and kisses and what can I get for you, honey, and do you need another drink, dear?

Mark loved his girls, but as they grew older, they took after their mother more and more until the three of them became a tormenting chorus. That was when he started running. It was hard in the winter because it was too cold to stay outside for more than an hour. But in the summer he could linger as long as he wanted. Sylvia barely looked at him anymore, so she never noticed if he was sweaty or not. And by the time she had a couple of cocktails, that coiled tension relaxed a bit, and the contempt softened to a general weariness. And Mark could make it through the night.

He looked out over the field with its splashes of extravagant color and let out a long breath.

Most of the time Anne didn't know what to do with herself. She didn't go to the club or see her friends. Every place was too public or too familiar, drenched in associations of Preston. And she was ashamed. The whole thing was a kind of personal humiliation. She was the one other women envied, the one whose approval most of them sought, and then suddenly to become an object of pity. The thought of it was unendurable. One afternoon she drove around aimlessly for more than an hour until she found herself in front of the nature preserve. She steered down a gravel road underneath the swaying trees until she came to a small, empty parking lot. Wandering through the trails, she came to a clearing with a bench, where she sat down and began to cry. She wept like a little girl until she exhausted herself and lay down on the bench and fell into a deep sleep. She woke only when she heard footsteps on the path. She felt as if she had been caught doing something inappropriate and looked around to see if there was someplace to hide. The steps drew closer until a tall man in running clothes stepped into the clearing and stopped. She hoped he wouldn't notice her and would jog off in a different direction.

Mark decided to stroll around the entire expanse of open field and turned to find Anne Winthrop sitting on a bench. He almost never saw anyone on his runs. He knew about her and Preston. Everyone knew. Of course, no one really knew anything. They knew only the basic fact that Anne had moved out. Preston hadn't said anything to his friends. The few who ventured to ask were rebuffed, and Preston Winthrop was not the kind of man you badgered about his personal life. Anne had simply disappeared. No one even seemed to know where she lived. Seeing her here was like a visitation from a ghost. When Anne moved out, it was a shock. The perfect couple. Of course, Mark knew how easy it was to hide a bad marriage behind a façade of public affection. Still, Anne and Preston. It was hard to imagine. Not that everyone hadn't enjoyed speculating about the causes. Mark didn't like these conversations. His own double life made it too uncomfortable for him to take part with any enthusiasm, and as he had stood quietly on the periphery of groups greedily dissecting the news, he was shocked by how much venom there was toward both of them. As if their previous perfection had been a standing affront to the community, and their separation was the obvious outcome for that kind of sham. After a few sympathetic words about how it would be hard on Baird, talk would turn to whether Preston had had an affair or if Anne was frigid. All of it seemed so wantonly cruel now that he saw Anne on the bench in front of him.

"Anne," he said uneasily. "What are you doing here?"

"I . . . I . . . don't know."

She looked as if she had just woken up. Her hair wasn't smooth, and her face was puffy. Mark had never seen Anne look anything but perfect. For no particular reason, he always vaguely associated her with Sylvia and with Sylvia's contempt. He was strangely comforted seeing her this way, and he sat down beside her.

"It's great here, isn't it? You feel like you could escape all the troubles in the world. I kind of feel like it's my own personal sanctuary. I run here every day."

Anne was fumbling with her purse. "I must look like a mess," she said.

He had never seen her so flustered. It made him feel gallant.

"Anne, you look beautiful. You're the most beautiful woman in town," he said, wondering at his own boldness.

Anne burst into tears.

CHAPTER TWENTY

Preston experienced a growing rage the time he found himself pushing his cart through the grocery store after Anne left and the housekeeper, Juanita, was away on vacation. He was a goddamn CEO, and here he was buying his own groceries. It was insulting, and he imagined that everyone in the grocery store was staring at him and laughing at the absurd picture of Preston Winthrop buying food. He should be at home reading a financial report or making important decisions, not deciding which goddamn frozen dinner to buy. Of course, if he had been home, he probably would have been having a drink, but goddamn it, that wasn't the point, was it?

He silently cursed his wife as he reached out and shoved anything that came to hand into his cart. Over the coming weeks, whenever he tried to eat one of these frozen dinners, something always went wrong. Either he didn't take off the foil before heating it up when he was supposed to, or he took it off when he was supposed to leave it on. Once an entire lasagna exploded, covering the microwave in a viscous red goo. He hadn't bothered to clean it up, and Juanita had not been happy about that the next day, although he didn't appreciate being scolded by his goddamn maid, who could barely speak a word of English. Later, after the remaining frozen dinners sat there for months and grew white with frost, Juanita threw them away. Later still, he would joke with his friends about how simple it was to shop and how he didn't see what all the fuss was about. How their wives were engaged in a vast conspiracy to make sure that their husbands didn't know how easy they had it. Years later, he liked to joke about the great female conspiracy. He embroidered and elaborated on it over time, and it always got a big laugh. Eventually he came to believe it was true, and he made fun of men who acted lost and helpless when they were on their own.

But that was a long way in the future. At that moment, as Preston stared into his freezer at the stacks of frozen dinners, at the Salisbury steak and chicken Kiev and fettuccine Alfredo, all he knew was that he was hungry and that none of the frozen dinners he had bought held the slightest appeal. He could hear Baird moving around upstairs, and he called out to him.

Baird came into the kitchen.

"Let's go get some dinner."

"I already ate."

Preston clenched his jaw in fury. "You already ate?"

"Yeah."

"Did you think that I might like to eat as well?"

"You weren't home."

"So you just thought you would go ahead and eat without me?"

Baird shrugged.

"And what did you eat after you decided not to have dinner with your father?"

"There were some leftovers from that casserole Juanita made."

"And did you ever think for one goddamn minute that your father might like some of that as well?"

Baird flinched slightly at the rising sound of Preston's voice. "I'm sorry."

"That's great. Just great. Maybe I will make a meal out of your sorrys tonight. How about that?"

"Dad, there's more left. I put it back in the fridge."

Preston walked over to the refrigerator and yanked the door open. A bottle fell off one of the shelves and exploded on the floor, splattering Preston's pants with oil.

"And did you think you should put things back so that they didn't fall all over the fucking floor when I opened the door?"

Baird stared at the ground. Preston grabbed the casserole dish out of the refrigerator. The bottom was still warm.

"And I suppose you didn't think that reheating the same leftovers again and again wouldn't be a problem! Let's leave aside the fact that this is going to taste like shit when I reheat it. We'll forget all about that because obviously what the hell does it matter what dear old Dad eats. Right? Let's just look at it from the standpoint of the fucking bacteria and God knows what else is growing in this right now. Do you really think I would put a piece of this in my mouth? Do you?"

Preston slammed the casserole into the sink, where it shattered, sending glass and chicken and noodles skittering across the countertop.

"Well, that's great, Baird. Thanks for thinking of me."

Preston stalked off to the bedroom to change his pants. Goddamn that boy! Preston had done everything for him! *Everything!* And what did he have to show for it? Goddamn son creeping around like a goddamn thief, sneaking into the kitchen to eat without him! He returned to the kitchen and found Baird on his hands and knees carefully cleaning up the floor. He felt a rush of shame and hurried out the door and into his car. He drove around for a long time. He kept approaching restaurants in town. But then he would catch a glimpse of a blurry face through the windows or see people walking down the sidewalk, and he would drive away. Finally, he drove two towns over to a dumpy hamburger joint sandwiched between a liquor store and a dry cleaner. He went in and sat at the bar.

"What can I get you?" the bartender asked.

"Burger and a double Scotch."

He looked around the bar. There was an old guy a few seats over, smoking and watching a baseball game on the television. A young couple sat at a table against the wall, whispering to each other. He should go home and apologize to Baird, he thought. But the boy could be so thoughtless. Why couldn't his son be a little more considerate? Was that too much to ask? He decided to stay and watch the rest of the game. By the time it ended in extra innings after midnight, he had had several Scotches, and he was a little unsteady when he got to his feet.

He walked carefully to his car. I'm fine, he thought, absolutely fine. Just have to be careful. He drove home slowly, staying under the speed limit and making a full stop at every stop sign. He relaxed as he neared Eden's Glen. A few more miles. The car was growing warm, and he stifled a yawn. Yes, just a little while longer.

He woke with a start when his head snapped forward and then back. Oh fuck, he thought! Fuck fuck fuck fuck fuck! He stepped out of the car and walked around to the front. He'd driven into a tree right by someone's driveway. Luckily, he had only been going about fifteen miles an hour when it happened. Fuck! The cops! What about the cops! He would get a DUI! His picture would be in the paper! A woman in an old bathrobe walked down the driveway toward him.

"Are you all right?"

Preston stepped back from the headlights into the shadows.

"Yes, I'm fine," he said, edging to the car door. If he could just get the damn car back home, everything would be okay.

The woman walked around the car to where Preston was standing. She looked up at him. "You're bleeding."

"Really, I'm fine," he said, putting his hand on the door.

She tilted her nose toward his face. "Have you been drinking?"

"Please, just let me go home."

"I think I'm going to have to call the police."

Preston crumpled to the ground. "Oh, God, please don't do that."

"Look, sir, you're drunk, and you just crashed your car, and you're bleeding."

"I know. I'm sorry. I'm not usually like this. Really. I've been going through a hard time."

He sounded idiotic. He put his head in his hands.

"Go ahead," he said in a strangled voice, "do what you need to do."

Vicky didn't know what to do. She still wasn't fully awake— she had been in the middle of a dream about her bakery. Row upon row of perfectly shaped lemon squares and brownies and éclairs. Everyone in immaculate white smocks. And then the crash awakened her.

God, he was a handsome man. He didn't look like a drunk. His skin was tan, and he had the most beautiful head of hair she had ever seen. Maybe he really was having a bad time. Or was she being ridiculously naïve? What did she expect? Some guy with the shakes and a bottle poking out of his pocket? Still, he was so good-looking. She couldn't believe it, but she was actually attracted to him. She could hear her mother's voice in the back of her head about how she always went after the wrong sort of man, and now here she was with a drunk who had just crashed his car.

"Why don't you come into my apartment?"

Jesus, Vicky! What are you thinking? Even as she invited him in, she was appalled at what she was doing.

"My car. We can't leave my car out here."

Vicky agreed to move it. She slid into the warm leather seat and eased the car into the driveway. They walked up the rickety steps to her apartment above the garage and sat down at a small kitchen table.

"So why don't you tell me about these hard times?" she asked, resisting the urge to reach across the table and run her fingers through his hair. God, he was gorgeous.

Preston recoiled when she asked the question. He didn't share personal information about himself. Certainly not with a stranger. But what choice did he have? He didn't want her to call the police.

"My wife left me," said Preston.

"You poor man."

She put her hand on his arm, and he began to cry. He hadn't cried in such a long time. Not when Anne left. Not when his father died. Not since he had been a young boy. Not *really* cried. Not like this with his shoulders shaking, struggling to catch his breath. Unable to stop for the longest time. When he finally calmed down, his reserve was gone. He told her everything then. It poured out of him in one long, incoherent jumble. Not just about the separation but about their marriage and what had happened with Baird that night and other random things that flickered through his mind. She put him to bed on her couch where he slept better than he had since Anne had left him.

———

Vicky stood in the living room the next morning, sipping her coffee and staring at the man sleeping on her couch. He looked even more beautiful in the morning, and she wanted to reach out and touch him. God, she was crazy! What was she doing with this man in her apartment? She could see the headlines: DESPERATE SINGLE WOMAN RAPED AND MURDERED AFTER SHE ALLOWS DRUNKEN STRANGER INTO HER HOUSE. Her mother would be quoted, telling the reporter how she had always warned her to be more choosy about men. Her friends would say that she had been a little flaky and lacked judgment. Preston stirred and opened his eyes. He looked around in confusion for a moment and then saw her.

"I'm so sorry," he said, starting to his feet. "This is . . . unconscionably rude. I should go."

"Why don't you get cleaned up first? You don't want to go home looking like that."

"I couldn't. I really have to apologize. I don't know what came over me last night. You didn't want to hear all that. I—"

"Preston, it's all right. Really. Now go take a shower. I put a clean towel on the sink."

Preston wanted to grab his coat and run through the door and somehow pretend that none of this had happened. But he found himself obeying her. After he shut the bathroom door, he looked at his face in the mirror. Vicky had cleaned up his cut and put on a bandage the night before, and he removed it gingerly. It didn't look too bad—just a thin line on his forehead.

He remembered the time he had cut his head on the stone ledge outside the kitchen door as a boy, and the blood had come pouring down his face and onto his chest. He went screaming into the house, thinking that he was dying, bleeding everywhere he went. Finally, one of the servants caught up with him and calmed him down and stopped the bleeding. He would never forget the look on his father's face when he saw all the places Preston had dripped blood. He had grabbed him by the collar and shaken him and told him to be a man, that it was womanish to be overcome by the sight of a little blood.

He took a hot shower. He tried to find a razor, but she only had a pink one that looked well used. He found himself staring at the shampoos and conditioners and lotions and makeup on her sink and bathtub ledge. Anne's side of the bathroom had always been neat, and now that she had left, it was empty. There was something comforting about this jumble of female products. He dressed quickly and walked back to the kitchen. Vicky was standing at the stove.

"I've made some breakfast."

"I've already imposed enough," said Preston, who had carefully rehearsed what he was going to say. "I really can't thank you enough. I should return home. I would be happy to pay you for all of this trouble. And if you—"

"Pay me?" Vicky laughed. "Sit down and eat your breakfast."

Preston sat and realized that he was ravenously hungry. After he finished, she took his plate and filled it up again. At first he was quiet as she walked around the kitchen and made little jokes or comments. But soon they were chatting away.

Whenever her back was turned, Preston studied her. She was attractive—tall and full bodied, with long chestnut hair that she had pulled back into a loose ponytail. Strands of it had come loose and fell across her face, and she tucked them behind her ears with practiced fingers.

After finishing the second plate, Preston stood up to leave.

"I really can't thank you enough. Are you sure I can't pay you something?"

"Only if you want to insult me."

They stood at her doorway.

"Last night," he said, "I . . . I don't know what to say. I can't thank you enough. If things had . . . Well, it would have been very embarrassing."

"I think I did the right thing," she said simply.

"Let me at least take you out to dinner," Preston said on a sudden impulse.

"All right," she said shyly.

"Good. How about next Friday? I'll pick you up at seven."

"Okay."

He started to walk down the steps when she called out to him.

"Your keys!"

She came down the steps barefoot to meet him.

"Sorry," she said, slipping them into his hand. "I was afraid you might wake up in the middle of the night and try to drive home."

Vicky couldn't stop thinking about Preston, although God knew she hardly had time for anything these days, not with picking up every extra shift she could at the bakery in an attempt to save some money. That morning had been the first one she had had off in two weeks. She tried to avoid looking at her bank statement for as long as possible each month. She already knew what it was going to say, but it was depressing to see the paltry sum expressed in all its decimal-pointed finality. She was working herself to exhaustion, but the number crept up with such agonizing slowness. She tried not to think about how long it would take to reach anything like the kind of sum she would need to open her own shop. To sign a lease and buy equipment and supplies. To hire people. The hundreds of details she would suddenly have to take care of. Sometimes the thought of doing it was so overwhelming, she wondered if it wouldn't be better to get a job as a paralegal. Or a nurse. She heard that paid well. It couldn't take that much time to get a nursing degree, could it? But she certainly didn't have any time to spend worrying about men. Her first marriage should have been enough to make her swear off men altogether.

There was no getting around the fact that she had terrible luck with relationships. Even before her first marriage, she had dated a string of losers. Like that artist in college. He seemed so interesting. Not at all like most of the boys. Until he moved himself into her tiny dorm room and sponged off her for a semester. And she had let him get away with it for months. Feeling sorry for him or guilty about breaking up or whatever. But certainly not because of love. The very word made her want to laugh. *Love.* People were always going on and on about love as if that was the answer to everything. She had had lots of men declare their love for her, and it hadn't led to anything but heartache and disappointment. *Love!* The word made her indignant. A swindle on naïve fools.

Still, thoughts of Preston kept flitting through her head. How handsome he looked sleeping on her couch. And his manners—there was something about him that made it impossible to imagine him ever saying a harsh word to a woman. And that unexpected soulfulness. When he had poured himself out to her the night before—she wasn't sure she had ever seen a man so honest and unguarded.

All that day as she rushed to do the errands that a normal person would have spread out over a week—only she couldn't, could she? Not when she was going to cover all of Mary's shifts next week while she was away on vacation—she would suddenly catch herself at a traffic light staring dreamily out the window and thinking about him until she grew annoyed and reminded herself that she didn't have time for this sort of silliness. And she could only imagine what her mother would say if she knew how she'd met him. For an hour or two, she would put him out of her mind, but later she would be waiting for the dry cleaner to find her blouse, and she would glance at a calendar on the wall with a smiling, golden-haired man, and before she knew it, she would be thinking of him. No, dreaming of him. And no matter how often she told herself to stop, his image would return unbidden to her mind.

CHAPTER TWENTY-ONE

Mark had never thought about having an affair before, never even fantasized about it. Not even when he would find himself in the house alone and sneak off to the bathroom to take care of those needs that Sylvia long ago decided she wanted no part of. That would have been enough for most men. The growing indifference of the woman sharing his bed. No, not just indifference. Actual disgust. He would snake a hand across the sheets, and she would brush it away without a word. Without even offering an excuse. The months gradually becoming years. And yet Mark remained stupidly loyal. He fantasized about other women, of course. What man didn't? But harmless fantasies. About movie stars or that cute weather girl on the local news. He never imagined himself having an actual affair. It would have been nice to think that there was something heroic in his dogged marital loyalty, but that would have been a lie. He was cowed, not courageous. An affair would be too complicated and messy.

But it had turned out to be the easiest part of his life. Every day, he would go for his run, and every day she would be waiting on the bench for him. At first, they just talked. She told him about Preston, about their life together, about her disappointments. Sometimes she seemed to think that her whole life was a lie, which he didn't quite see. Not that he condoned what Preston did. But her complaints were pretty small compared with his. Not that he said that. He tried to be supportive, tried to agree with whatever she was saying, and it seemed to help her.

He told her about Sylvia. The nagging and the bitterness. He could see from the look on Anne's face that his own marriage wasn't normal. That even a woman who was in the midst of her own crisis looked on the ruins of his marriage with absolute horror. And she didn't know how bad it really was, how Mark would meekly accept the latest nasty remark without uttering a word in his defense because that would only lead to a fight and to words that were far more wounding than whatever Sylvia originally said. When he told the stories to Anne, though, he always found himself embellishing a little bit, telling her that he had said things that he never said. Of course, he later wished he had said them when he had time alone and could replay the conversation again in his mind and craft the perfect reply, a comeback that would crush her with its exquisitely expressed disdain.

But soon their conversations led to more. Even then, it had been easy. By six, his office was deserted, and there was an unused room in the back with a large couch that had once been in the conference room. Anne would pick him up and park in the back of the building. Mark would let them in the service entrance, and that was that. Nothing could have been simpler.

He was happier than he had been for years. The affair made him glacially indifferent to Sylvia's little jabs, and now he would occasionally turn his own look of contempt on her. One night he saw something in her eyes when she looked at him that he hadn't seen in years. He saw uncertainty and worry and perhaps a touch of fear. And it made him happy.

After he and Anne had sex, they would lie on the couch

and talk about the future. Maybe move to another town. Mark would have to find another job—or maybe not. Given how much money Preston had, any settlement was going to be enormous. He liked the idea of being a man of leisure, sitting in a café and reading the morning paper. Of course, Anne had her own ideas about how they would live, and many of them had no appeal for him. But he wasn't that concerned about it. At this point, it was all pie in the sky anyway. Who knew where things would lead?

Anne was ecstatically happy. At least that was what she told herself. Mark was so different from Preston, and as far as she was concerned, different was good. Preston had been perfect, too perfect. It was as if he didn't need anything from anyone else. As if he was impervious. How could you love a man like that? Really love him? Admire, perhaps, but not love. She told herself that she liked Mark's bland good looks, despite his thinning hair and soft midsection, that his inexpert fumbling had an innocent appeal. That his constant complaints about his wife were the kind of thing Preston never would have shared. And he was so enthusiastic when she started imagining a future for them. Nothing like Preston, who always found something to object to whenever she had an idea. So cautious, so worried about how it would look.

Mark was as excited as she was to start a new life somewhere else. And that was the crucial thing, wasn't it? No one was perfect. Certainly no relationship. But two people who shared a vision of the future—you could count on that. You could build on it. She had once thought that she and Preston shared that sort of vision. But she had been wrong. She wouldn't be wrong again, though. Destiny had placed Mark in her path. Destiny was already pointing her in the right direction.

Not that she didn't have worries. There was something

vague about Mark's enthusiasm. When she pressed him on where he would like to live or what he wanted to do, he threw out an obvious fantasy like Fiji or Italy. But she told herself to be patient. At least he was willing to dream with her. They could settle on the details later. The hunger of his desire every time he saw her was reassuring. He needed her in a way that Preston never had. And that could only be a good thing. That was what she told herself as they lay on the couch, her head on his chest, rising and falling with each breath. Dreaming of a new life together as the old couch exhaled its musty fumes after their couplings.

CHAPTER TWENTY-TWO

Norman sat down at the oak table and was overcome by a rising giddiness. It was exactly how he'd always imagined it. The dark wood paneling. The leather seats with brass studs. The waiters quietly moving about in their short white coats. He felt like an English gentleman. He could picture long afternoons here smoking cigars and telling his rapt fellow members about his latest business triumph. He hadn't been able to wipe the smile from his face since he had driven onto the grounds and seen the enormous brick clubhouse rise up in front of him. It was as if he had arrived—at last—where he belonged.

Although, if he was completely honest with himself, he was a little disappointed in his playing companions. Truth be told, they looked just the slightest bit slovenly. John appeared not to have shaved that day. And Bill's shirt was faded. And that other guy, Tom something or other, wasn't even wearing socks! Norman looked down admiringly at his own shirt. Fucking beeeaaauuutiful! From the Nicklaus Collection. The thing cost more than a hundred bucks, which was ridiculous for a golf shirt. But it positively shimmered. A deep brown with gold thread running through it that sparkled. He looked like a

CLUB RULES \ 159

goddamn king in that shirt. Well, he thought, perhaps I have a few things to teach these old WASP blue bloods.

Norman glanced down at the scorecard and experienced a thrill when he read the words tucked at the bottom: "Members and their guests must observe club rules and show proper decorum at all times." Yes, he thought exultantly, a world defined by proper decorum. An end to the constant jostling and elbowing of daily life. It sounded like paradise.

The waiter glided silently up to their table. "Something to drink, gentlemen?"

"What would you like, Norm?" asked John.

Norman hated his name. His mother had seen a television show on the Norman conquest and thought it sounded regal. To him, though, it sounded too much like normal. Average. Not special in any way. And he hated being called Norm. He had already corrected John twice and only through a supreme effort stopped from correcting him a third time.

"I'll have a Heineken."

The waiter turned to the members.

"OLL," said John.

"Arnold Palmer," said Bill.

"Sam Snead," said Tom.

John whistled. "Expecting a long day out there?"

Norman was furious at himself for ordering first. A beer? A fucking *beer*? He didn't even drink beer at home, and here he was ordering a beer like a goddamn kid just out of college. What did he think? That ordering a Heineken was a touch of class? Because it was imported? He desperately wanted to change his order, but he would look like an idiot. He didn't know what their drinks were, and he damn well wasn't going to ask. He felt himself blush like a fucking teenager and asked in a meek voice if he could have an OLL instead.

"Ah, clean living," John said mockingly.

Norman's blush deepened. He silently cursed himself for changing his order. He had already made some sort of blunder, and what made it more infuriating was that he wasn't even sure what it was. He dropped his head and fiddled with some tees on the table. His glinting shirt seemed to be winking at him, mocking him.

John couldn't look at Norman without wanting to burst into laughter. Who did this clown think he was? A gold shirt? Did he think he was trying out for a dance troupe? John was already dreading the round of golf ahead. Norman had hardly spoken, but John could barely stand the sight of him. All tricked up in new gear as if he was off to a fucking ball. They were playing a round of golf, not practicing the fox-trot. And when he switched his order to an OLL—he didn't even know what it *was*—John could barely keep from mocking him openly. Was this guy that pathetic? What a loser. They could give him a cup of warm piss, and he would still drink it just to fit in. John wished he had ordered the Sam Snead because he was beginning to think that a few drinks were about the only way he was going to make it through the afternoon. How had he ever let himself be talked into joining the membership committee? Spending the whole afternoon with some idiot he already knew the committee was going to reject. He sighed and stared impatiently at the clock. They hadn't even gotten their drinks yet. It was going to be a long afternoon.

When Norman was safely ensconced in the tan leather of his Mercedes, he finally let himself relax. He couldn't help smiling. First of all, he looked fucking fantastic. There was no doubt about that. Those other guys—by the fourth hole, their shirts were untucked and their socks were drooping around their ankles. Tom spilled some of his Sam Snead on his shirt and played most of the round with a large splotch over his belly. Of course, in the heat it was no fun keeping your shirt tucked in and your socks pulled up. But Norman did it anyway. Hell, that was the way they did it on the tour. You never saw Nicklaus or Watson walking down the fairway with their shirts untucked. So whenever he'd had a moment to himself and the others weren't looking, he'd pulled and tucked. Not that he didn't feel slightly ridiculous. Still, it was important to make a good impression. That was the crucial thing.

And their equipment. Their bags looked like crap, and Bill's head cover had a hole in it. A *hole*! No one could fault his equipment. Brand fucking new! His bag had a metallic silver overlay, and the thing sparkled like a fucking suit of armor. John didn't even have a driver. Norman generously offered to let him use his own—an expensive new model with a special shaft that had set him back quite a bit—but John refused. And he didn't just refuse. He did it sneeringly as if he was insulted. It wasn't Norman's fault if the guy was too much of a half-wit to carry a driver.

Norman couldn't say that he had played all that well. He was too nervous. And he had always played on public courses with their slow, bumpy greens. But the greens at Oak Hollow—*Jesus Christ*! He'd rocketed his first putt right off the putting surface. The other three had burst out laughing, and he'd wanted to slink off in shame. But that had passed when Tom rammed his own putt so hard that it ended up about two feet from Norman's.

And no one could fault his etiquette. That was certain. The others were constantly putting, even though someone else was farther away. Or hitting out of order on the tee. If Norman hadn't been there, the whole thing would have been chaos. At least half a dozen times he'd had to remind them who should

162 / **Andrew Trees**

be teeing off. He was sure his efforts there hadn't been unappreciated.

Afterward he couldn't help noticing that everyone was friendlier than they had been on the golf course, and he began to think he hadn't been the only one who had been nervous, that they had also been trying to impress him—which made perfect sense in a way because they were asking him to plunk down $50,000 to join the club and then pay almost $1,000 a month just for the pleasure of belonging. And that was before he played a single round of golf or had a cheeseburger at the grill. Yes, that conviviality at the end—that was quite telling.

Norman was confident that the time was not far off when he would be getting a phone call inviting him to become a member of the Oak Hollow Country Club. And then he could rest content.

You had to laugh, John told himself. That was all you could do. Because if you didn't, if you actually chose to notice how insulting Norm's behavior was, then you would have to fucking kill the guy, wouldn't you? You would have to grab his driver and smash his fucking skull in, and then where would you be? No, you had to laugh about it. That was the only thing to do. The one consolation from the infuriating afternoon he had just spent was that at least he wouldn't have any shortage of stories to share for the next several weeks at cocktail parties. He was already shaping the material in his mind for comic effect.

First of all, every time Norm thought they weren't looking, he would start tucking in his shirt and pulling up his socks. It was hilarious. John felt as if he was in some sort of Benny Hill sketch. All of them were laughing about it, and by the end the three of them would pretend to be looking somewhere else so they could watch him go through the routine one more time. And his golf bag! The thing was unbelievable. The single most gaudy, tacky piece of equipment he had ever seen on a golf course. It was the kind of bag Liberace would have owned.

And the etiquette fetish! The fucking golf etiquette! What the fuck was up with that? The goddamn round took nearly five hours! Jesus Christ! It wasn't the fucking Masters! Every single time, Norm insisted that they tee off in the proper order. Every time, he made sure that the guy farthest away putted first, even if the poor bastard had to hump it from fifty yards away because he'd skulled a wedge. And Norm made them stand there and wait and watch the poor bastard huffing and puffing across the green. Norm standing there serenely, as if he were the master of ceremonies at the fucking Rose Bowl parade. And the practice swings! The goddamn practice swings! Three fucking swings before he would hit the ball.

He'd almost lost it when Norm offered him his driver. Fucking asshole! Did the guy really think he didn't have one? He didn't need to be reminded that he couldn't hit the fucking thing straight. And what made it more insulting was that Norm was a terrible golfer. A twenty-seven handicapper! He was a fucking twelve. He hit his three wood a good twenty yards past Norm. And that asshole had the nerve to offer him his *driver*! Unfuckingbelievable!

Yes, you really had to laugh. Otherwise you might kill the poor bastard.

Tom wondered why he bothered to play golf anymore. Did he enjoy it? No, he did not fucking enjoy it. He hadn't enjoyed it when he duck hooked his drive on the third hole into the weeds or when he skulled his chip on the fifth twenty yards over the green or when he shanked one so badly that he nearly killed one of the caddies. Why the hell did he bother?

And it wasn't as if he enjoyed the company. John was a terrible snob. He could be happy only when he was ridiculing someone. Tom had experienced the sting of his scorn on more than one occasion. Of course, Norm was ridiculous and annoying, but Tom kind of felt sorry for him. Poor schlub. Trying so hard. And he never stood a chance. He must have known, which would have made the round tough. By the end, John was openly laughing at him. Norm actually showed a certain strength of character by acting oblivious. And he managed to get his own back, albeit in a passive-aggressive fashion. Insisting on proper golf etiquette—Tom had to laugh when he thought about John's expression after Norm shooed him off the tee for trying to hit out of turn.

But then there was the thing that brought him back time after time. Those few sweet moments every round, brief instants when he loosed the chains of life and escaped up into the ether. Flushing that five iron on the fourteenth and rolling in that slippery twenty-footer on the ninth. He sighed. That was all it took. That was all it ever took. A couple of scraps from the golfing gods. Two fucking shots out of ninety-five. He knew he would be back out there next weekend and the weekend after that. And that even on his best day, those truly magnificent shots that made his face flush and his heart beat fast would occur only a handful of times. Golf was a cruel game. A very cruel game.

CHAPTER TWENTY-THREE

The first time Leanne took Paige to church, Paige didn't know what to expect. She and Norman had never really been churchgoers. The occasional Easter Sunday and once to the Christmas Eve service. And she had vague memories of going to Sunday school as a girl, although she couldn't recall what they taught her. Mainly she remembered getting to wear nice dresses and having her mother put pretty bows in her hair, and she would ride in the backseat to the church and finger the brass buttons on the front of her winter coat, the one she was allowed to wear only on special occasions. But none of those experiences had prepared her for this.

The church was less than two years old and held its services in a small community center auditorium on the edge of town. It had moved to the new location only a few months before, but it was already outgrowing the space. Folding chairs lined the back of the hall to handle the overflow. It didn't look like a church, at least not like any church she had ever gone to. The service was held in a large gym with backboards hanging down like stalactites. There was a small stage at one end. Men were running around setting up a sound system before the service. The minister was young and good-looking. When he wasn't carrying one of his children around in his arms, he was busy helping the other men set up. She knew it was silly, but she thought of ministers as old men or at least older men. Gray-haired. A little portly. Not this energetic young father rushing around the room in running shoes.

She was nervous about bringing the baby, but Leanne told her that no one would care. And it was true. The room was filled with new mothers like her, and they looked like her as well. Many were still heavy from their pregnancies, and a couple of them wore sweatpants to the service. Paige was wearing a navy skirt that she didn't quite fit into, using a safety pin to give herself a little extra room.

The service was much longer than she expected—an hour and a half—and her stomach was growling by the end. The baby was getting fussy and wanted to feed. She was bored during some of it, and the sermon went on and on. But there was one moment when the minister was speaking that touched her, one moment that spoke directly to her. Something about Christian charity. She wished she could remember what he had said because she found it so reassuring. But the rising heat in the gym and the baby's squirming made it difficult to keep her mind focused. After the service, Leanne pushed her into a group of new mothers, and she spent the easiest, happiest moments she'd had since they moved to Eden's Glen. The women gave her advice about where to shop and what doctors they liked. They invited her to join them for a new mothers fellowship group they had on Wednesday mornings.

And that was how it began. She would go to the Wednesday morning meetings and often have lunch with a few of the mothers afterward. And she would go to the Sunday service so she could chat with her new friends. Over time, she started to pay more attention to the sermon, and she went home filled with a vague sense of hope. Then she started attending one of the prayer groups that the other mothers liked to go to, and before she knew it, her entire social life revolved around the church.

She tried to get Norman to come with her, and he did—once. But he grumbled about the lousy acoustics and having to sit on a folding chair. On the way home, he complained about how boring the sermon was. That was the last time he came with her. She tried to make him a part of her new circle, but whenever she arranged a night out with another couple, Norman was surly and drank too much, so she gave that up as well. At first she worried about it, but she noticed that some of the other women didn't bring their husbands either. When she confided in them, they told her that women were always the ones who had to draw their husbands in and that she had to be patient and give it time.

Paige started to see her life in Eden's Glen with new eyes. All those women perfectly done up whenever they stepped outside their homes. All those expensive cars. It was so shallow and pointless. She would drive into the community center parking lot and be embarrassed about her own life. She started removing her engagement ring before she went inside because she thought it looked too showy, and she said a nightly prayer asking God to help her bring Norman to Him.

CHAPTER TWENTY-FOUR

The last person Baird wanted to spend time with these days was his father. Half the time he didn't seem to notice that Baird was there. Or he would suddenly look at him in this strange way, as if he couldn't quite place who Baird was or what he was doing there. They had hardly spoken after that awful night in the kitchen. Baird kept waiting for his father to come home that night so he could apologize, although he wasn't sure what he should apologize for. Earlier that week, his father had eaten without him, and Baird didn't start breaking dishes and swearing. Not that he didn't want to occasionally. One day he took one of his father's trophies and hurled it again and again against the stone wall that ran along one side of the property until the metal cup was dented into a misshapen lump like an artifact from a forgotten age, and then he threw it into the middle of the deep ravine behind the wall. He felt better for a little while. When he thought back on the episode later, though, he was ashamed. And it did nothing to stop the anger that would come over him for no apparent reason. Like that time when he was making himself a peanut-butter-and-jelly sandwich and he ended up throwing everything into the garbage. Not just the sandwich but an almost full jar of jelly and another of peanut butter and the plate and knife. Or another time when he was brushing his hair, and tears were suddenly stealing down his face. He smashed the brush against the side of the bathtub until the handle snapped in his hand.

And the guilt. The sense that somehow he was responsible. That never left him. He would lie awake at night and wonder if it would have been different if he had been a better son and done better in school and been more successful like his father. And he would feel bad about the way he treated his mother when he saw her. But when she was actually there, she would get teary and want to hold him, and he would sit there, stiff, and wish that he was somewhere else.

After that other night in the kitchen, though, he told himself he was going to try harder. He always waited for his father to come home before eating these days—not that his father noticed. Twice this week he got home late, and when Baird mentioned dinner, he said he had already eaten. But it was still better than going through a night like that other night.

Of course, tonight was Friday night, and that presented a problem. Friday nights were usually the nights that his mother and father went to a party or out to dinner with another couple. His father left the mail on a table in the kitchen, so Baird knew that there was a cocktail party that night. Neither of his parents had gone out since his mother had left, and he worried about what it would be like for them sitting at home and wondering what their friends were up to. So Baird decided that at least he could keep his father company. When one of Baird's friends asked if he wanted to go to a movie, Baird said no.

He waited for his father to come home, while he nonchalantly read the sports section in the kitchen as if he hadn't carefully planned the whole evening. He didn't want his father to feel like a loser. That would defeat the whole purpose. He heard the car pull into the garage, and a few moments later his father walked in, flipping through the mail with a distracted look on his face.

"Hey, Dad."

Preston nodded without looking up from the mail.

"How was your day?"

Preston tried to suppress a grimace. How was his day? What the hell kind of stupid question was that? How the hell did Baird think his day was? His wife had left him, and he could barely keep his mind on business. And he didn't know how the hell he was supposed to deal with everyone. He used to glide through life with a perfect sense of who he was and how he was supposed to act. And suddenly he was floundering around. He didn't know what was worse—the secretaries who had an overly solicitous air about them and talked in low, sympathetic voices or the men who stuck doggedly to the business at hand and avoided any personal conversation when last month they would have asked after Anne. Preston wished he could lock his door and hide in his office and lick his wounds. But the business of the bank ground on, and so did Preston.

"Fine," he said, loosening his tie and continuing through the kitchen.

"I was thinking maybe we could get a pizza and rent a movie tonight."

God, what was wrong with his son? Didn't he have any friends? It wasn't normal for a teenage boy to hang out with his father. He should be out with people his own age.

"I'm afraid I'm busy. Why don't you do something with a friend?"

He hurried out of the room. He hadn't told Baird about his dinner—he would hardly call it a date. The whole thing was too complicated. He might have to explain how he met Vicky, and that would lead inevitably to saying something about the accident. He quickly changed clothes and left through the front door so he wouldn't have to answer more questions on his way out.

Preston was actually excited about the evening. It was the first social encounter he hadn't dreaded since Anne left him. He pulled into Vicky's driveway and noted with relief that the tree he'd hit didn't look much the worse for wear.

It was dusk when he arrived, and he could see a nearly full moon rising above the treetops. The lights were on in the garage apartment and threw out a welcoming yellow glow. Preston suddenly felt like a much younger man just starting out in life and hurrying home to his quaint, cramped apartment. He took the steps two at a time.

He knocked, but no one answered, so he pushed the door open. Honey, I'm home, he almost said. But instead he just called out her name.

Vicky rushed out from the bedroom in a bathrobe, flushed from a hot shower.

"Preston, I'm so sorry," she said, giving him a quick kiss on the cheek. "There's liquor in the cabinet by the stove. I just need a couple of minutes."

She hurried back into the bedroom. Preston poured himself a small Scotch and sat down at the table. The whole point of tonight was to show Vicky he wasn't the kind of man who drank too much and crashed into other people's yards. Or was it? No, the truth was he was looking forward to seeing her.

He glanced around the kitchen at the mismatched glasses and the old pots and the dishes piled in the sink. He hated when Anne left the kitchen a mess, but in this apartment it was somehow cozy. Vicky came out of the bedroom wearing jeans and a black silk T-shirt that showed off her figure.

"Sorry about that," she said, bending over and sliding her feet into a pair of pumps.

She looked good, Preston thought, watching her as she hooked her finger into the shoe and guided in her foot. They chatted easily as they drove to the restaurant. He made a few jokes about their last meeting, and she teased him about his driving. It was fun, as if he were back in college.

He pulled up to a small French restaurant on a quiet street in a town several miles from Eden's Glen and handed the valet his keys.

"Oh, I've always wanted to try this place!" said Vicky.

Preston smiled and opened the door for her. It was one of the more expensive restaurants in the area. He wanted to give her a nice night after what she had done for him. Of course, he also didn't mind that it was out of the way and that he probably wouldn't see anyone he knew. The last thing he needed was for this dinner to become a source of gossip, especially when it was simply his way of thanking a Good Samaritan.

The maître d' saw Preston and smiled widely.

"Mr. Winthrop! How are you?"

They were ushered to a quiet table by the window. Vicky glanced around the room.

"I should have dressed up more," she said.

"Nonsense, you look great," said Preston, reaching across the table and giving her hand a squeeze.

Vicky looked down at her menu and tried to sort through her feelings. Being with him again was overwhelming. God, if he were only a little more average looking, she could catch her breath and stop acting as though she'd never been on a date before. But every time she looked up at him, and he flashed that easy smile at her—a little cocky, yes, but also reassuring, as if it held the key to any problem that might be troubling

her—she had to look down again at the menu and try to collect herself.

"What's the matter?" asked Preston.

You are what's the matter, she wanted to say. *You* with your
perfect hair and your neatly pressed shirt and your flash of a
smile. It wasn't that she hadn't figured it out. From the moment Vicky saw him slumped by his car, he looked familiar—
she vaguely remembered seeing a photograph of him in the
newspaper, and once he started pouring out his life story, it
didn't take her long to put two and two together. But somehow everything was different. Of course, the man by the car
was a total wreck. Drunk. Emotional. Blood on his face. Even
the next morning, he evoked more maternal affection than
anything else in his disheveled clothes with his stubble and his
sheepish smile. It was easy to daydream about *that* man because he didn't seem too distant. But the person who showed
up on her doorstep tonight was not that man. The person
who showed up on her doorstep was in total control. Confident, charming. And so good-looking. He was perfect—like
Robert Redford in *The Way We Were*. Definitely not the kind
of man she usually met. The kind of man who would break
your heart in a way that could never be fixed. Vicky feared
that tonight was a terrible mistake, that she should have politely
declined and at least left herself the small pleasure of daydreaming about the stranger who had briefly stumbled into
her life.

"Nothing," she said, keeping her eyes on the menu.

"Have I done something wrong?"

Although this was the same man who had drunkenly
crashed into a tree, she had trouble imagining that he ever did
anything wrong.

"I'm a little uncomfortable," she said.

"Look, if you are still worried about the way you're dressed,

I'll take you home and you can change. They'll hold our table."

"No, it's nothing. I'll be fine."

But Vicky wasn't fine. That was obvious to Preston. At first he couldn't figure out why—but then he remembered how awkward women used to become in his presence. Before he became a married man. Someone safe. Not someone they had to think about in that way. As he looked at Vicky chewing on her lower lip and staring at the menu, he found her endearing. More than endearing, really. He had worried all week that she agreed to the date out of pity. And now to find her so bashful in his presence. He reached across the table and took her hand.

"You know, I really am grateful for what you did the other night."

"I'm glad. Really, I am. But there is no need to do all this."

"But I want to do it."

"I just . . . you know, I don't usually rely on car crashes to get men to take me out. I don't know. Maybe this is a mistake."

"If I hadn't had the accident, I wouldn't have the pleasure of your company tonight."

A lock of golden hair had fallen over Preston's forehead, and he smiled at her. Vicky felt herself blush and had to look down again at the menu, but this time she smiled. There was something so reassuring about the way he looked at her. And also something flirtatious and playful about him. It was suddenly obvious that he was attracted to her. She had almost forgotten that she was still an attractive woman. She was so used to tallying up her worth in a way that could be presented to a bank, she had begun to believe that she had no worth at all. And it wasn't as if slaving away in a bakery all day covered in flour made her feel sexy. No, she told herself, this isn't a mistake. This is a good thing, a very good thing.

They had a wonderful dinner, laughing and sharing stories. After a couple of glasses of wine, she told him about her bakery idea and admitted that his bank had turned her down for a loan. He shook his head sympathetically and told her he would look into it. And although nothing would ever come from it, she appreciated the gesture. Even though she would never see him again, she had a wonderful time. He dropped her off and was a perfect gentleman, kissing her on the cheek. She wanted to ask him to come up but sensed he would say no. As she lay in bed that night, she almost wished he hadn't taken her out.

As Preston drove home, he wondered why she hadn't invited him up. He'd planned to say no if she had. But he wasn't so sure anymore. He had been married for so long that he no longer knew what the rules were. He thought he might seem too forward if he accepted her invitation. And how far did one go these days? Did people his age just make out? There didn't seem to be any step between a peck on the cheek and having sex. Still, it would have been nice to know Vicky wanted him to come up. Now he thought he might have said yes if she'd asked. But maybe it was better. They'd had a nice dinner. He had thanked her for her kindness, and that would be that. Anything more would have meant complications.

Preston was still thinking about Vicky the next morning when he arrived at the bank. He asked his secretary to find her loan application. When he looked through it, he saw immediately why she was turned down. No assets. No experience running a business. A spotty financial history. He was surprised the loan officer had gone to so much trouble when she clearly didn't meet the minimum criteria, although he noted that the final rejection was written in rather harsh terms. He sighed and pushed the folder away and went about the business of the day. During his meeting with Perkins, he found himself thinking again about her application. And later, during a phone call, he idly picked it up and flipped through it a second time.

She really wasn't asking for that much. Certainly nothing that would affect the bank in the slightest. When he thought about it, her discretion the night of his accident had actually saved the bank an enormous amount of money. He found the name of the loan officer and picked up his phone.

Matt had never been inside Preston's office. He adjusted his tie and ran his fingers through his hair on the way up in the elevator. The secretary—an ugly old bird who had been with the bank forever—gave him a cold smile as she ushered him in.

Preston sat at a large mahogany desk with an enormous window behind him framing a view of the city. A large portrait of Preston's grandfather hung on the wall above two sleek, modern couches and a coffee table.

Preston stood up and came around the desk to shake his hand.

"Matt, isn't it?"

"Yes, sir, Mr. Winthrop."

"Please, call me Preston."

He motioned to one of the couches, and Matt sat down.

"Would you like something to drink?"

"No, sir."

Matt placed his hands carefully on his thighs to keep from fidgeting. He was having a private meeting with Preston Baird Winthrop! In his office! This was it. He was finally going to be singled out from the herd and recognized for his special abilities.

Matt had to admit he was starting to feel a little impatient at the bank. Perkins didn't appreciate his talents. He was cut out for a better job than loan officer. He was going to business school at night, for God's sake! In a few more years, he would have an M.B.A. from the University of Illinois Circle campus. An M.B.A. from a Big Ten school! But all Perkins cared about was numbers. Always complaining about this or that irregularity. He didn't have the vision that Matt had—that Preston had!

He had actually asked Matt to call him Preston. His first name! Just as if they were golfing buddies, and Matt had strolled by the office and popped in. Hello, Preston, he might say, good weekend?

Yes, this was definitely it. He wondered what he would be asked to do. Maybe run one of the new branches. That would be a plum assignment. He would do a fantastic job. He was very personable. Everyone always said so. He would become a pillar of the community. Maybe not on Preston's scale but grand enough. Grand enough that he could join a country club and one day, as they were discussing branch business, casually suggest that Preston come out to the branch to see his latest innovations and play a round of golf with him.

Preston smiled inwardly as he looked at Matt sitting stiffly in his chair. He could imagine what Matt was thinking, probably worried that he was going to be reprimanded. Matt must have known that Perkins didn't like him. In fact, Perkins had complained several times about him and suggested that Matt occasionally approved loans based on the attractiveness of the applicant.

Of course, any similarity to what Preston had in mind was ridiculous. The woman had already done him a great service, and he was simply trying to show a little kindness and compassion. There was certainly nothing untoward in that.

"Matt, you were the loan officer on Vicky Thayer's application."

"Yes, sir, I was."

"A friend of mine recently told me about her. A bit of a sad story."

"Yes, I was sympathetic myself."

"Any room to reconsider?"

"Well, you know how Perkins is."

Yes, Preston knew. The man would deny a loan to his own mother without sufficient collateral.

"Perhaps we could get around that. There's no reason why you can't resubmit the necessary paperwork to me for approval."

"No, sir! There certainly isn't!"

"Good, I knew I could depend on you, Matt. You know I've got my eye on you, don't you?"

Matt sat up a little straighter. Preston suppressed a smile. He told Matt to get right on it. He had already decided he wouldn't involve himself any further. There was no need to call and tell her himself. She would know he was behind it. And he didn't want to make it seem as if he were angling for anything else. The dinner had been nice, but that was as far as it would go.

Matt's head was spinning with the possibilities. Of course, he was breaking about a dozen procedures by sending the loan directly to Preston, but what did that matter? If Preston asked him to do it, it was obviously okay. Everyone knew that Perkins was as sympathetic as a boiled egg. This was probably a test. Preston was seeing if he could depend on Matt, if Matt could be a go-to guy. Didn't Preston say he had his eye on him? He was confident he was about to move up in the world, out of the reach of an old turtle like Perkins.

And he would get to call Vicky with the good news. She hadn't been very appreciative when he'd tried to be nice before, but people always got upset when they were refused a loan. Matt tried not to take it personally. Yes, he was looking forward to making that phone call.

"Matt," Preston called out as he reached the door, "don't worry about calling her. I'll make sure she finds out."

CHAPTER TWENTY-FIVE

Preston lay in bed with his arm around Vicky, watching the leaves make sun-dappled patterns on the wall. He had called her that afternoon, and they had gone out that night. And almost every night since then for the past several weeks.

He loved spending time with Vicky, loved being in her apartment up in the trees. He was beginning to wonder if he didn't love her. It was a relief to be out of the bedroom he and Anne shared, out of their bathroom, out of their house, completely out of the life they had lived together. He hadn't gone to any parties, hadn't even played his usual weekend game of golf at the club.

He still thought about Anne at odd moments, and each time he experienced a sickening hollow feeling in his stomach. As long as he kept busy, though, the thoughts were infrequent. He began to think that all of this might be for the best. Vicky was younger, and it was nice to touch a round, firm, supple body. And the sex! He felt young and virile again. He and Anne had their routine, and the sex had always been fine. But now—the other day he was taking a shower before work, and she'd slipped off her robe and stepped into the shower with him. They had done it right there with the warm water sliding down their bodies and everything slippery from the steam. And she was still young enough to have children. Perhaps this was his chance to start over, to have more kids. Not that he didn't love Baird, but an only son of an only son didn't leave a lot to chance.

Of course, he felt guilty about Baird. He had barely seen him these past few weeks. But teenagers always wanted their parents out of their lives, so maybe he was doing him a favor. God knew that Preston would have loved that kind of freedom when he was Baird's age.

He usually woke up in the morning before Vicky, and he would lie there thinking about what their future together might look like. Was he crazy? He had known her only a short time. But everything was so comfortable and easy. At the very least, he saw no reason why they shouldn't keep seeing each other. That morning he made a resolution. He was going to introduce her to his world. There was a party that Friday night at the Swansons', and he was going to take her.

Vicky usually pretended to be asleep longer than she actually was. She could feel Preston shift his body to look out the window, but she continued to lie quietly against his chest, listening to the steady rhythm of his breathing. She liked to pretend that they were husband and wife as she lay there, and she built up an elaborate fantasy life for them involving children and in-laws and imaginary friends. Only it was starting to seem less and less like a fantasy.

God, she loved him. She loved the way he looked, and she loved the way he smelled and tasted. She loved hearing about his day. Before Preston, she could barely bring herself to understand her checking account, but now banking seemed like the most fascinating profession in the world. She was electric with love, as if she were always about to start giggling or burst into tears. She didn't need sleep. She was never hungry. She looked fantastic. When she got ready in the morning, she would stare at herself in the mirror. She thought she had never looked so beautiful.

But she worried sometimes. One night, he nearly had to cancel their date because of a late meeting, and she thought it was the beginning of the end. But he had shown up at ten P.M. with a pizza, and they had stayed up half the night. Now they didn't bother to make plans. It was just assumed he would come over after work. But every night she would begin to feel anxious an hour or so before she expected him, wondering if it would all come crashing down that day. He hadn't taken her to meet his friends. He hadn't even brought her to his house yet or introduced her to Baird—he sounded like such a sweet boy—but she couldn't blame him for that, could she? It was awkward with children. When was it appropriate to introduce them to your new girlfriend? Three weeks? Three months? She didn't know, and she certainly didn't think she had any right to complain. Of course, they hadn't really discussed the future, except to talk a couple of times about how they would love to take a trip to Paris, but what did she expect? He wasn't even divorced. She was being silly. No, she would tell herself, just slow down. Give him time. There was no need to push, no need to rush.

But then Vicky would fall into a reverie about their future together and imagine their children running around the yard—not that she wouldn't be a good mother to Baird. She told herself that she would never play favorites. And she would catch herself and remember that they had been seeing each other for only a few weeks. What did she expect? The poor man had just lost his wife. Well, not lost. She was still alive, of course. Vicky could feel her lurking on the edge of their relationship. And she could see the quick flash of pain in his eyes when he thought about her. She feared one night Anne would call and

tell him it had all been a terrible mistake, and he would leave.
And it would be over just like that.

But she had those thoughts only at night, usually when she
was waiting for Preston to arrive. She never had them in the
morning with her head on his chest and the reassuring thump
of his heart vibrating through her body. She had bought fresh
blueberries and was going to surprise him with blueberry pan-
cakes. And soon she was imagining a future weekend when she
would be walking through a field with Preston carrying a basket
filled with blueberries and watching their two children, a boy
and a girl, run ahead of them, laughing and playing and eating
blueberries right off the bush.

CHAPTER TWENTY-SIX

As the plane lifted off from the runway, Anne was giddy with excitement—and why not? She was no longer living a lie. She had anxious moments, of course. That was to be expected. It certainly didn't mean she had any reason to regret her decision. Mark reached for her, and she looked down at his large, doughy hands and found that she was nervous. Nervous! After all these years! Wasn't that alone a sign of how stale and wrong her marriage had become?

She hadn't slept with anyone but Preston her whole life. From the beginning, there had always been something deeply comforting about making love with him. Even the first time, when she was a little scared of the act, she felt safe. Not that she didn't occasionally find herself longing for more passion and spontaneity—at least that was what she thought now. She wasn't sure if she had thought that before she found out about the affair. It was as if the memories in her mind had become jumbled, and she was still struggling to piece together a timeline, to understand whether her disappointments with Preston had been there all along lurking below the surface.

Not that Preston didn't have his good points, although she didn't like to think about those. Not now. Not with Mark. One day she had found a book in the self-help section of a book-

store on how to get through a divorce, and the writer—a divorced woman—made it very clear that the worst thing to do
was to think about your spouse's good qualities. So she tried
to focus on his bad qualities. Only Preston didn't have many
bad qualities. He had slept with Maria, of course. Beyond
that, though, there wasn't much. When she really thought
about it, her biggest complaint was how Preston was always so
proper. But that was hardly a serious flaw. Some people would
say it was a virtue, and she supposed that was true for most of
life's relationships. But that didn't mean it was a virtue in a
marriage. No, in a marriage different virtues were called for.
Little daily tendernesses. Even small improprieties could carry
a kind of affection for a married couple. And Preston's unbending rectitude seemed to stifle things. It wasn't that he
stifled her, at least not exactly. He never told her not to do
certain things, but still she felt constrained. She would be telling a story at a dinner party, and he would give her one of his
looks. A brief grimace that no one else could see. And then
she would get flustered and wouldn't know whether to go on
or stop. In the early days of their marriage, it had happened so
often that she developed the habit of experiencing her words
from a distance, constantly monitoring whatever she was saying until she could police herself without Preston ever raising
an eyebrow. So, yes, he had stifled her. His whole manner was
stifling. Only she had lived with it for so long that she had forgotten about it. But then she would wonder if he had really
stifled her. Perhaps that was putting it too strongly. Constrained.
That was all. Her thoughts would circle back, though, and she
would vaguely remember some other incident. But she couldn't
recall exactly what she had been saying at the time, and she did
have a tendency to get carried away with a story. So she would
settle again on the idea that he had limited her in a way that she
found difficult to articulate.

Like the first time she had really lost herself in the pleasure of sex, she thought. It had been under the most unpromising circumstances. They had come home from a party. Both of them had had too much to drink. The dorm mother happened to step away at just the right moment so that Preston could sneak upstairs, and her roommate was away for the weekend. It wasn't the first time she had slept with him, but the other times had been so carefully planned. And she had been so nervous. Afraid of doing something wrong. Simply the idea of having sex had been scary. What it would feel like and if it would hurt the way a few of her friends told her it did. And what people would think—what Preston would think—after they had done it, although she knew she was being silly about that. Everyone was doing it in those days, as if the old rules no longer applied, as if girls like her were so behind the times. And that night it was as if she understood for the first time. It had happened so quickly. She was a little dizzy from the unaccustomed drinking, and the two of them had fallen into her narrow bed. They didn't undress all the way. But there had been a moment when he slid his hand up between her legs and she suddenly *wanted* him. When she stopped doing the things that she thought a girl was supposed to do at those moments, stopped thinking about what was going on, as if her body were no longer her body and was simply moving according to its own whims. Pulling him on top of her and then feeling him inside of her, her legs lifting up, up, up, and her breath coming in short hiccups. And suddenly an overpowering tension and the whole world tilting. When she had caught her breath, she smiled shyly at him; lost in wonderment at what had just happened, but she was met by a worried expression on his face.

"What's the matter?" she asked.

"You were so loud," he said. "What if someone heard us?"

Of course, he was right to worry. They were in her dorm room at Bryn Mawr. Someone could walk by at any moment. Being caught with a boy in your room was a serious violation of school rules. That was what she told herself at the time. That he was being a gentleman for worrying about her. Now she wasn't sure. She never questioned him back then. She had been swept away by it all. From the moment she had met him at a fraternity mixer, she had felt like the princess in a fairy tale.

And how was she supposed to judge? It wasn't as if she had really been with anyone else. She had dated a few boys before Preston. She even thought that she loved one of them until she met Preston, and then it seemed more like a crush. She wondered if she was being naïve about Mark. She had so little experience that it was hard to be sure how she really felt. Now here she was flying to Florida with him, and although she was uncertain, there was no turning back. So she tried to keep whatever doubts she had safely tucked away. She squeezed Mark's hand and smiled at him.

When the plane lifted off, Mark reached reflexively for Sylvia's hand, something he did every time they were flying together. But then he remembered and found himself holding Anne's hand. And he wondered if the trip wasn't a terrible mistake. What if Sylvia found out? He would have to be careful. Nothing unusual on the credit cards. Nothing too expensive. He would have to avoid the places he and Sylvia usually went to.

It had seemed like the perfect excuse to get away. He had to go to Florida on business, and it would be a chance for the two of them to spend time together. Not the hurried hour they spent in that back room at his office but real time. Just the thought of having sex on a king-size bed excited him. There wasn't much maneuverability on that narrow couch, and the one time they had tried it on the floor, the carpet had rubbed his knees raw. He'd had to wear pants for a week to hide it from Sylvia—not that she ever looked at him too closely. But he clearly hadn't thought the trip through. One day he'd just popped the question—"Hey, I have to go to Florida. Want to come along?" Anne was so excited that he didn't have the heart to cancel the trip once he realized how complicated everything could get. He pretended to read *Barron's* but kept glancing at her. He noticed fine lines around her eyes.

When they landed, he hailed a taxi and directed it to a small, nondescript hotel in West Palm Beach. He took Anne for dinner at Giuseppe's, a cheap Italian restaurant down the street. The door was guarded by a large plastic man in a chef's hat, endlessly twirling a sad-looking pepperoni pizza. The checkered plastic tablecloth was sticky, and the summer humidity made the bread spongy and damp. Of course, Anne was a good sport about it, laughing off her overcooked fish and insisting that their rotgut Chianti was drinkable. But he could tell she was as depressed by the whole thing as he was. And he hadn't given a thought to what they would talk about the whole time. Those stolen afternoons on the couch left only a few moments to dream about the future. Not enough time to get too specific. But sitting across from Anne at dinner was a different matter. He couldn't cut things short and say he had to get home. She wasn't exactly pushy. It was pretty clear, though, that she wanted him to start making some decisions. But she had to understand his situation. He had a wife and kids and a job with his wife's father.

Even the sex was depressing. He had envisioned a night of passionate lovemaking. That had been the one part he looked forward to, imagining the various things that they would suddenly be able to do to each other. Things that he and Sylvia had stopped doing long ago. Maybe a few things he had never done. And imagining Anne as his eager partner, seeing the look of ecstasy on her face. He worried occasionally that she wasn't as attracted to him as she pretended to be, but in his daydreams about Florida she was always gasping with pleasure. Nothing worked out as he planned, though. He had thought of a suave way to suggest what he had in mind, but when the time came, he was too embarrassed to say the prepared words. And the wine made him sleepy. Too sleepy to worry about any of those elaborate scenarios he had imagined. In truth, he could have just gone to bed, but after all that time thinking about it, he'd be damned if they went to sleep like an old married couple. He roused himself and kissed her and pushed her down on the bed without even taking off the bedspread with its faded sunbursts. The shiny cloth felt damp and unclean. He didn't bother to get completely undressed. He could feel his pants shaking around his ankles as the bed creaked underneath him. They left the lights on, and although Anne moaned and ran her hands along his back, the look on her face was nothing like what he had imagined.

Mark felt cheated and could barely bring himself to mutter good night before rolling onto his side and trying to go to sleep. What did the goddamn woman expect? He had been a fool to get involved with her, a fool to think he could compete with Preston. The man still looked like a fucking college football star. Whenever Mark found himself beside Preston, he felt flabby and clumsy, as if he were still struggling through adolescence. It was goddamn depressing. This Florida trip had been a terrible mistake.

Anne lay perfectly still with the blanket drawn up to her chin and listened to Mark snoring softly. She tried to stem the rising sense of panic that was making her breath come in short swallows. What had she done? Oh, my God! What had she *done*?

It was horrible. From the cramped economy seats on the plane to this tacky hotel to the brutal summer heat, which pressed on her as soon as she stepped outside. They shouldn't have come to Florida. That had been the mistake. This had always been where she and Preston had come, if they weren't going to Europe. The Winthrops had a lovely house on the ocean in Hobe Sound. She and Preston would come in January or February and go for a long walk on the beach. A quiet dinner of local fish and a nice bottle of wine—that Chianti had made her want to gag! And often skinny-dipping in the pool before they went to bed. Gliding around silently in the water, their limbs tangling and untangling. When they made love later, the salt and the sand would lightly chafe her skin, as if the ocean had infused her with its essence. The slightly raw sensation had made her feel alive to the world.

Mark felt bad about the night before. He went out early the next morning and bought Anne a racy bikini to make it up to her—paying cash, of course. He didn't want that charge showing up on his credit card. When he got back to the room, he insisted that she wear it. For a long time, she refused. They nearly got into a fight about it. But eventually she relented and slipped into the bathroom and put it on. When she came out, Mark whistled and acted as if he couldn't keep his hands off her. They ended up doing it again right then and there, and he was pretty pleased with his performance. Of course, they hadn't done any of the things he had imagined, but it had been a hell of a lot better than the night before. He propped her up on the pillows in a certain way that he had once liked to do with Sylvia, a way that gave him the sense of thrusting much more deeply than he normally did. He liked that sensation. It made him feel manly, powerful. And the quiet sigh of pleasure that escaped Anne reassured him, even if it didn't match the frenzied ecstasy of his dreams.

But a gnawing sense of worry had troubled him ever since she'd stepped out of the bathroom. He sat under a beach umbrella and sweated and watched Anne swim lazily beyond the break of the waves and tried not to think about how terrible she looked in that bikini. Not that she wasn't an attractive woman, but the thing made her look a little bony. Maybe it was the goddamn suit. But he wasn't sure. The light was pretty crappy in that back office during the late afternoon. He had never seen her in broad daylight standing practically naked in front of him. And when he finally did, he didn't expect her to look like *that*. Hell, in that light Sylvia was more attractive than Anne. Not that he saw Sylvia naked very often anymore. And she favored demure one-piece suits, which, he had to admit, she looked pretty goddamn good in. He wondered what she would look like in the suit he had bought Anne. It was made out of silvery fabric like something Barbarella might have worn. Just two little triangles of fabric to cover the breasts and not much more on the bottom. He had been tempted to buy one of those thong numbers that disappeared right up a woman's ass, but after seeing Anne in this one, he was glad he hadn't done that. No, he was pretty sure Sylvia would look better in this suit than Anne did, and that thought filled him with a vague discontent. Somehow he had been cheated again.

The waves pulsed under Anne's body as she floated on her back and squinted at the sun. She was happy for the first time on this trip. She had always loved the ocean, loved the vast serenity of it. And she felt young and sexy. She told herself she was glad Mark had gotten the suit for her. Of course, she hadn't wanted to put it on. It was the kind of suit that was

made for a teenager, some young thing whose body was untouched by time, and it was tacky. She was so nervous when
she came out of the bathroom. She worried that it made her
look old, as though she was trying too hard. But the way
Mark acted had reassured her, especially after the night before. That depressing episode on the bed. And that thing with
the pillows Mark had done—he'd seemed quite excited by it,
and she didn't mind if it made him happy. Now she was enjoying the feel of so much bare skin as she floated in the water.
She was half tempted to strip off the suit and float completely
naked for a while. No one would be able to see her out here.
She could never have worn a suit like this with Preston. He
would have frowned and said something that made her feel
ugly.

But Mark's excited fumbling had shown her that she was
still young and beautiful. It was exhilarating being liberated
from the stultifying atmosphere of Eden's Glen, and she fantasized as she floated in the water about where they would go
once they were married. She'd always wanted to try California. Perhaps a place in the wine country. Nothing flashy. Just
a little vineyard. She could picture herself pouring wine occasionally for the tourists, her hair back in a bandanna, wearing an old pair of jeans and cowboy boots. Or someplace else.
She didn't know if he really wanted to move. Or if she did. It
would kill her not to be able to see Baird, although he would
be going to college soon. But the details didn't matter. It
would all work out.

She floated for a long time and thought about her new life
with Mark and made a resolution. She was going to stop feeling anxious and trust her feelings, trust Mark, trust everything. And she was going to wear that bikini every day they
were there as a symbol of her new life.

———

One night after he returned from Florida, Mark ignored Sylvia the entire evening, not even bothering to respond when she spoke to him. That night, Sylvia's hand tentatively reached across the wide expanse of bed and rested lightly on his arm. Then she shifted her body closer, and the hand moved lower. Afterward, it was as if it had been a dream. He hadn't experienced such passion and intensity from Sylvia since the first year of their marriage. The next night, the same thing. And the night after that. On the following night, she cried softly as she moved on top of him and buried her head in his chest. And when she came, it was with a long, painful wail.

They stayed up the rest of the night and talked about everything—her disappointment with him, with their life, her feelings of guilt, his own hurt and frustration. Not the affair, of course. Not after so many years of cold war. He wasn't going to talk about *that*.

CHAPTER TWENTY-SEVEN

Preston should have known better than to take Vicky to the party. Or at the very least he should have talked to her, given her some idea what the night would be like. Not that he needed to tell her how to dress or what to say. But some sort of idea of what was expected of her. He had been going to cocktail parties for so long that the countless minor decisions involved had become instinctual. There were dozens of fine social gradations to the outfit alone—whether he should wear a tie with a sports jacket or just a sports jacket or only a button-down or perhaps a polo shirt. Slacks or something more casual. Maybe those outrageous madras pants if the occasion called for that sort of thing. Or those blue pants with green whales he wore every year to the Eversons' summer party because Fred would also be wearing them and because the pants themselves had become a part of the tradition, and people would comment if he didn't wear them. Socks and belts and cuff links and on and on—each choice calibrated for the specific occasion. And all of these decisions second nature. Like the club rules, many of which weren't even written down but were simply custom. A testament to good breeding and tact.

The point was that he no longer had to think about these

decisions. It was as if each party had its own uniform. There were a few people who refused to bow to these conventions and even insisted on flouting them, although they were the most image-conscious of all, their very rebellion necessitating hours of careful choices as they considered the fine line between enjoyable provocation and obnoxiousness.

And he didn't need to be told that a seven P.M. cocktail party at the Abbotts' was a more formal affair than an eight P.M. dinner party at the Sloans', even though their invitations suggested the opposite. Or that Eldridge Bellrod never wore anything but a coat and tie to his own cocktail party but would have been aghast if any of his guests thought they had to match his formality. Or even that one never wore one's nicest shirt to the Smythes' Christmas party, because everyone was forced to drink a lethally potent punch in tiny martini glasses, which meant that people were sloshing their drinks on you all night long.

The point was that he knew all of this and Vicky didn't. And he should have said something. When it was already too late, Preston realized he should have thought more carefully about the entire evening. Once he had decided to introduce her at a party, he had simply chosen the first available occasion and told Amelia Swanson he would be coming with a guest. He should have known then, by the small silence on the other end of the line, that he was making a mistake. But he didn't. Or maybe he heard it and didn't care. Perhaps that was the real problem with his relationship to Vicky—he had allowed himself to become cut off from the world of Eden's Glen, from the people who had surrounded him his entire life. A chorus of voices that defined what was and what was not acceptable. He knew Anne disliked that aspect of the town and chafed at the restrictions those voices imposed, but Preston found them comforting. Of course, he was less restricted

196 / Andrew Trees

by those voices than anyone else. Half the time, people watched him and only then determined what their own opinions were. He liked the murmur of that chorus in his ear. It offered a continual reassurance that the life he led was the right life, the proper life. Or he had liked the chorus until Anne left him, when he suddenly felt vulnerable and exposed to it. No longer its model but its subject. Looking back, he now realized that was part of Vicky's attraction. Those weeks with her were a retreat from that world, a cocoon where he could mend without prying eyes and sharp tongues commenting on his every movement. He cut himself off so completely that he almost forgot about them until he invited Vicky to the Swansons' and unwittingly thrust himself back under their scrutiny.

When that jackass on the train made a joking reference to his date, he knew everyone had already been gossiping about it. And then it was too late to back out, because it would make it seem he was somehow in the wrong, when he clearly wasn't. Anne had left *him*! Was he supposed to sit there and wait for her to come back? At least he didn't have to worry about running into Anne. She had turned down every invitation and kept herself carefully hidden—in some obscure way, Preston believed this proved that she was really at fault for everything that had happened.

But he should have chosen his ground more carefully. He could have picked a different party, one where the chorus didn't promise to be so loud and insistent. He had been impulsive, unthinking. Many of Anne's closest friends were going to be there. He supposed they would think he was trying to parade this new woman around so it would get back to Anne and make her jealous. Well, so what? He didn't mind that part of it. But it was at Amelia's house. And if there was any couple who delighted in pointing out the subtle distinctions and small infractions at any social gathering, it was Amelia and her husband, Julius. The party itself was an odd concoction. The invitations were always whimsical in a studied sort of way, carefully careless pen-and-ink drawings that seemed to say this was a last minute affair, just a few friends.

But anyone who knew about Amelia's summer party realized that was an affectation left over from the one semester she had spent drawing at the Lycée Français in Paris. Her friends joked behind her back that she was the only art student in Paris who managed never to set foot on the Left Bank since she lived at the Georges V and spent her time in the Ritz bar drinking Champagne with a variety of boyfriends from the lesser nobility.

Despite the casual invitation and the relatively early hour of the "cocktail party," it was an elaborately choreographed affair, which didn't draw to a close until well after midnight. Drinks around the pool followed by a buffet dinner under a tent in the backyard, a swing band and dancing after that, fireworks over Lake Michigan, and then around midnight a light supper.

No, he had not given nearly enough thought to this evening. He was wearing what he thought of as his formal casual wear—a blazer and an Hermès tie. And to give his outfit that hint of frivolity Amelia enjoyed, a pair of wildly patterned socks that clashed with his gray slacks.

He walked through the door and found Vicky in slacks and a cotton sweater, and he realized at that moment that the evening was going to be a disaster. Only his fear of what people would say about his sudden cancellation convinced him to go through with it.

"Perhaps you could wear something a bit more dressy," he said casually.

"Don't be silly. Going overdressed to a party is a terrible

faux pas." She batted her eyes playfully at him. "Besides, you told me you love the way I look in this sweater."

He suppressed a grimace.

"A skirt or perhaps a sundress," he said.

"I look fine." She laughed. "You don't find me telling you to change your socks, even though they clash with your pants."

He rubbed his eyes briefly. Even the thought of recounting the story of why he wore wild socks to the Swansons' exhausted him.

"Vicky," he said more forcefully than he intended, "you have to change your clothes and put on a bit more makeup."

His tone snapped Vicky out of her playful mood, and she stared at him as if he had just slapped her. Her lower lip started to quiver. And then he found himself on the couch with his arm around her, reassuring her that she was very beautiful and that he wanted nothing more than to go to the party with her, although he was already dreading the night ahead. All the while, darting discreet glances at his watch and realizing that they were going to be very late. By the time Vicky reemerged in a long skirt and a badly fitting blouse and wearing too much makeup, there really wasn't time to do anything else but hurry off to the party.

He had timed it perfectly. He would pick her up and drive into the Swansons' long circular driveway about twenty minutes after the party began. But when they finally arrived, they were an hour and a half late, and Amelia was not happy about that.

She greeted him coolly at the door, making it perfectly evident that she was offended. She did at least feign happiness at meeting Vicky and greeted her with a kiss in the air, but her expression changed when Vicky gave her an actual kiss on the cheek. The faint impression of Vicky's lips was visible on Amelia's carefully applied foundation for the rest of the evening, which she discovered to her horror only later that night when she was taking off her makeup in the bathroom.

Dinner had gone relatively well. They sat with Don Lufkin, a good friend of Preston's, and Don's wife, and the two were very gracious. Things went less well after that. Anne's friends made a point of coming over en masse and asking catty questions until he and Vicky escaped to the dance floor. He felt better until he saw two of Anne's friends in the corner pointing at Vicky. It was like being back in high school, only high school had never been like that for Preston. People did not point at him or at people he was with and judge them! He could imagine exactly what they were saying about Vicky, commenting on what she was wearing and mocking him for being reduced to going out with some bumpkin. It made him sick to his stomach, and during the fireworks, he made an excuse to Vicky about not feeling well. They left while the sky exploded behind them, and everyone else watched until the last ember had floated down and given off a dying hiss as it sank beneath the waves.

They left, but they were not forgotten. As the light supper was served, the chorus noticed that Preston and Vicky had disappeared, and they discussed them in clusters over plates of roast beef hash and poached eggs. The most vicious comments were directed at Vicky, but plenty of heads wagged in displeasure at Preston as well. More than one woman declared loudly, "He should be ashamed of himself, bringing a woman like that to Amelia's party." And the others chimed in with their disapproval, and many people shook their heads sadly and talked of "poor Anne." The men were mainly silent, but they made it clear with their sighs and their downcast eyes that Preston had behaved very badly. Preston, they all said, should have known better.

Later that night, Vicky lay in bed trying to sort through her feelings. All in all, she thought it had gone pretty well. Poor Preston. It wasn't easy going to a party like that without Anne. She had to be understanding. And he had shown a lot of courage and loyalty by taking her to the party. Good God, the way those friends of Anne's marched up to him and started asking questions! You would have thought that Preston had left Anne, not the other way around. No, it couldn't have been easy for him.

Not that Preston couldn't have done a better job of arranging things. I mean, my God! The man doesn't say anything about the party, and then he asks her to change the minute he walks through the door. Which would have been fine, except for the fact that what she would have worn if she had known— what she would have worn if he had told her!—was at the dry cleaner's. Between spending every night with Preston and trying to move forward with the bakery, Vicky had barely had time to run an errand in weeks. So she was forced to wear that skirt that made her look like a schoolmarm. And that blouse she didn't like because there was a stain on the one she wanted to wear. And he had told her to put on more makeup, so then she had put on too much. Good God, *men*! They could be so infuriating! If he had only said something to her a few days ago, none of this would have happened.

Still, she considered the night a qualified success. Amelia was perfectly nice. And that couple at dinner were quite friendly. Except for that group of hovering women, things had gone fine. She wished she had looked better. She wouldn't make the same mistake next time, that was for sure. After a few more parties when she actually looked the way she wanted to look, everyone would forget about tonight. This might even become one of those things she and Preston would look back on and laugh about. Those funny stories couples tell about themselves. At least that was what she told herself as she lay in bed awake late into the night.

Don Lufkin just wanted to sleep, but his wife wouldn't let him. This happened after every party. They had to spend at least an hour discussing the evening, which was fine when the party didn't end at one-thirty A.M. and he didn't have an eight A.M. tee time the next morning. But he listened as attentively as he could and offered an occasional murmur of agreement. From long experience, he knew that a failure to listen would only cause a fight that would last far longer than an hour and would probably end with him on the couch. She spent most of the time on Amelia, particularly enjoying the smudge on her cheek. Not that he could blame her. Amelia loved nothing more than going to a party and then regaling her friends with the failures in taste she detected, often not bothering to keep her voice down. As his wife wound down, she drowsily brought up Vicky. After cataloging a long list of faults with her outfit, she dismissed her with a wave of her hand.

"That will never last," she said.

CHAPTER TWENTY-EIGHT

After Florida, Anne noticed a change in Mark. He was more serious, somber even, and she hoped he was finally ready to talk about their future, to make some sort of commitment. He had asked her to meet him at the nature preserve bench, which was a good sign. They would plan their future at the place where it all began. The fact that they were finally going to talk about moving forward was a huge relief. Anne didn't like to admit it, but she was starting to feel desperate. No, not desperate. Anxious, perhaps. There was no need to use a dire word like desperate, especially when it would only force her to wonder if things with Mark . . . well, there was no reason to think about that. She was not desperate.

Of course, nothing had happened the way she thought it would. She had expected some act of contrition from Preston. A gesture to heal the breach. That hurt her more than whatever happened with Maria. It showed such a lack of remorse. An affair was one thing. But not apologizing for it—she didn't know how that was possible if their two decades of marriage had meant anything. Men fell into affairs for lots of stupid reasons. Even Preston. Too much to drink and a certain type of woman was all it took. Someone who was easy, although that word struck her as archaic, a word her mother would have used. Maybe that was the problem. Nothing meant what it once did. Her mother would have said she was easy for sleeping with Preston before they were married, but women's magazines made it sound almost quaint that some women slept with only one man their whole lives. As if the line between being a good girl and being easy had simply faded away. Not that any of that excused Preston's behavior, although she had convinced herself that it was all Maria's fault. She could imagine what Maria had done to get him into bed. Anne realized that she had never liked Maria, that flirtatious tone she always took with men. The way she leered at them and told them how good they looked in whatever overpriced golf shirt she was trying to sell them. The woman was little better than a whore. Still, Preston should have apologized. He should have been contrite. Not forever, but for a decent length of time. None of that had happened, though, and she had stumbled into this affair with Mark. She worried that it had all happened out of a misplaced desire for revenge. Even if it had, so what? Didn't she deserve revenge?

But now what was she supposed to do? She couldn't go back to Preston without an apology from him. It would be humiliating, and how could she object to anything he did in the future if she crawled back now? Too late, she realized that it had been a terrible mistake to move out of Winthrop Hall. It had given a kind of permanence to their rift. But she couldn't imagine being a single woman and raising Baird in a depressing little house. Or going on dates. Or getting a job to keep busy. When they divorced, Anne wouldn't be able to set foot inside the club, except as a guest. It was a long-standing policy that membership stayed with the husband in the case of a divorce. Everything was designed to belittle her. For all of her hesitations and doubts about him, Mark had come to seem like the only way forward. She told herself that she had no doubts about Mark himself. It was only their situation that gave her pause. The complications of marriages and children and the interlocking friendships of Eden's Glen.

When Mark emerged from the woods wearing his usual running clothes, she was disappointed. No flowers or Champagne. No grand romantic gesture. Still, the important thing was the future.

Mark sat down beside Anne and took her hand.

"Anne, you know how special our time together has been for me."

"For me, too," she said, barely able to contain her excitement now that her life was going to move forward again, that this awkward, awful purgatory she was stuck in was finally going to end. A new life away from Preston and Eden's Glen! She was almost giddy, and her mind instantly turned to the future—a beautiful house in the mountains. Or perhaps by the ocean. It didn't matter. She knew she would be happy wherever they went. Weren't they happy now?

"And I don't regret anything about our interlude," he continued.

"Interlude?"

Mark was pleased with his choice of the word. He'd been thinking about what he was going to say all day. "Affair" made it seem so tawdry, but "relationship" sounded too permanent. He had to walk a fine line. He needed to make it clear that things were over, but he wanted to let her down easy. He wasn't a cad after all. He still cared about her and wanted to see her happy. And he wanted to shuffle her out of his life as quietly as possible so that Sylvia would never hear anything about this. All in all, he thought he was being quite gentlemanly about the whole thing. I mean, my God, the woman couldn't expect him to upend *his* life just because she had upended her own.

"Well," he said gently, "it doesn't matter what we call it. We knew that this could never last. Our kids, this town, it's too complicated. I wish that wasn't the case, but what can we do?"

He waited for Anne to speak, but she simply stared at him with her mouth slightly open. It wasn't her most attractive pose, he thought.

"Anne?"

"But . . . but . . . the future . . . Our future. Together."

"You must have known that was pure fantasy. It was a fun indulgence imagining some other life for ourselves, but we both knew that was never realistic. We have to be grown up about this. We have to deal with this as adults. We have to take responsibility for our lives. We can't just walk away from all of our commitments. You wouldn't want that either. What about Baird? You wouldn't want to walk away from him, would you?"

Yes, he had worked on that bit for a long time. It was very important that she see this his way. Adults didn't throw fits or make threatening phone calls to your house or tell your wife. Besides, he had never actually promised her anything. He had never said he was going to leave his wife or move away. What did she expect? So he had let her dream a little bit on that tired couch in his office. It wasn't as if he had signed a contract. What did she expect?

"But Sylvia—you said you were unhappy."

"Every marriage has its ups and downs. You know that."

He wasn't about to tell her that things had changed in that area. No, that would be disastrous. Anyway, it was true. Every man complained about his wife. Half the shows on television were about infidelity. She couldn't really have thought he was doing anything more than voicing the usual complaints.

Anne's halting questions continued for several more minutes, and Mark thought he handled them very smoothly. But finally he grew impatient.

"Anne, I think we've said all we have to say," he said tersely. He stood up and walked toward the woods. "Really, this is the only way. And maybe this is an opportunity for you to take a good, long look at your life and make some positive changes. I know that's how I view our time together. Good luck."

He moved off into the woods and smiled to himself. He had been so nervous. He didn't like to admit it, but after all those weeks together, he was still a little in awe of Anne. Of course, the glamour had worn off the physical fact of Anne's beauty. The first time he had seen her naked, his whole body had tingled in anticipation, and he had lasted an embarrassingly short length of time. But the Florida trip had cured him of that. And it wasn't easy for him to keep up the pretense now that he and Sylvia were fucking like a couple of horny college kids. My God, he was in his forties. It was no mean feat doing it with Anne in the afternoon and then with Sylvia in the evening. And he had come to a realization one night as he curled around Sylvia's back and cupped his hand between her legs the way he used to do when they were first married. His fingers had grazed lightly against her pubic hair, and he was struck by how similar it felt to Anne's pubic hair. That same curly, prickly sensation. That same slight dampness. And he realized that fucking Anne was not that different from fucking Sylvia. And although he wasn't that experienced, he thought that fucking any woman would not be that different. There was a basic biology after all. A certain way things went together. He had mistaken the excitement of being with someone new for the excitement of doing something new. Once he thought this through, he was quite proud of himself. It struck him as a mature attitude. Wise even. In that sense, he was glad of the affair. It had given him a newfound perspective. A certain depth. Yes, Mark really was quite pleased with himself.

But that didn't make things with Anne any easier. It wasn't as if he could share his newfound wisdom with her. Although he was no longer in awe of her physically, he was still pretty goddamn nervous about telling her. He wasn't too worried that she would do anything. Anne wasn't that kind of woman. Too much pride. It would be humiliating for her to tell Sylvia. But she was still Anne Winthrop. Mark knew it was silly. She wasn't with Preston anymore. From the way she talked, she would never go back to him, but there was still something about her. A kind of dignity that was more than just pride. It was almost regal, although that sounded a little grand for a woman who was about to get divorced and who lived in a dinky little house.

Now that it was over, and he was walking back down the path to the parking lot, he felt sorry for her. Throwing it all away because of some stupid affair between Preston and Maria. My God, he shuddered to think about what his life would become if Sylvia ever found out about Anne and made the same choice. He wouldn't be living in his own house like Preston. *He* would be the one living in a depressing little apartment. It was so stupid. He wanted to run back up the hill and tell her that she was making a big mistake, that she should go back and make the best of it. Of course, he had given her the opposite advice while they had been together, had enjoyed egging her on in her complaints about her husband. Not that he blamed himself. Preston was a goddamn prick. All the women in town, including Sylvia, treated him like a god. It was nice hearing him brought down to size, especially by his own wife. But he knew that going back up the hill would only make his life more difficult. Besides, Anne would figure it out. Eventually.

So he kept walking. It was a lovely afternoon. The shade from the trees along the path made the late August heat bearable as a soft breeze swayed the overhanging branches, shaking the leaves and making a sound that to his ears was like hands lightly clapping, as if the world itself were applauding his newfound perspective. And not just that. Applauding him. For ending the affair. For saving his marriage. Mark was a good man. Not like other men. Even that . . . interlude had only made him a better person. But now he was free of it.

Yes, that had gone remarkably well.

CHAPTER TWENTY-NINE

Preston reluctantly walked up the steps to Vicky's apartment. The old, rotting wood creaked under his feet. He sat down at the kitchen table and waited for her to get ready. His chair wobbled, and the tabletop was sticky underneath his drumming fingertips. He looked around the room and wondered what he had ever found charming. The pile of mismatched dishes in the sink with dark bits of food stuck to them struck him as deeply depressing, and the fluorescent light over the sink flickered on and off like a warning sign.

Vicky hurried out and gave him a quick kiss. Her wet hair was pulled back in a ponytail. She was wearing the same outfit Preston had made her change out of for the party.

"How do I look?" she joked, spinning around as if she were flaring out a ball gown.

Vicky hated the way she kept chattering away during dinner. It was obvious Preston had something on his mind. But she couldn't stop herself. Every time the conversation threatened to flag, she launched onto another topic. She didn't know what she was saying half the time. And she was drinking too much. One glass of wine had been followed quickly by another and then another. She could feel the warmth from her flushed face, and her words were spilling out so fast that she kept getting mixed up and having to repeat herself, looping back and hoping to pick up the thread of her own conversation.

She wanted to stop. But every time she looked at Preston's somber face, she rushed on. What was she so worried about? It wasn't as if one party were going to change things. He probably wanted to apologize. Maybe he felt guilty for not preparing her well enough. God, every time she thought of her outfit that night, she cringed. He must feel bad about that. He must know that she would never have gone to the party looking like that if she'd had some advance warning. If she could just stop talking for a moment.

This was always her problem, she thought, remembering her mother's voice calling out to her as she hurried off to meet some boy. "Don't be too eager to please," she would say, "let him be the one who is eager." That time they had sat around the television and watched the Miss America pageant, and the announcer was reading out the various categories in a rich baritone voice. He had come to poise, and she had thought, Yes. Poise. As if all of her problems could be fixed with that one thing. Doing better in school, for instance. It wasn't that she was dumb, but on a big test, she would grow so flustered and have so much trouble putting down what she knew. Or when it came to men. Doing what her mother said, which seemed silly at the time but would have saved her a lot of trouble. But poise had never been one of her talents. Warmth, yes. Kindness. But not poise.

But her wineglass was refilled again, and she was hurrying through a complicated story about how she'd found her apartment. And all the while Preston nodded his head slowly and silently, as if marking time.

Preston kept his sleepless eyes trained on the ceiling. He didn't want to look around the room and be reminded of Anne. That was the problem with his house. Everything in it reminded him of her. She had found his dresser at an antiques sale in Wisconsin. And she had replaced the drapes with fabric she'd bought when the two of them were traveling in France. Even the goddamn sheets reminded him of her!

He almost wished he hadn't ended it with Vicky just so he could continue to sleep at her apartment. God, that had been awful. The tears and the pleading and the accusations. The breakup had been longer and louder than when Anne had left him. Was that possible? Nearly twenty years of marriage, and his wife walked out the door after one fight. A few weeks of dating, and he had to wade through a two-hour emotional breakdown.

And it had seemed so clichéd—as if they were both playing parts in some poorly written television show. He found himself saying things that had nothing to do with how he actually felt but that sounded like the things one was supposed to say at that moment.

Vicky begged him to give her another chance. Literally *begged*. Her face smeared with tears and snot leaking down her face too quickly for her to wipe it away. It was repulsive. Not just the physical part but the actual begging. It was so unseemly. Didn't she realize how it made her look? If she had stayed calm and talked to him about the other night in a way that made it clear she understood, then he would perhaps have reconsidered. He probably wouldn't have changed his mind, but at least they could have talked about it like two adults. And then when begging didn't work, she started yelling that it was all so easy for him. But none of it had been easy. Didn't she realize what he had risked by going out with her? Didn't she realize how she had let him down at the party? And he wouldn't be doing her any favors by letting things drag on for a few more weeks. No, he had done the right thing. The decent thing. It hadn't been easy, but it was the only thing to do.

CHAPTER THIRTY

When Nancy saw Anne hurrying to her car late one evening, she ran outside with a solicitous smile and coaxed her to come inside the store for a moment. She cooed over her until Anne was seated uncomfortably on a love seat. Nancy sat next to her and took her hand.

"Darling, I've been so worried about you," said Nancy, noting happily that the separation had already taken a toll on Anne. Her roots were showing, and she needed a haircut. And there was a new look around her eyes. A hunted quality, as if she had just been slapped and was still skittish.

"How are you holding up?"

"I'm fine. Really."

Nancy could see her chin begin to tremble.

"Anne, you know you can talk to me."

She smiled inwardly when she saw the tears start to trickle down Anne's cheeks.

After she cried and Nancy coaxed out of her a few of the less embarrassing details about what her life had become—certainly nothing about Mark—Anne felt a little better. Up until that point, she had cut herself off from everyone at Eden's Glen, including her friends. She had thought it would be a week or two at the most before she returned. And a mixture of shame and pride had kept her from talking to them as one week slid into the next. In part, she feared they would take his side. All of them had told her more than once how lucky she was to have Preston as a husband. Then Mark came along and absorbed her days. By the time that ended, she had avoided everyone for so long that it was hard to start back up again. Today she had waited late enough in the day when she could be fairly certain she wouldn't run into anyone. And now she found sympathy in the most unlikely place—Nancy, of all people. Acid-tongued Nancy.

She was so grateful at finally being able to unburden herself that she allowed Nancy to talk her into buying an expensive jacket she didn't like. Still, the woman had listened to her. For the first time, she thought she could see a way forward, a glimpse of what her life could be without Preston.

"Nancy," she said, clearing her throat, "there's something I'd like to talk to you about."

Nancy was thrilled. Enjoying her newfound position of confessor, she had browbeaten Anne into buying a ridiculously expensive jacket. Anne's story was going to make delicious gossip at the Barclays' party that week. Every eye would be on her when she casually remarked that Anne had stopped by her store, although she wasn't sure she could wait that long to talk about it.

"It's about the store," Anne continued. "You remember we spoke at the beginning of the summer about my becoming a partner."

"Yes, of course."

"Would you still be interested in that?"

"I won't lie to you, Anne. The store has been doing very well."

The store was an ongoing disaster. No matter what she did,

214 / Andrew Trees

it lost money. Frank had actually carried out his threat to cut her allowance. She awoke each morning feeling a dull dread of the day ahead. The store had become her prison.

"But for you," she continued, "I would be willing to share my success."

"Oh, Nancy," Anne said, "I don't know how to thank you! That would mean so much to me."

"Of course, we'll have to figure out what a half share in the store would cost, and you will need to pay for your part of any merchandise in the store. But it's nothing you can't afford."

"Of course," Anne said.

"And it's not like you need to pay me today."

"Actually, about the payment . . . It might be a while before I would have the money. Not until . . . everything is sorted out."

"How long?" Nancy asked a little more coldly.

"I don't know. Months. A year at the most."

Nancy didn't know what to do. She wasn't sure she could put up with the drudgery of the store for months. She had held on this long only out of stubborn pride. She didn't want to close the store and give Frank the satisfaction of telling her he had been right. But Anne would continue to confide in her. She would have a ringside seat for the whole divorce. She could imagine what that would do for her social position in town. No party would be complete without her.

Even now, though, she despised Anne. The thought of having to pretend to be nice to her for months at a stretch almost made her gag. She couldn't forgive her for coming to her only in a moment of need and not earlier when Anne could actually have done something for Nancy. She blamed Anne for her allowance. Every time she noticed her own roots showing because she had to cut back on her visits to her stylist, she silently cursed her. If Preston hadn't forced Frank's firm to cut its fees, everything would still be fine. Frank hadn't actually told her that was the reason, but she knew. And now Anne was coming to her for charity! Nancy's smile hardened into a phalanx of glittering teeth as she made her decision.

"I'm sure we can work something out."

"Nancy, you are such a wonderful friend." Anne grasped her hand. "I don't know how I can ever thank you."

"Of course, until you have the money, you will simply be an employee of the store. You'll have to work for minimum wage."

She could see *poor* little Anne's chin begin to tremble again.

"How much is minimum wage?"

"I think it's three-fifteen an hour or something like that."

Anne despised herself for being so foolish and weak. Why had she ever confided in a shrew like Nancy? She had been right to cut herself off from everyone. They all loved seeing her humiliated, loved seeing her brought down to their level. It was so unfair. She was the one who had left Preston. Shouldn't he be the one who was humiliated by all of this?

And $3.15 an hour! Was that how much people were paid? It was scandalous. How did they live? She wasn't sure what they paid the servants who worked for them, but she was certain it was more than that. She realized she would rather die than have to abase herself before the likes of Nancy, and that realization only increased her anger.

She could feel herself tearing up again, but this time they were tears of frustration. She wasn't going to give Nancy the satisfaction of seeing her cry a second time, though. No, she would never make that mistake again. That bitch!

Nancy could see that Anne was about to cry again. She had already consoled her once today. She wasn't going to be consoling the likes of Anne Winthrop twice in one day.

"Well, Anne, I'm quite busy," she said. "You think about it, and let me know."

She watched Anne leave the store with the crumpled shopping bag clutched to her side. Nancy couldn't decide if she should phone people right away or wait until the party.

CHAPTER THIRTY-ONE

Matt hadn't ever seen Perkins this angry. It wasn't even a big loan. It was true the woman met none of their usual criteria. But Preston had asked him to do it, and he had done it. He kept waiting for Preston to call and thank him, maybe tell him about the promotion that was planned for him. And now Perkins had pulled him into his office and was dragging him over the coals. He kept his mouth shut, though, because it was obvious Preston wanted him to be discreet, was perhaps using the entire incident as a way to test him.

"If you can't give me some reasonable explanation of why you went against the bank's policies in approving this loan, Matthew, I'm going to have to dismiss you."

Perkins noted with pleasure that Matt's feigned indifference finally disappeared.

"Fired?"

"Yes, if that is the word you prefer," said Perkins, smoothing the strands of hair across his forehead back into place.

Perkins was enjoying putting Matt in his place. He knew he had a reputation for being a tough boss, even a cruel boss, which was grossly unfair, but it was a useful reputation nonetheless. Useful in helping him run the bank as efficiently and

218 / **Andrew Trees**

profitably as possible. And he was enjoying himself at this moment, although not, he would have argued, because of any innate cruelty. He was enjoying this moment because Matt was causing his bank to run inefficiently, and when parts of the machine failed to function properly, it was his job to fix them or replace them. It was all done in service to the bank. No one could doubt that if they looked at the matter in the proper context.

For instance, hadn't he treated that one loan officer with as much solicitude as if she had been his own child? Hadn't he given her extra time to recover from her chemotherapy? And when she still had problems remembering things, hadn't he offered her a new position that didn't require her to work with numbers? Of course, the job was a significant demotion, but he was running a bank, after all. It was difficult to find many positions that didn't require working with numbers and a careful memory. If she chose to do something else, he could hardly be blamed for that.

He also didn't like Matt's easygoing manner, but that was not, as some people might think, because of any sort of social envy. In point of fact, he didn't like it because banks ran more efficiently when employees were punctilious. A casual attitude was bad for the bank and bad for the bank's business. This loan was just one more in a lifetime of examples that had proven this to Perkins's satisfaction.

He himself had nothing against unbending a little—as long as it occurred in the proper context. There was nothing wrong with Matt going out for a drink or two after work and letting his hair down. Nothing wrong with that at all. Perkins himself often enjoyed a drink before dinner with his wife. But not on the bank's time.

Perkins leaned back in his chair and waited for Matt to speak after he had gotten over his initial shock.

"But I had approval for the loan!"

"You didn't have approval of the loan from me. And as even you must know by now, any loan must be routed through my office for approval. It's basic procedure, Matthew. If you can't remember something like that after all this time, I'm afraid that does not give me a great deal of confidence in you as a loan officer."

"But Preston signed off on it!"

"Mr. Winthrop signed off on it," Perkins said pointedly. "That is true."

This was nettlesome. He had no idea how Preston had become involved in this business, and it only strengthened his conviction that Preston had no idea how to run a bank. You couldn't give a loan to every Tom, Dick, and Harry because some loan officer bothered you. He had likely signed off on it simply to get rid of Matt, whose cavalier attitude probably grated on Preston as much as it did on Perkins. But Perkins knew how to handle such matters. No, you couldn't sign off on something like that to make the problem go away. You had to deal with it directly. You had to fix the machine.

"Just because you somehow managed to circumvent bank procedure does not make any of this all right. In point of fact, bothering Mr. Winthrop about this only makes your error look more egregious. Much more egregious, I'm afraid."

"But—but—"

"No, Matthew, I'm afraid you and Winthrop Trust are going to have to part ways."

"But Mr. Winthrop called me about the loan!"

"I find that unlikely."

Perkins was almost amused. It was incredible what people would say when they were in trouble. Preston would never bother himself with something like this. That was one of his problems. He didn't realize that a bank was nothing less than the sum of these small decisions in aggregate, that he should care about each and every one of them.

"It's true! He told me to send the loan directly to him."

"He told you not to send it to me?" Perkins was aghast at this flagrant breach of procedure.

Matt nodded.

"And you can prove this?"

Matt nodded again.

"Fine," Perkins said, "prove it to my satisfaction, and I will perhaps reconsider."

Matt hurried out of the office, and a slow smile spread across Perkins's face. Was it really possible? Had Preston purposely circumvented bank procedure? If so, how far could Perkins take this? At the very least, it would be embarrassing for Preston, but what if the board was made to see this gross breach of procedure in its proper context? What if they could be made to see just how pernicious this type of activity was?

The first faint outlines of a plan began to form in Perkins's mind. The vague inklings of a vast shift in which it would no longer matter that he was losing his hair and that people at the bank made fun of him, a shift that would make people like Matthew show some respect when he walked into a room. President Perkins had a nice ring to it. Crisp. Efficient.

And as any objective observer could not fail to see, he was doing it in service to the bank. Fixing a problem like Matt was like oiling a rusty hinge, but fixing a problem like Preston Winthrop was like rebuilding an engine. Yes, under Perkins's steady hand, Winthrop Trust would finally run like an efficient machine.

CHAPTER THIRTY-TWO

Norman had always known the receptionist at his office liked him. And why shouldn't she? He was one of the top people at the firm. Then there had been that little incident at the Christmas party when Marjorie had pushed up against him wearing that tight scoop-necked sweater with her tits practically falling out of it and kissing him right on the mouth, even darting her tongue past his lips for a moment. She had whispered something about mistletoe and giggled before wandering off to the bathroom.

And it wasn't really his fault, was it? He and Paige hardly ever had sex anymore, what with the baby and her church groups. Even when they did, it was no good. Paige complaining about how tired she was and Norman humping away like crazy to try to get her excited. Half the time she would tell him to go ahead and finish because she was too tired. It made him feel pathetic, hurrying his thrusts and trying not to notice the vacant look in her eyes. He would come with a quiet sigh and roll off of her and hand her some Kleenex. She would pull on her underwear and nightgown and go to sleep as if they had just turned off the local news. And he would lie there feeling spent and dissatisfied. Simply watching her pull on her underpants was depressing. She used to wear these sexy little thongs, but now she wore large white cotton underpants that reminded him of his mother.

So he started to flirt a little more with Marjorie. Nothing wrong with that. A few words from someone who laughed and smiled at what he said. They started having the occasional lunch together or a drink after work. One night, when he stayed late, she walked into his office and they started joking around, and the next thing he knew, his pants were around his ankles and they were doing it right there against the wall. What had they called it in high school? A knee trembler. Every picture on that wall was askew by the time they were finished. And there was such a look of gratitude in her eyes. Jesus Christ, was it too much to expect that from his wife once in a while?

That was how it began. They were discreet. The occasional late night tryst in the office, or they would go back to her apartment and fuck there. The funny thing was, he didn't feel guilty about it. He figured Paige wasn't interested in sex anymore, so what did it matter if he found someone on the side? He wasn't hurting anyone. That was how Norman saw it.

CHAPTER THIRTY·THREE

Preston used to look forward to a round of golf with Costas. He would play better than usual, as if Costas's swing magically rubbed off on his own. And Costas was one of the few people in his life who didn't want anything from him. They had a nice, easy camaraderie. They would play for a few bucks, and Costas would usually take his money. But Preston didn't care. He liked hearing Costas's stories about playing the semipro circuits and hustling guys like him when he was a teenager. And Costas could always make him laugh. He would tell filthy jokes with a choirboy face. And when everyone else broke up around him, he would look at them innocently, as if the words had never passed his lips. But things had changed over the last few years. It was possible he had found out about Maria, although Preston doubted it. Even if he had, Costas had left her, so he could hardly be jealous of what she did these days. My God, she still ran the shop, which would have been masochistic if Costas still had feelings for her.

He watched Costas walk briskly up the small hill to the first tee.

"All right, Preston, are you ready for me to take your money?"

Preston gave him a tight smile.

"How about fifty bucks a side and a hundred for the eighteen? Automatic press if you are more than two down," said Costas.

"No press," said Preston.

"What are you worried about? Don't be such a tightwad."

They used to play for $5 a side and $10 for the eighteen. Jesus Christ, the other week Preston had lost $200. And it wasn't just the money. It was the way Costas gloated about taking it from him. In the old days, when Costas won, he was almost apologetic. I mean, Christ! He was the pro. He was supposed to win. But now he liked to rub it in Preston's face.

And it wasn't only the betting. He picked at Preston the whole round. He stuck him with the young caddies who didn't know what they were doing and gave himself old Scooter, who had been caddying there for thirty years and was worth at least three shots a round. Then there were the snide remarks. Every time he thinned an iron or missed a putt, Costas was right there to jab him. Preston could feel anger welling up in his chest, a spark of rebellion against his usual quiet civility.

"All right, but I'm taking Scooter as my caddy," he said.

Costas gave him a condescending smile. "Hell, Preston, I'll give you two caddies if you think it will keep you from slicing your long irons."

Scooter gave Costas a nervous look.

"Go on, Scooter," Costas said. "If he feels like he needs a babysitter, I'm not going to deprive him."

Preston positioned himself over his drive. He ripped the ball with a barely controlled fury and sent it rocketing down the fairway.

Costas's lips curdled into a halfhearted smile.

"Nice drive."

He liked playing with Preston. It was therapeutic. He took his money and went right up to the edge of being insulting, always keeping just on the side of acceptable banter among friends. The rich fuck! The guy had everything handed to him in life, and the bastard still had to go and sleep with his wife. Not that other members hadn't done the same thing. They all bothered him. Every single last motherfucker among them. But Preston made him angrier than any of those other assholes. The guy had everything! And it wasn't as if his wife had ballooned into some Orca, or he couldn't have found a nice piece of ass somewhere else. No, the fucker had to sleep with his wife. And what made it worse was that he had thought Preston was a friend. Not a friend you actually invited over to your house. He understood the rules about that sort of thing. But he enjoyed his rounds of golf with Preston. They had a good rapport, and he had thought Preston felt the same way. Then that fucker goes and sleeps with his wife! As if Costas were the hired help! Just some greasy punk there to do his bidding. It was unforgivable. And Costas was looking forward to making him pay for it again.

He felt the first flutter of worry on Preston's second shot when he drilled a three wood right between the bunkers, and Costas had to watch the ball nestle up to the flag for an eight-foot eagle putt. Preston got a stroke on the hole, so by the time Costas chipped it close in three, Preston was already one up. It was a tricky putt, but Scooter knew those goddamn greens better than Costas did. As he watched Preston's ball curl into the cup for a three, he realized he was in trouble. There was something different in Preston's eyes, a coldness. He barely spoke to Costas, none of the usual chatter or even an occasional nice shot. Nothing.

Usually, no matter how rich the members were, if you put a little money on the line, they folded. It didn't take much. Decent golfers suddenly got the yips over short putts when they were worth $20. Preston was better than most, but even he wasn't immune. At least he wasn't until today. Costas watched him launch another perfect drive on the second. His caddy, a young kid who had just started working there that summer, handed Costas the driver, although he always hit a three wood on the second hole.

"That's the wrong goddamn club," he barked, throwing it away in disgust.

His anger threatened to overwhelm him. His heart was thumping, and his mouth was dry and chalky. He swung too hard at the ball and yanked it left into the weeds.

"Fuck!"

By the fifth hole, he was three down and had to press on both the nine and the eighteen. He had to press again on the back nine. By the time they reached the last green, Preston had already won more than $300, and if he made his putt on eighteen, he was going to win another $100. Costas stalked around the green like an angry bear. He hadn't spoken for the last six holes, except to curse his caddy at regular intervals. He watched Scooter carefully lining up the putt, a ticklish ten-footer. The kind of putt an average golfer knocked eight feet by and three putted. A three putt would at least salvage a little of Costas's dignity and his money. They would tie the nine, and he would win the press. Scooter continued to study the putt and talked to Preston in a low murmur.

"Goddamn it, Scooter, I haven't got all day! Why don't you just hit the fucking putt for him!"

Scooter flinched and stood up hesitantly. Preston put his hand on Scooter's shoulder.

"We're going to take as much time as we need," Preston said levelly. "If you need to hurry off to your duties, we'll be happy to finish the round without you."

Goddamn that rich fucking son of a bitch! Costas folded his arms over his chest and glowered at Scooter. Preston and

Scooter took a last look and murmured a few more words. Preston stood over the putt and stroked it so gently, it was more of a nudge. The ball quickly picked up speed. By the time it reached the cup, it was moving so fast that it shot across the hole, banged into the back, popped straight up in the air, and fell into the hole, where it rattled around definitively. *Motherfucker!*

Preston walked over and held out his hand.

"It was just my day today."

Motherfucker!

Costas pulled out his wallet and started to count out the money.

"I'm short. I'll have to grab some cash from the pro shop," he said.

"Don't worry about it," Preston said breezily. "It doesn't matter."

Costas's fury boiled over.

"I pay my goddamn debts! All right? I don't need your fucking charity!"

Costas could see the coldness again in Preston's eyes and worried that he had gone too far.

"All right," he said, "go get it."

Preston turned to Scooter and gave him the money Costas had just handed over—more than two hundred fucking dollars!

"Here you go, Scooter. You earned it."

Scooter glanced nervously at Costas.

"That's very kind of you, sir. But it's too much."

"Nonsense," said Preston as he looked at Costas, "it's not that much."

Motherfucker! Costas stalked off to the pro shop. When Maria asked him how much he was taking out of the cash register, he told her to shut up and mind her own goddamn business.

After the round, Preston took a long, hot shower in the men's locker room. He didn't normally do that, but he was in no hurry to return home. He went through each shot in the round, savoring every last one of them. He'd shot an even par seventy-two. He hadn't shot a round that low in years. What made it sweeter was that he had taken Costas's money. He had loved stuffing it to him—watching him swear at his caddy and throw his clubs and kick his bag. It was as if they were engaged in a deeper, more elemental struggle, that it was far more than simply a game of golf. There had been something primal about this encounter. And Preston had absolutely crushed him.

Even so, Costas's behavior was appalling. He thought he might make a complaint to the golf committee. Perhaps it was time to encourage Costas to move on. The club could hire a younger pro, maybe someone who was more of a gentleman, a little more polished. And it would be a relief to have Maria out of the shop.

CHAPTER THIRTY-FOUR

Paige had originally gone to the church to make some friends, but over time she experienced a growing sense of belief, a conviction that there was something more to life that she and Norman were missing. She bought a special edition of the Bible for housewives and studied it in bed before she went to sleep. She tried to talk to Norman about it. He would listen impatiently and then make a sarcastic remark and go back to whatever he was doing. She told herself to be patient. That was one of the things the Bible counseled. But she was worried. Her Bible group's discussions about how to lead a Christian life as a family didn't seem to have much to do with her family. So she schooled herself in patience and waited for God to reveal His plan.

Then one day as she was pulling the laundry out of the hamper, she noticed a trace of blood on Norman's boxer shorts and looked at it in confusion. It wasn't time for her period. Besides, she and Norman hadn't had sex for weeks. She wasn't happy about that. A good wife should have regular sex with her husband, but she felt so distant from Norman. It was as if he couldn't be bothered to make an effort. He would roll over and press himself against her and pinch her nipples roughly and rub her briefly down there, and then he was on top of her, pushing against her as if she weren't even there. If he would slow down. If he would just do more for her. Not even sexual things. Just talk to her. That was all she wanted. But they never talked anymore. At least not about anything that really mattered. Patience, she told herself. This is a phase. We'll get through it. God has a plan for us.

She stared at the blood for a long time until a dull, unwilling comprehension stole over her. The pit of her stomach fell away, and she was suddenly dizzy and had to lean against the doorway to keep from falling down. She picked up the underwear and buried her nose in the folds of cloth and inhaled a loamy odor.

The first phone call she made was to her pastor. He came right over and told her that this was God's way of testing her and that a lot of couples emerged from this stronger than ever, that Norman's repentance could ultimately be the doorway for him to find God. When she confronted Norman, though, he wasn't repentant. He started yelling at her and telling her it was all her fault, that she was a bad wife and had driven him to it. When the pastor came to talk to them, Norman wouldn't let him in the house and accused him of turning his wife against him.

Everything moved quickly after that. A member of the church helped her find a good lawyer. Norman was forced to move out of the house and pay her a monthly sum. Soon her friends were introducing her to all sorts of men. Good men. Christian men who were happy to go to church with her. Her path had been made smooth just as the Bible promised, as if this were indeed part of God's plan.

Norman eventually married Marjorie and moved to another suburb. He never quite achieved the success he had hoped for in life, and after their initial months together, Marjorie developed a shrewish tongue and a stern sense of her own rights. Often, after she had flayed him for some failing, he would think back wistfully to his life with Paige. Occasionally, when he had too much to drink, he would brag to his neighbors about how he had once been a member of the finest country club in the Midwest. If Marjorie was in a good mood, she would let it pass. If she wasn't, she would fix her eyes on him in a way that made his insides shrink and say very firmly, "Norman!" And he would fall silent.

CHAPTER THIRTY-FIVE

Perkins waited nervously in one of the chairs at the bottom of the conference table. He hadn't put himself on the agenda because he didn't want to commit himself too far. He wanted to see how the board reacted to Preston's financial indiscretion. He knew most of the members fairly well, and he was confident that a few of them would be outraged at his behavior. But would enough of them be upset by it? It would do him no good to upset Preston without wounding him in any significant way. So he planned to introduce everything in a neutral tone and then see how it played out. If the board was still behind Preston, he would act as if the matter were of no great importance but did perhaps require a slight reworking of bank policy so that Preston could have more leeway to do that sort of thing in the future. He could even spin it so that it looked as if he were trying to protect Preston. If, however, the board saw it the way they should see it—the only way to see it, as far as Perkins was concerned—then he would impress upon them not only the financial impropriety of it but also the ethical impropriety. He had asked around and discovered a personal relationship as well, an adulterous relationship, and he was confident he could paint the entire thing in a lurid, unseemly light.

And then, who knew? Uncharted vistas unrolled before his

eyes. Perhaps a major expansion of Perkins's role with a com-
mensurate increase in salary. Or perhaps more. He didn't want
to get ahead of himself, but if the board saw this matter in its
proper light, Perkins might soon find himself at the head of
the table. And Preston would be eased prematurely into the
figurehead role of chairman, where he could no longer foul
up Perkins's well-oiled machine.

Preston usually enjoyed board meetings. He experienced a
sense of mastery, as if he were a general whose every order had
the power to create and destroy worlds. But he was having
trouble focusing today. He had glanced at the board packet the
night before, but it all seemed so unimportant. Whatever they
decided, the bank would trundle along comfortably as it always did. For the first time in his life, the work of the bank
struck him as pointless.

And Perkins simpering away at the bottom of the table. He
was so finicky that he usually insisted on having his items
scheduled on the agenda, but Preston could tell from the way
he was fidgeting in his seat that he was going to introduce
something under new business. It would undoubtedly be some
piece of bank procedure that Perkins would insist on laying
out in mind-numbing detail until the board was ready to ap-
prove whatever he proposed simply to shut him up so they
could go to lunch.

Preston kept his eyes trained on the papers in front of him.
Normally he had a friendly word for just about everyone
around the table, but today he was quiet and withdrawn. All
of them knew, of course. He and Anne were good friends with
many of these men and their wives. A couple of them pulled
him aside before the meeting to offer a kind word, but Preston found himself unable to do anything more than nod ston-
ily in return. He felt ashamed, as if all of this were a sign of an

inadequacy on his part. He couldn't escape the degrading sense that he was becoming an object of pity, so he withdrew.

The board was laughing about something, but Preston had missed the joke. The secretary taking notes in the corner coughed discreetly.

"And now for new business," she said.

Perkins raised his hand. Preston suppressed a sigh.

"I have something I would like to bring to the board's attention."

Preston turned to see Jonathan Summers looking at him with excitement. Summers was the board member closest to Preston in age. He had been a protégé of Preston's father, but when it became clear that Preston would become head of the bank, Summers moved to another company with his father's blessing. Summers had shot to the top of the corporate ladder and become an enormous success. He had made the front page of the *Journal* the previous summer. Preston and Summers had always been friendly and still played the occasional round of golf together. Summers lived one town over from Eden's Glen with his second wife and his three sons.

Preston remembered what a mess Summers had been when he went through his own divorce. Drinking too much. Sleeping around. Then he met his current wife, and he slipped right back into the harness as if it had never happened. Summers was one of the ones who knew, and he had called Preston last week to let him know how sorry he was. But Preston couldn't escape the sense that Summers was gloating—as if he had one over on him. And now, as Summers directed an excited smile at him, he experienced a wave of loathing so powerful, it nauseated him.

"You see, my old college roommate works at U.S. Fidelity and Trust and we were talking the other day. He was telling me how they want to get into the midwestern market, and the more we talked about it, the more we realized that Winthrop Trust would be a perfect buyout candidate."

Jonathan paused and glanced at Preston. The man looked as though he had aged a decade in the past couple of months. He understood all too well how that could happen. When he thought back on his own divorce—which he tried to do as little as possible—it still made him cringe. But Jonathan also knew it would pass. He had gotten through it, and Preston would get through it. Men like Preston Winthrop weren't knocked off course by a divorce, and if they did wobble a little, they righted themselves soon enough, although he had to admit that he liked Preston better this way. They had always been friendly, but Jonathan had never particularly warmed to Preston. It wasn't because Preston had blocked his path at the bank. That was perfectly understandable. Hell, his family name was above the door, and anyone could see that Preston was a smart, capable guy. Too capable. As if he weren't touched by any of the things that pressed upon the rest of them. It was hard to feel any warmth for a guy like that, but this thing with Anne had humbled him. When Jonathan looked at Preston, he realized he had never liked him more than he did right now.

"Now, of course, there are a lot of stumbling blocks," he continued, "but—"

"Sell the bank?" asked Preston with disbelief.

Jonathan expected this. No one ever wants to give up control of his own company, and he might never have brought it up if Anne hadn't walked out. With Preston distracted by his home life, though, Jonathan thought he could get Preston and the board at least to consider it. And it was a good deal, maybe a great deal. All of them would make a lot of money from the sale, especially Preston. And they could probably get Preston a good job at U.S. Fidelity and Trust. Something perfectly respectable.

"I know this seems a little sudden. I wanted to tell you earlier, Preston, but you've been . . . distracted lately," he said. Preston sank back into an embarrassed silence. "If you look at the numbers, though, this is worth considering."

Jonathan briskly laid out what it would mean financially for them, and he could see a few of the other men nod. By the time the meeting broke up, Jonathan was confident that a good portion of the board was behind him.

"Any other new business?" the secretary asked.

Perkins tucked his folder back into his briefcase. The board was too distracted to focus on anything he would say at this point. Besides, this merger opened up a whole new area of possibilities for him to consider.

As they left the room, Summers put a condescending hand on Preston's shoulder.

"Preston, give me a call if you want to talk. I know what you're going through," he said.

Preston wanted to bite his hand, but he only smiled wanly and turned to walk down the corridor alone.

In his office, he thought over Summers's proposal. The money would be immense. Preston couldn't believe how much U.S. Fidelity and Trust was willing to pay. Even the most extravagant projections of growth could hardly justify the price. It would be a financial coup. There was no doubt about that. Of course, they were paying as much for the foothold as anything else. It would make them a major player in the region.

But he didn't want to sell. The increase in his wealth wouldn't change anything about his life. And he didn't like the idea of having to answer to a boss in New York—or, worse, being eased out after a few years for some young, fresh face from the home office. What if he found himself retired at the age of fifty? What was he supposed to do then?

But he also worried about what would happen to the bank after he died. Would Baird take it on? Would the board be willing to place him at its head? It was hard to imagine his son ever becoming the president of Winthrop Trust.

CHAPTER THIRTY-SIX

Costas smiled lazily at the teenage boys waiting for their group lesson. He liked to arrive a little late. To let them know he could keep them waiting. Not so late they would complain to their fathers. Just a few minutes. Because that was one thing he could never do with the members themselves. He was forced to wait on them. But here the tables were turned. And Costas liked that.

The boys were pimply and awkward, and Costas enjoyed bullying them. Not in any way that could be called mean. More like a demanding drill sergeant. So he would make fun of them and tease them and yell at them. And they would leave the lesson demoralized and ask their fathers if they could stop going. It didn't actually make up for all the shit he had to take from members, but it helped. The tightness in his chest lessened a little bit, and for the rest of the day his breath came easier.

They were a sorry group of golfers. Chilly dipping their wedges and shanking their irons and shaking over three-foot putts as if they were trying to win the Masters. No, Costas didn't need to pretend when it came to expressing disgust for their games. All these kids getting lessons from the time they were five or six, and the little shits couldn't even play a decent round of golf.

Of course, if Costas were completely honest with himself, his classes were not helping them improve. It hadn't always been that way. He was a pretty good teacher, and when he'd first come to the club, he had taken pride in the junior golf program and worked hard at it. A few of those kids became good golfers. As soon as they showed real potential, though, their fathers would come to his office and start explaining why their son was going to work with some other pro, how they had to take the next step. As if it were obvious that Costas could never be good enough to coach their goddamn precious sons. Who the hell did they think had gotten them to where they were?

Costas could have lived with that. It didn't make him happy, but he could have accepted it. Grudgingly. But what really got under his skin was the ragging from those same goddamn fathers. Constantly needling him about the low round that their sons had shot. They never let up. And so gradually he stopped being a good teacher. He didn't tell the kids to do anything that was actually wrong. He simply learned to give them advice in a way that was more likely to screw them up than help them. Like instead of telling them something simple about how to sweep their arms back, he would give them a complicated explanation about swing plane that meant the same thing but left them wondering about weird stuff like what direction their club heads were pointing at the tops of their backswings. He didn't do this with the members. He still gave them good lessons—not that it mattered. Most of them never changed a thing about their goddamn swings no matter how many times he told them. But the members left their lessons thinking Costas was a very good teacher. And every time their sons would ask to stop taking lessons from Costas, the fathers would frown and shake their heads.

Costas lined up the seven boys at the lesson that day and began to put them through their paces. One kid wasn't wearing a proper shirt. Costas chewed him out and sent him off to the pro shop to buy a new one. The thought of that tidy profit put a smile on his face. During the next hour, he managed to yell at each of the boys about something, and he noted with satisfaction that they were all hitting the ball worse by the end of the lesson than they had been at the beginning. He decided to finish off the day with a demonstration of his superiority.

"Okay, boys, get out your wedges." Costas pointed to a red flag on an elevated green a hundred yards out. "I'm going to hit three balls. If any of you can get inside of my closest ball, I'll buy you a Coke. If you manage to get more than one ball inside of mine, I'll buy you a new golf shirt."

He took a couple of practice swings and then clipped his first ball neatly off the turf. It had a nice, high trajectory, bounced once just behind the pin, and then spun back seven feet from the hole.

"Aw, hell, I better stop there, or you boys are never going to have a chance."

The kids stepped up one by one, and each failed miserably. A couple of balls came close, but far more often they skulled the shot and sent it rocketing over the green or hit it fat or lost it off the toe. And Costas stuck the needle in. Every. Single. Time. He couldn't remember the last time he had enjoyed himself this much, and he was already thinking about how he was going to tell the story to some of their fathers later.

Baird was the last one to hit. Costas was looking forward to this. He was still burning after that fucking round of golf with Preston.

———

Baird couldn't stand these lessons, but he had stopped asking his father to let him quit a long time ago. He hated Costas. He hated everything about him. He hated how loud he was, and he hated the bullying. It was as if Costas took pleasure in tormenting them. They would be ready to play, and Costas would stroll out and tell them they couldn't play until three. And then at three he would tell them to wait until four. And then at four he would tell them they could go out at four-thirty but that they could only play nine holes. And Baird wasn't sure why, but the lessons never helped anyone get better. So he didn't pay much attention to what Costas said. He tried to play just well enough not to get yelled at but not so well that Costas would notice. When he got up to hit, he planned to leave his balls well outside of Costas's shot.

"Okay, mama's boy, let's see if you can manage to hit the green," Costas said.

Normally, Baird wouldn't have cared. Costas called all of them mama's boys. But not today. His face flushed, and he wanted to swing his wedge right into Costas's big, flabby gut.

"Well, don't stand there all day, Your Highness," Costas said with a laugh.

Baird suddenly stopped pretending and settled over his ball with a confident air. He clipped the ball perfectly and watched it float toward the flag. He noticed that Costas had grown quiet. His ball bounced once and settled just inside of Costas's ball.

"Well, well, well, what have we here? Will miracles never cease?"

The boys looked at each other nervously. Costas's tone of voice was one they had all grown to fear.

"Don't just stand there, Baird," he said quietly, "you might as well get those two shanks out of your system now."

The moment Baird made contact with the second ball, he

knew that one was going to be inside Costas's ball as well. Costas's face reddened.

"Congratulations, Baird. I guess even baboons get lucky once in a while."

Baird walked back to his bag to put his wedge away.

"Where the hell do you think you're going?"

"I put two balls inside of yours already."

"Get back here, and hit that goddamn third ball!"

Baird would normally have done what he was told and missed badly on purpose. Costas would have laughed and made fun of him. And everything would have been all right. But not today.

"I'll hit it," he said with a tight smile, "but if I get another ball inside, I want another prize."

He didn't really mean it, and he wasn't planning on making Costas give him the golf shirt. As soon as he saw the look on Costas's face, though, he knew he had gone too far.

Before he knew what he was doing, Costas ran over to Baird and grabbed his arm. Grabbed it hard. And leaned down into his thin, pathetic face and began yelling at the top of his lungs.

"Goddamn you! You hit that goddamn ball right now!"

"Fuck you!" Baird said.

"Fuck me! Fuck *me*? We'll see about that."

Costas squeezed his arm more tightly and saw a look of pain flash across Baird's face.

"Let go! You're hurting me!"

"What? Little mama's boy can't take it?"

Costas squeezed harder.

"Let go!"

"Are you going to cry? Is the mama's boy a crybaby? Is that it?"

"I'll hit the fucking ball!"

Costas dropped his arm. "That's all I wanted."

Baird's hands were shaking so badly he could barely hold the club. Costas smiled.

"Tell you what, Baird, we'll go all or nothing. You put that third ball inside of mine, I'll give you a new set of golf clubs. You miss, you don't get anything."

Holding back tears, Baird tapped the ball with the club and moved it a few inches.

"There, are you happy?" Baird said.

Costas shrugged.

"Lesson over, boys," he said, walking away.

Piggy watched it all with greedy eyes. Maybe he didn't have to be Piggy any longer. Before Baird even hit the third shot. Piggy was already shaping a story in his mind and imagining how he would tell it. He already knew the punch line— Crybaby Baird.

CHAPTER THIRTY-SEVEN

Although Blanche was one of her oldest friends, Anne almost didn't accept the invitation to tea. Driving those familiar streets past those familiar houses was a reminder of what she had given up. Blanche's house had always been one of Anne's favorites, and that made the visit even harder. She couldn't even decide what to wear. She tried on one outfit after another until a pile of blouses and skirts and pants and shirts spilled off the bed and onto the floor. She felt unmoored from her place in the world and couldn't find her bearings. Her friends had always envied her taste, her ability to glance into her closet and unerringly choose the right outfit. And now she found herself immobilized as she stood over a jumbled pile of colors and patterns and fabrics, which seemed like obscure hieroglyphics designed to humiliate her. Even then, she could simply have shrugged it off and slipped on a pair of jeans and a polo shirt. But a part of Anne couldn't escape the feeling that this social call was a test, that Blanche would take one quick look at her and decide whether Anne's self-imposed banishment should become permanent or not. At last, she gave up and put on a clean pair of khakis and a light blue cotton shirt, only remembering after she was nearly there that her outfit was a perfect match for the uniform worn by the florists at Zellinger's, minus the plastic name tag. The Anne from a few months ago, the confident Anne, would have made a joke out of it, and that in itself would have lent a certain charm to the resemblance and made it seem not so much a faux pas as a clever tweaking of social mores. But the new Anne kept plucking at the shirt as if the blue would take on a different hue if she worried it with her fingers enough.

Gracefully curving trees flanked the long driveway, and when she pulled in front of the house, the flowers made her stop and stare. Bright bursts of red and blue and white from the neat rows of impatiens. Pots of geraniums flanking the walkway like Praetorian guards. And a crowd of tall sunflowers nodding their heads in approval at the scene. Two gardeners were working at the side of the house, and she thought of the untended yard in front of her house with its sparse grass and empty beds.

Baird sat silently beside her. She was glad he was there, glad that Blanche had invited him to come and see Tim while they chatted. It made everything more normal, as if this visit were more for the boys than for her. She could see Baird wasn't thrilled to be there, but it would be good for him. He needed more friends. She worried about how much time he spent alone. Not that she knew what to say to him anymore about it—or about anything for that matter. Although she still tried to see him whenever she could overcome her dread of visiting Winthrop Hall, the visits rarely went well. She wasn't comfortable going to the house as a visitor, the two of them sitting stiffly at the kitchen table, making small talk in a mockery of conversation. It made her feel like a stranger in her own life, and the visits would leave her depressed for the rest of the day. And the one time she brought him to her house, he never said anything, but she could see how uncomfortable he was.

"Why are you wearing a long-sleeved shirt on such a hot day?" she asked in what she hoped wasn't a nagging tone.

Baird shrugged and continued to stare out the car window. She didn't even know how to begin a conversation with him anymore. She used to know every detail of his life, and now she hardly knew what to say to him.

Baird was dreading this visit. He'd agreed to come only after his mother had asked him repeatedly. Then he'd almost told her at the last minute he couldn't go. Now he regretted ever saying yes. Just sitting next to his mother made him tense, as if someone were standing on his chest and forcing his breath to come in quick gasps. Baird opened the windows in the car and turned on the radio so she wouldn't talk to him.

But other times he found himself wanting to talk, *desperate* to talk to her. If only they could have an actual conversation, he thought he might understand what was going on and if she was going to come back and if it had somehow been his fault. Questions multiplied in his head, but when they did talk, he was tongue-tied and didn't know how to ask the things that crowded his mind. Instead, they talked about stupid things like how his summer school classes were going or if he had seen any good movies. Seen any good *movies?* The world was falling apart, and his mother was asking about *movies.*

He could tell that she didn't like coming to the house for some reason, but the one time she'd had him over to her place had been a disaster. She couldn't stop apologizing about the way everything looked. He didn't care. It was better than hiding up in his room, listening to his father roam around the house. But then she started crying in the middle of dinner, and he didn't know what to say. Afterward, they watched television, but she sat right beside him and kept hugging him. It creeped him out, and by the end he couldn't wait to leave. She could tell, and it hurt her feelings. And she never asked him to her place after that. She still stopped by the house occasionally when she knew his father would be at work, but something always went wrong. She would start crying, or he would get upset about something stupid. At first, he felt sad about it. But then he started to grow angry. Very, very angry. His parents were supposed to be the adults. They were supposed to have some sort of fucking *idea* about what to do, but they were clueless. No fucking clue whatsoever.

Then he would suddenly be overcome by guilt. Like he should be doing something more. Being a better son. Comforting his mother when she cried. Finding a way to talk to his father. But he didn't know how to do any of that. And the only people he could ask were the people he was no longer able to talk to. If only he had had a brother or a sister.

Then his mother would ask some stupid question like why was he wearing a long-sleeved shirt, as if that *mattered*. His mother didn't feel comfortable setting a foot inside her own house, and she was asking him about what he was *wearing*. It was as if he were caught in some bizarre world where everyone was in on a conspiracy not to talk about the only things he wanted to talk about. Besides, he was wearing a long-sleeved shirt for a reason—to hide the bruise where Costas had grabbed him. His mother had enough to worry about without seeing *that*. Of course, it looked weird wearing a long-sleeved shirt in August. He wasn't an idiot. But what was he supposed to do? If she saw the bruise, she was going to ask about it, and she would get upset. Maybe she would yell at Costas. And what good would come of that? He could imagine the scene. His mother would look crazy, and everyone would gossip about it. So he wore a long-sleeved shirt. A large sweat stain had already formed on his back, and he felt like a dork without his mother asking about his shirt in this tone of voice that made him feel like an even bigger dork.

He should never have agreed to come.

————

Blanche greeted them at the door. Anne looked at her trim figure and her perfect skin and her neatly coiffed blond hair. Was that the way she used to look, to? An immense weariness stole over her, and she wanted to get back in the car and drive away. To drive forever, as if she could outrace time itself and make her current life into a bad dream. But she forced a smile and hugged Blanche, as if she were genuinely happy to see her. Blanche told Baird that Tim was out by the pool. Then she took Anne by the hand and led her to a quiet sitting room overlooking the garden. Afternoon sunlight filtered through the leaves and the wooden slats of the shutters and created a shimmer in the room as the shafts of light shifted and danced across the floor. It looked so beautiful to Anne that she wanted to cry.

"Anne, what would you like to drink?"

"An iced tea is fine."

Blanche looked at her and smiled.

"I'm going to have a gin and tonic, and I think you should have one, too. It will make everything easier."

Blanche couldn't believe how different Anne looked—older and plainer and something else that Blanche couldn't place at first. Then it struck her. There was something about the way Anne was sitting on the couch. She looked tentative, almost mousy. And what was she wearing? She looked like one of those girls at the florist's. Well, Blanche could hardly blame her. This visit would fix all of that, if Anne would only listen to her.

"How are you?"

"I'm fine."

Blanche wasn't surprised by her answer. After that horror Nancy had gossiped about Anne all over town, Anne was probably afraid to talk to anyone. After a couple of drinks and a little gentle coaxing, though, it all began to pour out, and soon Anne was weeping in Blanche's arms.

Baird wandered back to the pool. He could see Piggy lying on a towel reading a magazine. His fat belly spread off to either side as if he were slowly melting. Baird used to come over here all the time as a kid, and Piggy had been one of his good friends. That was before he was Piggy, though. When he was just Tim. Before the sleepover when Piggy made him watch some weird movie about two friends in high school. And that night when Piggy kept rolling up against him as if they were on a hill until Baird yelled at him to stop it, and Piggy freaked out and started crying. Before he started acting weird around Baird. Staring at him all the time.

"Hi, Tim."

Piggy grunted but didn't bother to stop reading his magazine. Baird wished he could turn around and leave. Although he and Tim weren't friends anymore, he tried his best to be nice to him. He was the only one at school who didn't call him Piggy. But Tim only seemed to hate him more because of it. Those dicks who sat at the cool table never stopped ragging on him, and he just lapped it up. Laughed and smiled as if they were the best of friends. Like that time when one of them had dumped spaghetti sauce all over Tim. Bright red streaks dripping down his shirt like blood in a cheap horror movie. Baird found him in the bathroom later, cleaning himself up. He had brought a shirt from his locker for Tim to wear. Tim was standing in front of the sink, wiping at the stains with those crappy brown paper towels that always fall apart. And he was crying. Baird didn't know what to say. He patted him on the back and held out the shirt. Tim was so upset that he hadn't noticed Baird come in, and when he looked up, he gave Baird a horrified look. "Don't look at me!" he had screamed over and over again until Baird put the shirt on the sink and left.

Not that Tim appreciated any of it. He still tried to hang out at the cool table whenever he could. No matter how much they laughed at him or made fun of him. And he was still a jerk to Baird, although Baird had no idea why. The other day he found out that Tim had been telling people at school about how Baird cried because he didn't win a new set of golf clubs. Tim was an asshole. That was all there was to it.

Baird peeled off his shirt. He could see Tim glance at the bruise on his arm before looking away. He dove into the water and paddled around until he got bored. After he dried off, he walked around picking up the various games and books that were lying around near the pool.

Piggy pretended to be reading, but the whole time he watched Baird out of the corner of his eye. Fucking asshole! Baird must have known Piggy hated him, but he still came over. It was like he was taunting him. It wasn't as if Baird didn't have his own swimming pool, which was twice as big as Piggy's. It was infuriating.

Piggy couldn't stop watching him. Baird's long, lithe body slipping easily through the water. The drips that fell off the bottom of Baird's suit as he walked around the pool looking at Piggy's things. Piggy felt a strange sensation well up inside of him.

"Stop touching my stuff!"

"Fine," said Baird, dropping a copy of *Sports Illustrated*.

Piggy hurried over and picked it up. "You got the pages wet!"

"Tim, it's just a magazine."

Piggy hated the way Baird still called him Tim. It was like he was mocking him in a nastier way than everyone else. As if he couldn't even be bothered to tease him. As if Baird had forgotten how they had once been friends. Why did he come over here? He would never be friends with Piggy again. So why did he come? They would never horse around or sleep together in a tent in the backyard the way they did when they were little. Rage welled up inside him, and he shoved Baird hard so that he fell back into the pool. Baird's head popped back above the water.

"Take it easy!"

But Piggy could barely see him now. His anger was so overpowering that his vision had blurred, and he threw himself into the water on top of Baird. His fat fingers closed around Baird's hair and one of his arms, and he pushed down with all of his might.

Baird didn't have time to react before Tim was on top of him, and the shock of Tim's body knocked the breath out of him. He had been under for only a few seconds, but he already felt he couldn't hold his breath for another moment. He kicked out wildly with his legs and managed to knock Tim's hand from his arm and get his head above water, where he gulped a breath. But Tim pushed back on top of him and shoved his head down again. Baird's lungs ached, and he started to fear that Tim wanted to kill him. He lifted his right leg and jammed it into Tim's crotch with all the force he could muster.

Soon, they were both lying on the side of the pool, gasping for breath.

"God, what's wrong with you?" Tim whined. "Are you gay? Do you like touching other boys?"

"Fuck off, Piggy," Baird said.

He stood up, wrapped a towel around his shoulders, and walked into the house. He didn't know what he was going to tell his mother, but he knew he wasn't going to spend another minute alone with Tim. He was outside the study when he heard his mother sobbing. He had heard her cry before, but he had never heard anything like this. This was more like wailing than crying. He stood there for a moment and then turned around and went back to the pool.

"What? Had to run to your mommy?"

"Shut up, Piggy."

"Did you cry, Baird? Did you? Did you?"

Baird feinted at Tim as if he were going to hit him, and Tim scurried to the other side of the pool. Baird deliberately picked up the magazine he had been looking at before and sat on a chair to read. Tim glared at him and then settled in a chair on the opposite side.

After Anne finally quieted down, Blanche took both of Anne's hands.

"Did I ever tell you that Rick and I separated?" she asked.

Anne looked at her with such raw need that Blanche had to turn away.

"It's true. It was a few years ago, and we kept it very quiet, pretended that I was away to help my mother through her illness."

Then she told Anne about Rick's affair. It was so clichéd that it was laughable—clothes smelling of perfume, pretending to work late at the office—and when she confronted him, he confessed. Later, that was the part she found hardest to forgive. That he was so weak and cowardly about the whole thing and hadn't tried to protect her from the knowledge of it. Instead, he poured out every last detail about his stupid little affair with a secretary at his firm. Blanche had vaguely remembered the woman from some Christmas party—big boobs and bad hair.

Rick begged her to stay, but that made him seem more pathetic. So she packed a bag and took the next flight to the Golden Door in California. She decided she would treat herself to the spa until she figured out what she was going to do to Rick. Then he hired a lawyer and canceled their credit cards. God, the humiliation! Begging Rick on the phone to pay her bill. And then, still full of pride, renting a cheap one-bedroom apartment in L.A. rather than returning. The month she spent there was the longest of her life. She felt like an exile. She had no money and no friends, and she wanted to kill herself half the time.

Then she made a decision. She scraped together what money she could, went to a beauty salon, and took the next flight home. For the first week after her return, she never said a harsh word about anything, let alone the affair. She acted as if it were her greatest joy to have Rick in her bed again, and she did things for him she had never done before she left.

Finally, when she thought it was safe, she talked to him about the affair. Not to berate him, simply to establish a few ground rules. He couldn't have a mistress, and he couldn't sleep with anyone locally. But what he did when he was away was his own business. As long as he wore a condom, she didn't want to know about it.

Before Anne could protest, Blanche turned the conversation to Preston, how no man cared more about propriety than he did, how he wanted to have her back if only he could overcome his own pride, and what Anne would have to do to make that happen. When she finished, she sat there silently and waited for Anne to say something.

At first Anne was horrified. Her pride rebelled at the idea of such a degrading arrangement, but in the golden afternoon light she softened. By the time she had finished her second gin and tonic, a pleasant drowsiness enveloped her, and she began to imagine that the whole matter had already been arranged, that she could drive to Winthrop Hall and walk through the door as if nothing had happened.

After a while, Baird grew hot. He took off the towel and dove into the pool. Eventually he forgot that Tim was there.

He thought about his mother's sobs and felt an overwhelming sense of guilt. He had managed to disappoint both his mother and his father. And he hated himself. He tried to come up with something he could do to make things better, but he couldn't think of anything. What if his mother and father never got back together? The thought of living alone in Winthrop Hall with his father made him shiver. Not that he didn't love his father, but he couldn't talk to him. Not the way he could talk to his mother, or at least the way he had once been able to talk to her. And the house was so quiet without her there. She used to hide notes in his room so that he would pull out a T-shirt and a little piece of paper would flutter to the ground telling him how much she loved him and how special he was. He had hated it when his mother pestered him with questions after school, but now he arrived home to an empty house and found that he missed it. He would have given anything to walk through the door and find his mother standing in the kitchen waiting to ask him about his day.

Piggy hid behind his magazine and pretended not to notice what Baird was doing. Gradually, Baird drifted closer and closer as he swam until finally he was near the edge of the pool, staring off in the other direction toward the back of the yard.

Piggy jumped out of the chair and launched himself at Baird. He could feel his knee smash into Baird's skull with a satisfying crunch, and he fastened onto his shoulders and shoved Baird's body down with all of his might.

Baird gave a halfhearted struggle, a couple of twitches, but Piggy wasn't going to be fooled a second time. He watched Baird's legs and made certain that they were nowhere near him. He could feel his fingers dig into the smooth flesh, and he smiled. Eventually he noticed that Baird wasn't moving, and he let go. Baird's body floated just below the surface.

Then Piggy felt a stab of fear, and he dragged Baird over to the steps in the shallow end, desperately digging his fingers into the soft flesh of his limp body. He pulled him out as far as he could so that Baird's chest and head were resting on the cement, and his legs were wedged on the concrete steps. Piggy stood over the body, terrified and uncertain what to do.

As the slanted rays fell across the floor and dazzled her eyes, Anne thought Blanche sounded perfectly reasonable. In fact, nothing about their life had to change. It would go on just as before. Blanche even seemed to suggest that Preston did not have to be the only one to enjoy greater freedom. But she didn't need to think about that now. It was as if a great weight had been lifted, and she wanted to lie down on Blanche's couch and sleep for a week. As if the past summer had been a bad dream that was now coming to an end.

"What are you doing dripping all over the floor? Go out and dry yourself off!" Blanche yelled.

Anne looked up and saw Tim standing outside the room. A puddle of water was growing around his feet, but he didn't move.

"Didn't you hear me? Now move!"

"Baird," whispered Tim.

"What? Speak up," said Blanche.

"It's Baird. He . . ."

"What?" Blanche said impatiently.

He wasn't a very articulate boy, Anne thought. Maybe it was his age.

"He's not breathing."

It took a second for the words to register, and then Anne leapt off the couch. Her glass bounced and then shattered against the parquet floor. She ran outside and saw Baird's body lying on the cement like a gutted fish. She grabbed him and began shaking him.

"Baird! Baird!"

CHAPTER THIRTY-EIGHT

When he came home from work, Preston received a phone call from Blanche telling him there had been an accident at the pool. He arrived at the hospital and saw Anne sitting on a hard plastic chair in one corner. Her fingers twisted her wedding ring around and around, and one look at her ashen face told him all he needed to know. He slumped into a seat across from her and waited.

Dr. Thornton hurried over from his office as soon as he received the call from the emergency room. By the time he arrived, the doctor on call had stopped his attempt to resuscitate Baird Winthrop and pronounced him dead at 6:12 P.M. Dr. Thornton looked down at Baird's lean adolescent body, already beginning to wither like a bud prematurely cut from the stalk, and shuddered. He had been Baird's pediatrician, had given him his immunizations, teased him about whether or not he had a girlfriend, seen him often at the club. He shook his head, disgusted at the waste of it all.

Out of habit, he examined the body. A contusion at the back of the skull that was roughly consistent with what the other boy had told the emergency room doctor about Baird falling on the cement. A few scratch marks and the early signs of bruising around the shoulders and neck, probably caused when Baird was dragged from the pool. He also noticed a bruise in the shape of a handprint on Baird's arm. Perhaps one of the parents. Dr. Thornton knew about the separation, of course. You couldn't live in Eden's Glen and not know. Although surprising to see the signs of child abuse, one could never predict how people would react to the stress of the breakup of a marriage. It was difficult to imagine Preston losing his composure like that. He had heard some stories about Anne, though, and it was possible that she had done this in a fit of rage. It certainly wasn't consistent with her personality, but it wasn't easy going through that sort of thing. The boy was dead, though, so there was no need to inquire any further, certainly no reason to add to the parents' suffering. If Anne caused that bruise, she would punish herself far more severely than Dr. Thornton would.

He and the other doctor spoke for a few moments about whether or not an autopsy was necessary. Dr. Thornton knew the parents would want an open casket and would resist the idea of cutting up their son. He looked down again at Baird, at the smooth skin and the young limbs, the flat stomach and the first signs of manhood.

"Goddamn shame," he muttered.

There was no easy way to tell parents they had lost a child, but there was no point in prolonging their anxiety. He walked into the waiting room. Anne and Preston looked up and could see immediately that his face held no comfort for them.

"Baird! My son! My son! Baird! My beautiful boy!"

Anne began to scream and didn't stop screaming until Dr. Thornton administered a sedative.

Preston listened silently to what Dr. Thornton had to say. Dr. Thornton patted him on the shoulder, but Preston didn't seem to notice. He stared, stony-faced, out the window, but his jaw continued to work convulsively as if he were trying to grind something down.

Dr. Thornton said what he could to comfort Preston and eventually left him, still standing silently in the middle of the room. The only change was that he had turned his gaze from the window to Anne, and he stared at her with a malevolence that frightened Dr. Thornton and made him hurry out of the room.

CHAPTER THIRTY-NINE

At the funeral, Anne wept until it seemed impossible for anyone to weep more, murmuring Baird's name over and over. Preston stood rigidly by her side as the casket was carried into the family crypt. The reception afterward was a brief, cheerless affair held at the funeral home after Preston made it clear he did not intend to let Anne set foot in Winthrop Hall again for any reason.

The mourners crowded into the drab rooms to sip coffee and speak in low voices about the boy. One of his classmates was so distraught that her parents had to take her home. She was crying loudly, and she kept repeating a confused story about being his lab partner and how she knew he didn't mean to do what he did. She seemed to feel in some obscure way that it had all been her fault.

Although he was in the midst of a divorce and had moved back temporarily to an apartment in the city, Norman Bond cleared his calendar and made sure to attend. He found a place near Preston's side as Baird's casket was carried into the marble vault. Later, he saw Preston standing alone staring blankly out the window, and he thought the only polite thing to do was to offer his condolences. He hurried over to him and stood silently for a moment, his eyes lowered in an affecting show of grief.

"Your son," Norman said, wagging his head, "seemed to be such a fine boy. Terrible what happened. Absolutely terrible."

Preston's eyes slid over him in a manner that unnerved Norman. They seemed almost reptilian, and Norman stumbled on nervously.

"Didn't know him well, of course. Perhaps I met him at the party. Such a grand party. Honor to be invited, really. Never thanked you properly." Preston's cold eyes slid over him again, and he shivered. "Not the moment, of course. So sad. So sad. Poor boy. Can imagine how you feel. I have my own son. He's . . ." The cold eyes stopped. Terrifying in their blackness. "Not the time, of course. Just wanted to pay my respects. So sad, so sad."

Norman took a large gulp of coffee to give himself a moment to collect his thoughts, but some of it spilled down his chin and onto his shirtfront. The brown stain agonized him.

"I'll just go and clean myself up," he muttered and hurried away.

He left in embarrassment soon after, and when he received a letter a few weeks later notifying him that his membership application to the Oak Hollow Country Club had been rejected, he blamed that inadvertent spill. It all seemed so grossly unfair, he told himself, especially after he had gone to such trouble to attend the funeral.

When Blanche approached Preston later about getting back together with Anne, he sent her away without a word in response. He seemed so certain in his fury about who to blame that others began to assume that Anne was somehow at fault, and gradually the idea solidified in town that she bore some hidden responsibility.

CHAPTER FORTY

Nancy liked to hold forth at cocktail parties, dropping hints about what she knew. She continued to dine out on the strength of her presumed intimacy with Anne, and some of the best houses in Eden's Glen, houses that had been closed to her and Frank, invited her to join them at small dinner parties. She acted as if discretion restrained her from sharing more than a glimpse of what she actually knew, but the truth was that even the few things she did tell people were almost entirely fabricated, or it was information she had managed to glean from mutual acquaintances.

But her welcome was wearing thin. People began to realize that despite a great deal of breathless exclamation on Nancy's part, they left conversations with her knowing no more about Anne and Preston and Baird's death than they had before. As Nancy's luster faded, they once again became aware of those elements of her personality that were grating and unpleasant, and the invitations dried up. Baird's death had given her new currency, though, and she was determined to secure her place in those houses by the end of the summer.

Dr. Thornton found himself seated next to Nancy at a party in early September. He had drunk too much and listened in a surly silence as she prattled on about Anne. It had been a hard summer. First Baird's death. A few days later, a local boy and girl were killed in a car accident. The boy's blood alcohol level was through the roof, but Dr. Thornton had helped keep the whole thing quiet. What would airing the truth have done for the grieving families? His own wife had recently miscarried in her third month. Yes, a hard summer. Too much death and disappointment. Dr. Thornton noticed he was drinking more when he got home from the hospital and also at parties. Too many mornings he woke with a low throb in his head and a dry mouth. He told himself it would have to stop. Not yet, though. He still came home too often to find his wife sitting at the kitchen table and staring silently out the window, or he would wake up in the middle of the night and see one of those young, slender bodies splayed out on the slab at the morgue. It was too soon for him to give up the comfort that alcohol offered. Things were too raw. Maybe in another month or so.

So he sipped his drink and listened to Nancy. It was obvious this woman knew nothing about Preston and Anne, yet she acted as if she were their closest friend. Why didn't someone tell her to shut up? He looked at the other faces around the table, but they all seemed engrossed by what she was saying. They had finished their drinks, but they remained perched around her, fearful of missing a single word.

"And I don't have to tell you what it was like at the hospital."

"You weren't at the hospital," Dr. Thornton said quietly.

"What?" Nancy said, blinking rapidly.

"I said you weren't at the hospital."

Everyone's attention turned to Dr. Thornton.

"Of course I wasn't there," said Nancy, quickly recovering her composure, "but Anne told me about it."

"I doubt that," he said.

Dr. Thornton was as shocked as anyone else at what he'd said. Maybe he'd had more to drink tonight than he realized. He had already said more than he should have, and if he had been able to, he would have slipped away, found his wife, and gone home. But everyone was staring at him. Nancy was looking at him with contempt to cover her fear of falling back to her usual rung on the Eden's Glen social ladder.

"Oh, and I suppose you've seen Anne," she said dismissively.

Dr. Thornton looked down into his drink and tried to think of how he could politely excuse himself. He *had* seen Anne. He was worried enough that he had gone to her house twice. She was virtually catatonic. She had hardly bathed or eaten since the day of the funeral, and she sat at the kitchen table and stared listlessly out the window as he tried to talk to her. He was seriously considering having her committed until she got through this. He wasn't surprised by her reaction. She had lost her only son. There could be no greater tragedy. But he couldn't just let her starve herself to death. Each visit, she had roused herself long enough to plead with him to write her another prescription for sleeping pills, and each time he'd reluctantly given it to her. On the second visit, he'd told her it was the last time. He had given her the number of a grief counselor, but Anne hadn't called. He phoned Preston to talk about it, but Preston simply hung up without replying.

"Yes, just as I thought," she said. "Of course, Anne was an angel of a mother. When I think of the sacrifices she made . . ." She trailed off and remained silent as if the sacrifices were too intimate to be shared so publicly.

Why did no one tell this fatuous woman to shut up?

"And the stories she told me about Baird . . ." Nancy trailed off into another pregnant silence.

"You know nothing about Anne and nothing about Baird!" Dr. Thornton snarled.

He felt dizzy, but he couldn't sit there and listen to the woman for a moment longer.

"Surely you're not trying to suggest that Anne was a bad mother," Nancy said.

He thought of the bruises on Baird's arm. He had thought of those bruises every day since the accident. He didn't know anything for sure, but those bruises kept coming back to him at odd moments when he didn't expect it—when he was giving a small boy a tetanus shot or drawing blood from a baby. No, he didn't really know anything, but he couldn't stop thinking about those damn bruises.

"No one knows anything about anyone!" he said fiercely. He pushed himself unsteadily out of his chair and walked off to find his wife.

By the time the party had ended, Nancy had convinced everyone that she was the source of this new revelation, and she embroidered it so artfully over the rest of the evening that everyone went home convinced that the fault for the tragedy lay in some obscure way with Anne.

CHAPTER FORTY·ONE

By the time the board met formally to discuss the buyout, Preston and Anne had buried Baird. Preston arrived looking haggard. He hadn't shaved properly since the funeral, and his hair was matted on one side as if he had just woken up. Board members quietly approached him one by one to offer their condolences. He sat silently in his usual chair and absently shook the hands that were offered to him.

He no longer had any reason to reject the offer. There was no son. No family tradition to continue. No family. There was nothing but a bleak future in the empty, echoing expanse of Winthrop Hall.

He let the words of the board members wash over him as he sat there. He wasn't really listening, although he would occasionally catch a phrase. Fiduciary responsibility. Obligation to the stockholders. Responsibility to the community. Protecting their employees. But none of it mattered. Preston was the largest shareholder. Any deal was unimaginable without his approval. And the board would follow his lead. These speeches were a collective throat clearing as they waited to find out what he would do.

Eventually the room fell silent, and everyone looked expectantly at Preston. He thought about his father and his grandfather, of what they had built over the years. He recalled long speeches about what Winthrop Trust meant to the family and to the community. He remembered the mayor coming to his father for help refinancing the city's debt. He could even remember one cold, crisp November day riding with his grandfather in an old carriage down State Street in the city's Thanksgiving parade and people cheering for his grandfather and calling out his name. But what did all that mean now?

The board was still waiting, staring at him intently.

"Sell it."

They began to ask questions about the details of the sale, compensation packages, protection for the employees, his own position in the new bank.

"I don't care about the details. Just sell it."

He stood up and walked out of the room.

CHAPTER FORTY·TWO

At first, Perkins bitterly regretted the proposed sale. Just when he had found his chance, everything turned against him. After more careful consideration, though, he realized this could be a better opportunity. Convincing the board of the severity of Preston's fiscal malfeasance was never going to be easy. Not that he should have had to convince them. It should have been obvious to anyone. But far too many board members were chummy with Preston, Yes, technically it was still Preston's name above the bank's doors, but the board's first loyalty—in fact, its only loyalty—was supposed to be to the shareholders. Admittedly, Preston was the largest shareholder. But Perkins was himself a shareholder with a significant part of his wealth tied to the bank's fortunes. And as a shareholder, he was entitled to exactly the same consideration as any other shareholder.

Now that the bank was being sold, though, Perkins could leapfrog the internal loyalties and go right to U.S. Fidelity and Trust. There would be no problem with chumminess there, and Preston couldn't charm his way out of the whole mess over drinks at the club. No, Perkins was fairly confident that the people at U.S. Fidelity and Trust would view things with the severity they deserved.

Not that he wanted anything but the best for Winthrop Trust. As he said to himself many times, rules were there for a reason, and it didn't do anyone any good—including Preston—if they were broken. No, not just broken but flouted! Of course, if U.S. Fidelity and Trust saw everything in the proper light, they might very well decide that they needed a steadier hand to run the ship, and if Perkins happened to be that steady hand, then so be it. In any merger, the most difficult order of business was getting things running efficiently, bringing all the pieces together so they worked as a single unit. Who better for that task than he?

And U.S. Fidelity and Trust could count on his loyalty. He knew where the deadwood was in the bank. He had already informally worked out a list of people who could be let go so that everything would run more efficiently. They could count on him not to get sentimental about things.

CHAPTER FORTY-THREE

Gordon Talcott was not happy with the price he had agreed to pay for Winthrop Trust, but he accepted it as the cost of doing business. U.S. Fidelity and Trust had waited too long to get into the Midwest, and now they would have to pay top dollar if they were going to catch up with their rivals. It didn't help that the family was still involved. These family companies were a tricky business. There were all sorts of issues—family tradition, pride, fear of losing their role in the community. That was another reason he had made such a high offer. It had to be too good to turn down. And he couldn't afford the rejection, not with Wall Street breathing down his neck about the bank's lack of presence in the region. Failing to complete the deal would have knocked 20 to 30 percent off the stock price. But none of that meant he liked the price he was paying.

Still, it gave him a small thrill as he stepped out of the limousine and walked through Winthrop Trust's imposing entrance with his entourage of advisers and executives. In one fell swoop, he had put U.S. Fidelity and Trust into seven additional states with more than a hundred branches. This was more than a toehold. He had planted the bank's flag firmly in the only territory it hadn't yet conquered. Yes, this was quite a coup. There was probably much gnashing of teeth in rival boardrooms around New York.

There was one difficult piece of business remaining—
Preston Winthrop. He had expected the deal to include iron-
clad protection for Preston or at least an outrageous severance
package, but Preston hadn't made any demands. Although the
deal was going to make Preston unimaginably rich, Gordon
was still surprised. He couldn't figure out what sort of game
Preston was playing. Despite himself, Gordon had developed
a grudging respect for the man.

This was their first face-to-face meeting, and he expected to
be disappointed. The fact was that these sons and grandsons of
founders were usually a feckless lot, coasting along on their
family name and fortune. He was probably going to have to get
rid of him, which would be an unpleasant business even without any contractual guarantees. Many of the employees would
be loyal to Preston, and the local business community would line
up behind one of its own. The last thing he needed was to create ill will at a moment that should be his crowning glory.

No, he would have to find a way to ease him out gently or,
better yet, convince him to choose an early retirement. There
were plenty of ways to make life unpleasant for Preston Winthrop. It was simply a question of patience and persistence.
There was already something about a loan that had been
handled improperly. Who was that annoying man who had
brought it to his attention? Peterson? Well, it didn't matter
who it was. The loan was a helpful first step in the process, a
clear reminder to Preston that he was no longer in charge.

He swept into the boardroom feeling like a conqueror.

"Remember—he just lost his son," an aide whispered to
him as people stood up and began introducing themselves.

Preston sat at the end of the long conference table, staring out
the window at the city below. There was a giddy energy in the
room—most stood to make a fortune from the takeover—but

Preston remained silent. He was indifferent to everything around him.

He had forced himself to pull it together for the meeting. He owed that to his father and grandfather and to all the people who worked at the bank. He owed it to them to put his best foot forward. He showered and shaved and put on a charcoal suit with a sober blue tie. After getting ready, he had stared at himself in the mirror. He looked tired. And old. As if age had suddenly descended on him over the course of a few weeks. His hair was grayer around the temples, and the lines on his face had deepened. And his eyes—to him, they looked like the blown-out windows of an abandoned building.

When Gordon Talcott entered with his people, Preston stood up and tried to smile pleasantly. He was silent for most of the meeting as various people laid out timetables and discussed the broad details of how the operations would be merged. After the meeting ended, Gordon asked him to remain behind. The two of them sat together at one end of the table. They were joined by an attractive young blonde who was going to be the temporary liaison between the two banks.

The woman reached across the table and placed her hand on Preston's.

"I'm so sorry for your loss," she said.

Preston looked down at her hand and experienced a brief flicker. For the first time since Baird had died—admittedly it was just an instant, hardly a passing thought—Preston's indifference to life thawed.

Gordon bubbled with excitement. Of course, he didn't show it. He kept his face a mask of serene contentment. A good deal for all concerned, his expression seemed to say. But inside he was positively bursting because Preston Winthrop had just gone from his biggest problem to his biggest asset. Here he was worried about how he was going to get rid of him, and now he was wondering if he should promote him. His manner was so sober. There was something about his entire bearing that was . . . well, he didn't know what it was, but it was impressive. Gravitas! That was the word. The man had gravitas. He was movie-star good-looking. God, that head of hair alone was worth a 5 percent bump in the stock. Gordon had already decided that the next annual report would feature a prominent picture of Preston Winthrop on the cover.

And clearly he was the man not just to manage the branches but to spearhead the expansion. Even from their brief conversation, it was obvious Preston had contacts with every major player in the region. This whole thing was a slam dunk! The only question in his mind was whether he should try to get Preston more involved in the bank's New York office, maybe convince him to relocate. If his gut instinct was right, he had just met a man he could groom to be his successor.

There had been one unfortunate moment with that Perkins fellow, who had accosted him as he was walking through the lobby. The man's obsequious manner was ridiculous, and the way those long strands of hair kept falling down on his forehead. He had gone on and on about that loan. What was it for? Maybe $30,000? Gordon had spent that much on a new rug for his office. No, Perkins would have to go. Once the two banks merged their operations, there would be no need for someone like Perkins.

His only worry was that grief might ruin the man. Gordon detected an emptiness in Preston's eyes. Not that he wasn't sympathetic. He couldn't imagine what it would be like to lose a son, but Preston was still a young man. He could start over. Gordon had to get him back in the traces. It would do no good for Preston to cling to his grief. Back to work as soon as possible—that was the answer.

CHAPTER FORTY-FOUR

As the final scenes of *Anna Karenina* unfolded on television, Anne wept. She wept for Anna. And she wept for Baird. And she wept for herself. And she wept for what might have been. Then she drew a hot bath and poured a large glass of red wine and climbed into the tub. The steam filled the room, hiding the cheap white tile. In the silence, she could almost imagine she was back in her own bathroom in Winthrop Hall, back amid the piles of plush towels and French fixtures and Carrara marble.

She sipped her wine and thought about Anna. Throwing herself under a train was unimaginable. Too horrible to consider, although she tried—and failed—to see herself crushed beneath the wheels of the five forty-five commuter train. It was an unnecessarily nineteenth-century sort of death—violent and industrial and gruesome. There were so many easier ways to slip away today. Hardly even a suicide, more like a final sigh.

As she soaked in the bathtub, her mind floated back over her life, and she tried to understand where she had made the wrong turn. As if in understanding, she could find her way back to that place before everything had happened. But it was too late. As the water grew cold, Anne blanched at the terrible realization, and her frightened gaze fell on the large bottle of sleeping pills.

Was it cowardly or brave, she wondered? A Roman falling on his sword? Or a panicked flight from justice? She wasn't sure. She wasn't sure about anything anymore. It was as if her life had been stripped of any guiding light, as if she were floating not in a bathtub but in a dark ocean with no sense of which direction she should swim.

Her hand reached for the bottle. The plastic was reassuringly solid and real. She turned on the hot water to warm the bath, and the steam began to fill the room again, to hide the misery that reflected back at her from every surface.

As the scalding water poured into the tub and the steam rose around her like a cloak, she tentatively opened the bottle.

In a few minutes, her eyes fluttered gently and her hand let fall the glass of wine into the tub coloring the water a pale pink. A half-smile played on her lips. This is what it's like, she thought. Not a painful tearing but a gentle slide. And death came not as the avenger she feared but as a warm embrace, like that day when Preston held her after they won the Benedict Cup. How many months ago was that? It didn't matter. Her hand drowsily circled the surface of the water before slipping under.

By the time the paramedics arrived the next day the water was spilling out from under the front door. They pulled Anne from the tub and did all that modern medical practice required in a perfunctory and competent manner.

Her funeral was arranged in an embarrassed, hasty, unacknowledged way. No one knew who picked the music or the flowers or even who paid, although not much was spent. Just enough to avoid any unseemly cheapness. She was buried not in the Winthrop family crypt but in a small plot in a quiet corner of the cemetery. A modest stone with only her name was placed on top, as if the carver had stopped midway through his work.

Not many people came to Anne's funeral. And the few who did were drawn as much by the gossip as anything. For a while, there were whispered conversations at every party about what happened. But eventually people moved on. Only Nancy couldn't leave it alone. She never forgave Anne for her suicide. Her death put an abrupt end to Nancy's social climbing, and she spread malicious lies about her whenever she had the chance.

Did a man occasionally visit that out-of-the-way corner of the cemetery? If he did, his face was always hidden in the half-light, and he didn't stay for long.

EPILOGUE

For many years after Preston moved to New York, Winthrop Hall was closed. There were no summer galas, and the Hall—with its darkened windows and furniture draped in white cloths—was quiet and still. During the summer, the grass grew high, and weeds pushed into the flower beds and snarled the hedges. In the autumn, leaves were left on the ground until they formed damp piles in odd corners.

The biting wind of fall with its promise of winter sent leaves skittering across the cracked tennis court and through the broken window of one of the French doors by the terrace. They spun with lovely grace across the smooth marble, dancing through the finely carved legs of the furniture and gathering in far corners like revelers at a party. And the leaves fell through the air and down to the lake. A slow, pirouetting, graceful descent, utterly indifferent to the watery grave awaiting them. Falling and flying and spinning dizzily before disappearing beneath the black waters. And falling. Always falling.

ACKNOWLEDGMENTS

I want to thank my family for all of their love and support over the years and for being nothing like anyone in the novel.

I also want to thank Judith Riven, who has been unfailing in her encouragement. And I am extraordinarily grateful to Elizabeth Beier, who is an editor of impeccable taste and good sense. To say that she improved the book in countless ways is an enormous understatement. In addition, everyone at St. Martin's Press has been a pleasure to work with from start to finish.

Although he is relatively new to this world, thanks are due to my son, Spencer. I cannot claim that he is much of a reader yet, but he has managed to provide a great deal of emotional sustenance nonetheless. As always, my greatest debt of gratitude is owed to Heesun, who puts up with a remarkably large amount of complaining for a remarkably small amount of words produced. Despite being married to me, she remains my biggest fan.